The Pit

Andrew Griffiths

ISBN: 978-1-918240-06-1

For S and S, my daily inspiration

CONTENTS

ACKNOWLEDGEMENTS

Thanks to everyone that made this possible and allowed me the time to get on with it, the evenings and weekends, the time spent editing and proofreading and all the little changes.

Thanks also to the brave men and women of our police force who have to deal with this stuff day after day – this is for all of you..

ONE

Seamus awoke with the usual feeling of dread that another day brought him. He lay motionless for a few more minutes, enjoying the relative quiet of his new home and the comfort of the position he had been sleeping in just seconds before. He stared up at the ceiling thinking about the last few months and where he now was: new house, new post, new town. It was still all a little surreal. The steady hum of the traffic outside was building which was an indicator it was time to get up.

Getting out of bed with a sigh, he padded across to the bathroom and leaned on the wall above the toilet. So, this is what they call a middle-aged all-nighter, is it? Seamus thought as he was still there after what felt like ten minutes. Having finally finished he got the shower running and fumbled about looking for pants and socks that vaguely matched. You could get run over and it would look better – you never know; his mother used to say when he was young. After a warm and refreshing shower, he dressed and made his way downstairs to the kitchen.

He switched the kettle on to start the morning routine after the momentous occasion of not having to get out of bed for seven hours - it made him sound as though he were talking about his kids when they were babies. The kettle's sound drowned out his thoughts for a moment as his focus moved from sleep to the day ahead: what would be going on at the office, and how much extra paperwork might have piled up on his desk over the weekend.

Click – he was snapped back into the present by the kettle's unsubtle notification that his water was ready, so he pottered across the kitchen to attend to the most important task so far that day, getting some breakfast. Strong black coffee and toast, preferably not the same colour as the coffee. Although this morning it was just coffee, because somehow the knob in the toaster had moved and it had come out the wrong side of destroyed and was destined for the bin. One sweetener in the coffee and the crumbs from toastageddon neatly cleaned up and deposited in the bin too since Seamus preferred to keep a clean house.

He flicked on the TV to see what was happening in the world and see who was presenting today – decent presenter, excellent! Usual shite on the news, weather looked awful, some distant conflict and a bunch of whingey folks on some subject or other, nothing local to note. Should be a reasonable day, if a little quiet, like pretty much all of them were these days, since his move here. He sipped his coffee.

The quiet mornings were a deliberate choice, the small victory of the new Seamus, trying to prove he was more than just the job. Hopefully also making more progress towards demonstrating there was more to him as a father and husband too. Due to the toast incident there was a gap where his breakfast should have been, but thankfully, via the slightest of detours, he passed a shop on his way to the office. He parked just around the corner after having scanned the streets for a suitable spot and joined the usual out-of-the-door queue, thankful that for the first time in what seemed like weeks, it wasn't raining.

Another benefit of having moved here was that his mind was clearer; he wasn't encumbered with constant work-based distractions, pulling his attention away from the task in hand, in this case using his time in the queue to decide on whether a bap or baguette would be the vessel of choice for his sausages and bacon. No question on the sauce, though - brown all the way.

A short time later, in the car on the way to the office, coffee in the cup holder, croissant crumbs across his lap and moaning about every other person on the road - why can't they drive properly, can they even see? – the usual morning complaints, he was prepared for the day ahead. Somehow when he got to the front of the queue, the freshly-cooked croissants that had just been placed on the counter were too good to pass up, so two of them and a large black coffee found their way into his car. Probably better than a mass of processed meats and a big stick of bread, although much less contained in terms of their ability to cover every surface.

"Morning!" came the booming voice of Jim Pallister from across the office. "French breakfast again there?" Seamus took a look down at his clothes. He was part pastry to be fair, that stuff really does get everywhere, to the extent he was considering how many calories he had managed to consume, versus how many were still attached to his crotch. He missed nothing, that man, nothing where food was involved anyway. "Why, did you want to hoover up my crumbs, Jim?" Seamus replied without the slightest hint of a smile, "and stop looking at my balls." Jim simply grunted in recognition of this response and continued his meander to the group of desks that he and Seamus usually occupied. Seamus fell into a chair with a sigh. Another day of this shitty case. "Jim, did you get anything from the old fella in the market?" Jim shrugged a negative reply. "Nah, he can't remember his own name, never mind what happened last month, I mean, he's probably more pickled than Desmond Hirst's pet shark". "Damien," Seamus corrected him. "Who now?"

Over the last month the two men and their wider team had been investigating a series of reports pertaining to market sellers. The prevailing thread related to underage workers, and one informally obtained statement from a stalwart of the markets which alluded to 'foreign lads telling me they don't get paid', so they needed to get hold of this guy to follow up and get more details, and in a more formal manner.

"Never mind, so we still have no witness statement, no evidence gathered and the boss riding us for answers on a case that has less weight than a vegan bikini model.

What's the poi-" He was interrupted by the phone ringing. "DCI Corrigan, can I-" His face turned pale, his eyes going from their usual blue to a steel grey, a deep frown gathering across his forehead. "What do you-" he stuttered out then winced, shook his head slowly and began to regain colour until he was almost scarlet.

"WTF?" Jim mouthed at him. Seamus ended the call, shaking slightly and now ashen again. "It's Wilson; he's been found up at Sykes Farm and, he's, ummmm- in boxes." Jim just stared at him in disbelief for almost a minute. "Are they sure it's him?" he asked, eyebrows hitting his hairline. "I mean he was only here on Wednesday, his irritating cocky self, parading about the place with his usual swagger."

Reg Wilson was the guy the term 'serial offender' had been created for. He'd been in the station more times than most of the coppers, so much so he almost had a loyalty card for the coffee machine and his own mug. "Yeah, definitely him – the first team onsite recognised his face straight away, even though it was… Christ, I can't believe this… it was in a box." said Seamus, turning very pale at the mental image he now had, thinking of those response officers arriving on scene and seeing that. It was bad enough when a more seasoned officer was first on scene, or even just attending once the victim had been discovered, but he was thinking of the impact this would inevitably have.

Discovering a dead body is one thing, that first one never leaves you – looking at a person who is no longer alive. Coming to terms with that is something you never forget, and you do have to try to desensitise yourself to it otherwise the job becomes unbearable, but a person, in boxes… that was a whole other level. Reg was just a petty criminal, car theft mostly, no real aggro, never anything physical. Just a pain in everyone's arse, and a bit of menace on the roads during his joyrides while antagonising the Roads Policing Unit. But he knew the system and was happy to spend the odd night in the cells and get a good breakfast out of it. He'd never paid a single fine despite having many thousands levied against him; he'd smile at the custody sergeant; he'd nod in court while his charges were read out like he was having his experience played back to him in an interview. Then in no time at all, he was back in someone else's car giving the traffic guys a run around the streets.

"What do you mean, boxes?" Chief Superintendent Dawn Bowler almost spat out. "Plastic boxes, ma'am - seven of them with various parts in each, different sizes and the kind you put stuff into to keep dry, just laid out on the ground, but the one with his head in," Seamus paused as he mentally processed what he had just said, "had some odd writing on it; 'I've saved you all' then some numbers, followed by 'You're welcome'. The CSIs have taken some photos."

Jim took his phone out and showed Bowler the photos he had been sent from the scene. Seamus looked at them again, not really able to make much sense of the situation, while Bowler, seeing them for the first time, was trying to understand how Reg Wilson, petty car thief and irritation of the RPU team, had ended up as a human jigsaw. "You and Jim get over there as soon as you can, please. Let me know what you find and catch up with

Bina and see if her and the team have anything yet," said Bowler, still staring at the space where Jim's phone had just been, displaying the unbelievable images. "Seems like he may have stolen the wrong car this time," she suggested, to which Seamus nodded distractedly, trying to work through possibilities. "Yeah, maybe. Do we know the last few vics who lost their cars to him recently? We ought to start there, since he's never been into drugs, nor actually hurt anyone so this just looks like this is revenge, although it's pretty extreme for a bit of metal," Jim thought out loud. It was now Seamus's turn to nod slowly and thoughtfully. "We'll get there within the hour, ma'am, and let you know what's going on."

Even though Reg was a royal pain in the force's backside and annoying as he was, he didn't deserve that. Chopped up and put in boxes is off the scale for some small-time guy, well anyone really, and Seamus couldn't help thinking - what did he stumble into?

The drive over was used to try to work through a few scenarios. Fortunately, mid-morning traffic was light as Jim was distracted by thoughts of what he'd seen and what they were going to expect when they arrived. Who and why were the key questions, but neither Seamus nor Jim had got to anything concrete by the time they arrived at Sykes Farm. "I'm still not sold on this being something like mistaken identity," said Seamus when they got out of the car. "Maybe Wilson just has - well, had - 'that look', you know, and got caught up in the crossfire," Jim added. "This is a weird place too - why here? This place is in the middle of nowhere, and Wilson's name has never had any connection to here, so what's the story? I don't get it."

Seamus's brow was deeply furrowed, and he looked around slowly, taking in the wider scene before walking any further.

Both men walked towards the cordoned-off area to the site officer that Seamus noticed as they drove in. She looked a little unsteady, that anyone outside the force may have put down to having been on her feet for a while, but Seamus recognised that look on her face and realised she must have been one of the first ones to attend. They signed their names into the log and ducked under the tape surrounding the scene, but before walking further Seamus made eye contact and gave a slight nod and smile, enough to let PC Gregory know he understood.

And there they were, seven plastic boxes with parts of a person in them with what looked like a huge pool of dried blood under and around them. Neither man had ever witnessed anything quite like it before. They had both seen dead bodies - the victims of a stabbing, the ones who had succumbed to an untimely death by natural causes or the odd accident - but this was extreme. The macabre scene took a moment or two to really process. It was so abstract to see body parts in clear plastic boxes, just assembled on the ground like that – head at one end, feet at the other.

"Christ!" Jim almost choked. "I mean, that's just, fucking hell- it's -" and he blew air out of pursed lips, a curious look on his face that fluctuated between disgust, curiosity and shock. They stood there for what felt like an eternity just looking at what used to be Reg Wilson - petty crook, bit of a dick but mostly harmless, and now in bits in plastic tubs on an old farm. Seamus walked slowly closer to the arranged boxes, noticed that there was no smell, not the usual sweet and slightly metallic smell of blood, the unmistakable stench of decay, nothing at all. "These must be good boxes, you know – good seals on the lids, not cheap shite, nothing's leaking out." Jim just nodded from a few feet away, still struggling with the scene in front of him. Seamus carefully and thoughtfully walked around the display, bending to get a better view of the contents. What he thought was odd was that Reg still had some clothes on.

Not that Seamus was particularly experienced in the discovery of folks chopped to bits and stuffed into plastic boxes, but there had been plenty of reports of mutilations in his old place, and all of them were naked. Probably made it easier to chop up if you can see where you need to cut, he considered while staring at one of the larger boxes with what was once Reg's torso inside. The box with Reg's head in it had some writing on, just like the CSI had reported from the site earlier, and Seamus bent over a little more to read it. 'I've saved you all £5,5??, you're welcome.' The writing did appear to suggest that whoever had put Reg into this state had saved someone some money. Some of the characters were not clear, could have been £5.5k, maybe more, but the message was certainly about money saved. The question was, who had saved the money for whom? Was it a message to someone who had ordered this to be done, had the killer done it on the cheap, or was it a final note to Reg, or to someone else? But that wasn't what caught Seamus's eye. The CSIs had been instructed to leave the boxes as they were, exactly as they had been laid out by whoever had put them there. Aside from Reg's clothes being mostly present, there was something that wasn't. His thumbs were missing. All the effort to cut up the body, keep most of the clothes on, including his shoes, put everything into different boxes, but then remove the thumbs – maybe they were in the bottom of one of the other boxes. Seamus took some time and peered around them all but couldn't see them. "Jim, get over here. See if you can find his thumbs," said Seamus, in a tone even he didn't recognise. Jim looked up, clearly lost in his thoughts. "What?" he asked, uncertain as to whether he had misheard or just couldn't quite correlate the question with the bizarre array he had been looking at. "His thumbs, Jim – they're missing." Jim's face went from thoughtful to confused in a heartbeat. "What- do you mean, like in a box or something, or just gone?" asked Jim, still in a slight daze. "I don't know, I can't see them anywhere," Seamus said, with an air of detachment still in his voice.

He called Bowler to apprise her of the situation. "Chief, it's definitely Reg and the message looks very much like something to do with money, but I think we need to get this lot into the lab and start looking at this in more detail." Bowler was quiet for a moment. "Your call, Seamus, but the sooner the better, please. This is still low-key for now, but I have a feeling it won't stay like it for long." She let out a long breath. "Poor Reg." Seamus ended the call and walked over to Bina Mistry, the lead forensics officer. "Bina, can we get these boxes down the road and see what's going on?" Bina smiled thinly. "I thought you'd never ask," she said and gestured to the team who got to work putting Reg into their van. "You ever seen anything like this?" asked Seamus to Bina, keen to get her take. She scanned the scene in front of her and sighed slightly, clearly affected by such an horrific way to display this kind of work. "Not like this," she said quietly, slowly shaking her head, but due to the mask she was wearing it was hard to see the look of sadness on her face. Bina had been doing this job for over twelve years and had attended some scenes that would shock anyone, and whilst she had acclimatised herself to seeing what others were capable of, there were extreme cases that took a lot more to contemplate. This was definitely one of those.

She didn't know Reg, never even heard of him, but the way he had been dealt with, and that was the only way she could really see this, was violence beyond the spectrum she and the team would usually see. "Guv, we've got the boxes loaded and are heading down to the lab. We've got site photos of everything in-situ, we've got some initial swabs and ground shots so if it's OK, we'll get going." Bina had a way with her patients, as she called them, never offhand, never any humour at their expense, they were still people and they had a story to tell her, and she respected them throughout their time together.

"Thanks Henry. Please take care of him, drive carefully and I'll see you down there," she said to her team lead.

"Thanks, Bina," said Seamus, and away they went to take Reg, in his seven boxes, to the lab.

TWO

It was just another day as far as Adrian was concerned: another day at work, another day when he came home to his family and they ate together while sharing stories of what each had been up to. His kids telling him of their day at school, not so much about their lessons, but more about the other kids, the break times and conversations that took place. Who was now going out with who, and which of the teachers looked like they had been out drinking all weekend. It was a different world to when he was at school, tennis ball football, kiss-chase and tag. Adrian smiled as he listened to what was important to them and never undermined it. He asked them questions that were related to what they were talking about, didn't patronise them and instead encouraged them to be confident to talk about anything at all.

His wife Lisa had been busy both at work and at home, and he wasted no time recognising this, and making sure she knew her efforts were valued. Her job was something she really enjoyed, the hours worked for school, and it gave her real satisfaction being part of something outside the home. Not that she wasn't happy there, not at all - it was a close household and she knew she was surrounded by those who appreciated and loved each other. Lasagne tonight - his favourite and something that took some time to prepare.

He walked across the kitchen and gave Lisa a gentle squeeze and a peck on the cheek. "You are wonderful," he whispered. There was also a nice glass of red to go with it – he didn't really care that it was Argentinian and not Italian. He wasn't a wine snob, he just thought it was a nice accompaniment to the meal, and very welcome after quite a busy day. He'd dabbled with trying to learn more about wine a few years back, got a few bottles from here and there and tried to determine their make-up, but all he really got when holding the glass to his nose was the smell of, well, wine. So, rather than try to keep up any pretence that he had the vaguest idea of different grapes or fruits added to the mix, when others in the group had groaned a little too many times about his 'ooohh, I'm getting athlete's nostril' jokes, he just accepted that he was partial to the odd glass of red and that was that. Tonight's was nice though, quite smooth so it must have been one of the more expensive ones - so at least £7?

Yes, that was what counted as a more expensive bottle at the Burch household, not the world's biggest spenders – not that they didn't have money, just that they would rather use it for more important things. Adrian still bought most of his new clothes from a supermarket, and the nicer items were more often than not second-hand, either from eBay or Vinted or some app or other. Lisa was much the same - one of the many things that brought them, then kept them, together. Neither was particularly extravagant, and neither bothered by the Joneses – they can have what they want, but we have what we need. Following dinner he washed up after stacking most of the stuff into the dishwasher. He usually did the washing-up if Lisa cooked, always when he cooked, so that Lisa didn't need to add anything else to her day. She worked hard and didn't deserve to be expected to do household chores as well as everything else. They both settled down in the living room while the kids vanished, probably into their bedrooms to watch something on TV, play online or whatever made them content.

For Adrian it was the usual evening diet of police documentaries – Interceptor repeats, the Traffic Cops, always breaking their backs to apprehend these arseholes only to see them the following week or month doing exactly the same thing, like their brush with the law was just a passing glance. He was never sure why he kept watching these things. It only annoyed him that so many people had so little respect - not just for each other, but for the police. Where did that come from? These men and women who had dedicated themselves to our safety, just treated with such contempt. All the time, the effort, the stress to get these scumbags off the streets - and for what?

Millions of tax pounds every year down the drain, he thought, as they would be back out there doing the same thing the next day, and the police would have to catch them again. By the fourth or fifth time, they had a certain swagger about them, an arrogance that could only come from knowing that they would get away with it. Again. More recently he had started on the many forensic series, how the science played its part in detection of criminals, all these people involved in each stage of the process, and again, to see their efforts wasted as the human rubbish walks free to repeat the same steps. How did they stay sane? These programmes fascinated him. He loved science, he had been good at it at school and maintained a lifelong interest in aspects of it, which probably explained how he had ended up in IT. He would use that expression when asked about what he did. "Oh, I just ended up in it," he would reply and would simply say he 'worked in IT' rather than go into any detail. He used to until he could see people's eyes glaze over, so just left it there. It was easier not to try to explain it.

"I don't know how they don't just chuck them in a big hole in the ground and cover it up, like landfill," he said after an episode featuring multiple persistent repeat offenders. Lisa looked at him the way only a wife could, a combination of resignation mixed with a little pity. She offered a faint smile and returned to Facebook. He shrugged and carried on watching as the team on another documentary talked about cell site identification and how it allowed the police to locate people and track their routes, even using built-in vehicle tracking now available on a lot of modern cars – you can't move without someone somewhere knowing about it.

'We were able to identify each of the group by their mobile phones, not just from the calls made and messages sent between them, but from the cell analysis to show where they met up before the theft, to where they hid the vehicle and how they dispersed when the

police arrived.' Amazing, thought Adrian – but I bet they won't get charged, lack of evidence or some similar rubbish, and even if they do it will be a driving ban and a slap on the wrist.
"Are you coming to bed?" Lisa said for the third time from the stairs.

"Sorry, I was miles away," Adrian replied. "Yes, I'll be right up."

So, no phone, older car, generic shoes in a generic size, and clothes that didn't stand out seem to be the go-to wardrobe of choice for the criminal about town this season, he thought to himself as the TV show did a recap of the evidence they found that finally led them to the suspect. I wonder how many career criminals actually watch these shows - they must be able to learn something from them?

Adrian mulled this over for a while as he swilled the last of his wine around in the glass. Anyway, Lisa was waiting upstairs and had seemed quite playful - must have been the wine, but even so, there could be a nice night ahead unless she'd fallen asleep already. So he rushed up to check and saw that she was very much awake, and looking every inch the seductress she could be when the mood, or level of alcohol, dictated.

THREE

May 2019

It had only been six weeks since Seamus had to move out as things were - how did she put it? - untenable between them. She blamed him, he blamed himself or more accurately his work, but ultimately himself. There was only so much he could blame on the job, hard as it was, although he was offered support but chose not to accept it. He was moved to a different team over the last few years but still he didn't really seem able to leave the noise in the office. He'd seen people do unspeakable things to other people. He'd had to unpick vile cases, interview people with no decency or consideration, bare-faced liars, those that were happy to twist everything to help them attempt to get away with some of the worst behaviours. These past weeks, though, made all he had seen and dealt with out there pale into insignificance. The terror he felt now was so much more than he had ever experienced while hunting a criminal, and the fear was unimaginable.

She was right to ask him to leave of course, but that didn't make it any easier, nor that they had reached some sort of agreement between them - mainly what was best for the girls but, in reality, what was best for all of them. He was unbearable all the time, you couldn't talk to him and he wasn't much of a talker either so there was no chance to get to the bottom of it, so it festered away until she simply had to put some space between them. But despite all the discussions and the nodding he hadn't taken it well when it finally happened, when they actually separated and he ended up in a flat by himself while she stayed in the house with the girls.

His whole world had imploded that day. The days that followed were darker than any others he could remember, the sense of loss and lack of meaning were all-encompassing. One day a husband and father, in the house with his family, going on holidays together - well, sometimes - and sharing a bed, a breakfast table and a sofa. The next, staring at the side of the bed-: a different bed in a different room in a different house. An empty bed. No sleeping wife beside him, no kids running in to wake him up, no cereal to clean up from the worktop, no sounds of a family home, just the abyss of loneliness. Sleep was elusive, despite his utter exhaustion. Even the level of depression he had become enveloped by made no impression on his ability to get any rest, which is most likely the reason that it happened.

The op had been difficult to start with, a lot of preparation and a lot of hours to spend on surveillance to understand the routine and the habits of their targets. Weeks of focused efforts, pushing the whole team to their limits of patience and tolerance with each other, Seamus being almost unapproachable. Too much time cramped into small rooms, vehicles and places not conducive to comfort, but necessary to get the results they needed. Night shifts, day shifts, weekends and any and every available hour consumed, to make sure the operation was watertight. They were not going to let this group slip through their fingers this time. Their main target was a key player in the wider drug game in the county, he had led them on a merry dance for months, moving product and people around so his location was always changing, always a step ahead.

It got so bad Seamus had become convinced there was a mole in the team. It was too much of a coincidence that just when a raid was planned, they would receive intelligence that the target location was empty and the team would have to stand down, again. But that night, everything had lined up. No updates to suggest they were anywhere else, no intel that the product had been moved, everything was ready. Everything, that was, except for Seamus. Five days without sleep and his mind in turmoil was not ever going to lead to a good result. The team needed their leader to assert the necessary authority and keep the operation on plan and keep everyone focused. It all came down to this – the pinnacle of months of hard work and letdowns and their DCI was to be front and centre. But he was not present, not mentally or emotionally, just physically. As the night went on, the wider team swept the site, picked up some less important members, seized as much product as they found, and kept the control room updated. They worked through the plan as it had been presented back at the HQ, each breakout team executing their specific role. The net was closing and he was cornered, and it seemed it was his last night on the scene. All Seamus had to do was block his exit.

Hours later, when they found Seamus, they thought he was dead. Unresponsive and crumpled at the doorway to the building, he was cold to the touch and covered in blood. He remembered the ambulance, the shouts from the paramedics and his DI, but little else. He didn't remember Bariu leaning over him, the knife in his hand and being told he was a marked man now, he could never escape, never hide from his fate.

The next two days in hospital were a haze of busy medical staff, the odd police officer checking in on him and the noises around the ward, but nothing to really provide answers. He lay in bed trying to organise the thoughts and images swimming around his head, trying to find something to focus on that might explain why he was there, and what was going on. The food was appalling, that much he had been aware of. By the time he was discharged to his empty house a few gaps had been filled, some by colleagues, others by his own mind. His main issue was whether he could trust his own recollections, and whether it was from exhaustion, pain relief or trauma, Seamus really didn't know what was real. He could hear the voices over the radio, giving updates on his location, the status of each sub-team and the feeling that things were finally going right. He could see the door, the cars beyond and the shouts from those chasing their quarry towards him, and then they were face-to-face. His first opportunity to sleep in what felt like weeks had been shattered, he sat up in bed covered in sweat and – yes, he was crying. His emotion caught him by surprise. It wasn't like Seamus to cry or show any feelings, but clearly the events of the past few days, layered onto his new living arrangements, had cut a hole through his usual wall. There was nobody there to offer any comfort, the girls would not burst through the door with pictures they had created, and his wife wouldn't come to check he was OK.

He had never felt so alone in his life, and the tears burned his eyes and would not relent.

He didn't dare close his eyes, partly because of the absolute darkness that enveloped him and partly because that face was always there, but he couldn't understand the expression on it. The look in those eyes - was it anger, hatred or fear?

FOUR

Present day

The pathology lab attached to the large general hospital had recently been refurbished and had the feel of an ultra-modern facility about it: Gleaming walls, lots of stainless steel and LED lighting that left no shadows, wherever you stood. Although even with all the investment and hard work that smell was still there - the cloying odour of chemicals that were only ever associated with death. Bina was really pleased with the work; she and the team had all been consulted on what they felt was really needed and been required to attend some of the meetings where the overall project had been discussed. It was great to be part of the process as well as to be able to see first-hand the bureaucracy that her senior leadership had to deal with in order to get anything done. It made her appreciate their efforts a great deal more. The old lab was not really conducive to the team size or working patterns, and for some time now Bina had worried about potential issues seeping into their results. Walls were starting to crumble, the ceilings were showing signs of damage and the equipment wasn't quite at the standard it should be. But now, with all the new gear and the way the place had been set up, there was a real feel of renewed energy and professionalism about the place. Bina had been part of the path lab team for a good few years before graduation, so felt more a part of the history and took much more interest in every aspect than some of the newer members.

She was pulled out of her reverie by the sound of someone at the door, knocking at the door to be precise, which annoyed Bina since there was a bell to get attention, and it was clearly labelled – I guess you can't fix stupid, she thought to herself. Fixing her best 'I'm not really cross' smile she walked purposefully out and down the hall. Perhaps it was the new lights, or her sunnier-than-usual air, but Jim looked different today - slimmer, perhaps? Not that he was overweight per se, more the comfy side of athletic. Maybe his hair had been tended to? That wasn't it, he was still sporting his usual mop – he's in a suit! Bina took a minute to absorb this before opening the door, checking for evidence of an overnight session at some posh bar, or wedding reception, but he was clean and tidy and looked fairly fresh, for Jim. "Morning, Jim," she said. "You look- smart," she added, trying hard to keep the surprise from her voice and worrying that she had failed miserably. "Good morning, erm- thanks," said Jim, his cheeks turning almost the same red as his hair. Jim Pallister, embarrassed? thought Bina, he never gets embarrassed about anything, all I said was he looked smart, oh... Bina turned away to stride back to the lab with Jim trailing somewhere behind, hoping he hadn't noticed the slight smile on her face. She'd checked his shoes too - clean and shiny, he really had made an effort. Very impressive.

"What time's the ceremony?" asked Seamus on arrival at the lab, looking at Jim with a quizzical expression. He couldn't ever remember seeing Jim in anything smarter than Next jeans and a reasonable shirt - maybe once he had a blazer on but that was for someone's birthday party at Faizan's, the restaurant in town. Not that he was a mess, just not often tidy. "It's to your mum," said Jim over his shoulder, "and good morning to you too, Sir." The two men signed in at the main desk and Bina escorted them to the main lab where Reg had been arranged on the clean steel benches. Seamus still couldn't quite come to terms with a person in boxes, and this was all the more difficult since he had only told Reg to 'piss off and get a proper job' a few days ago, yet here he was. It seemed Jim was having a similar internal consideration, the way he paced up and down the benches just looking with a mixture of shock and disbelief still. Then he stopped and stared at Bina with such a serious expression she nearly took a step backwards. "What do you think was used to cut him up?" asked Jim, still almost staring at her. She moved away slightly; his gaze was making her feel somewhat uncomfortable. "Are you OK, Jim - do you need some air?" She asked without getting to his question. He shuffled a bit where he stood, looked across at Seamus, and passed out.

If Jim had been embarrassed by the earlier compliment, it was nothing in comparison to that little episode. As much as he really wanted to blame it on a lack of sustenance or a long and alcoholic night out, the reality was he just couldn't deal with what was in front of him. He'd been to many trips to the path lab in his career, seen enough people on 'the slab', but this was just too much. Reg was such a regular there that the notion of him not being back in the morning, added to the sight of what had happened to him, just tipped Jim over the edge. Both Bina and Seamus hauled his feet up off the floor and managed to get them onto a seat and keep him still until he came back round, and even then he looked like he would puke. But there were no jokes from either of them. They knew he was usually much stronger than this, so there must have been a good reason for such an extreme reaction. "Here you go, mate," said Seamus, offering him his hand to get Jim onto a chair and handing him a glass of water and checking his eyes for signs of concussion, as his descent had been rather rapid. "Cheers, guv, and I'm sorry - I just-" Jim looked across the room at the boxes and teetered a little in the chair. "I think I'll sit this one out, if that's OK," he said meekly to Seamus, almost under his breath. "Of course. Just take your time - we'll handle the first bits and see how you're feeling later," offered Seamus, realising that he too wasn't feeling quite as well as he could be. This really was way more violence than he'd witnessed, and that it was someone he sort of knew made it even more difficult.

Bina made sure Jim had a wall to lean on to prevent any further visits to the floor, picked up some fresh gloves and made her way back to the bench to open the first of the plastic boxes. "Hang on a sec," said Seamus, very much back in his stride, "what can you make of the writing first? I couldn't quite see what was said."

Bina looked over to the box containing Reg's head. On the lid the characters were unclear. The message did appear to suggest that there was a figure of £5K something, so she went to the cupboards containing some of the chemicals used to extract evidential information and tried one. The result was less than satisfactory, at least to start with. After a few more seconds though, the fainter characters came up a little clearer - £5,500. "What's that about?" she asked out loud, "£5,500 for what, can't be for the job, surely, and why say that it's been saved. Saved from what, for what? Well, I suppose that's for you two to find out." She looked over to Seamus then across the room to Jim, who was by now starting to regain a little colour and composure. "There is the possibility that it's got nothing to do with what's in the boxes," mused Seamus, "and maybe it was in there before and just that the lid was the only one that would fit - and whoever did this didn't bother to clean it off."

"We can check that," said Bina, looking for a kit to carry out ink-aging tests. "Let's get a sample of the ink and get that analysing, then we can open a box and sample the contents to see if we can determine a time of death."

Open a box. Seamus looked over to where Jim was sitting and tried to gauge how he was, and how he had received that update. To be fair, Jim had looked better, but he also looked somewhat stoic and tentatively got to his feet. "I can't spend the whole day on my arse," he said with what he hoped was a smile, but to Seamus looked more like he had wind.

The moment the lid came off it hit them - the smell was overwhelming, even with the strong air extraction system in the lab. "Oh my, Reg," Bina exclaimed, "maybe I shouldn't have started with your feet."

Jim immediately returned to his seat but this time buried his face in his hands. Slowly shaking his head, he muttered through his fingers, "you poor, poor bastard." A mass murderer, child killer or a rapist would never have received this level of sentiment, but this was harmless Reg, for Christ's sake - he'd handed him a shitty cup of coffee only last week.

FIVE

Breakfast at the Burch household was often a frantic time of the day, albeit just on weekdays. School was looming, and Adrian and Lisa always made sure the kids had something to eat, preferably something wholesome and good enough to set them up for the day. There was an array of cereals to choose from, or toast, and today even crumpets. Adrian grabbed a mug of tea and checked that the kids both had their shoes on and bags ready, and that Sam had his packed lunch. The radio was on in the background and Lisa was almost dancing to the latest offering by Hozier, or was it Coldplay? God, she was feeling old - she used to know every song by every band, now she feared she was turning into her mum with comments like 'well, it all starts to sound the same' but stopping short of adding 'these days'. She didn't have a blue rinse and bifocals just yet.

"Come on, Sam - those are Shreddies not sharks in there, stop making them chase each other and gobble them up,"

Adrian said jovially, in an attempt to get his youngest son a little closer to the front door. "Daddy" said Sam, in almost a whisper. This was not a good sign. He only called Adrian 'Daddy' when he wanted something, turning on the child-charm offensive, knowing very well his dad was much more of a pushover than his mum. "Yes, sweetheart?" Adrian replied, turning to look at his almost-8-year-old son.

"I don't want to go to school," Sam said, with an expression of sadness and defiance. "Why not, kiddo, what's wrong?" asked his father, with genuine concern. It wasn't like Sam to not want to go to school, by all accounts he seemed to love it there. He had some good friends, kids that lived on the same street that he'd known most of his life, and he showed a genuine interest in the lessons. "My teacher is a bum head" came the response. It was all Adrian could do not to jettison his tea across the kitchen floor, and he fought to maintain a degree of composure. "Right, OK – why is your teacher a, uh - bum head?" It could have been worse, thought Adrian, I mean, bum head – not what he was expecting at all. He'd met Mr Clarke at the last parents' evening and he seemed OK, cheery and dedicated as many younger teachers are, full head of hair too if memory served, so didn't look as though his head resembled that part of the anatomy. "Why is he one of those?" he asked, trying to diffuse the need to repeat the comment. "He said that Charlie's hair was silly, but it's actually the same as Will Stuart's, so it's cool." Adrian knew when he was out of his depth, as he hadn't the slightest idea who Sam was talking about, but didn't want to seem like an idiot in front of someone so young. "Well, perhaps Mr Clarke is jealous and he wants the same haircut but can't really express himself very well?" he suggested, in an attempt to recover his grasp of the conversation. Sam pondered this for a short while, then smiled. "You're probably right, Dad. His hair is a bit rubbish actually." Crisis averted, time for the school run.

The route to the school was mercifully short, not giving Sam enough time to rethink his now revised opinion of his teacher, but long enough for Adrian to become slightly obsessive about other drivers on the road. This was a daily issue for him, and it wasn't because he felt he was a superior motorist but was fuelled by his fascination with police documentaries and following traffic police TV programmes with such fervour. He'd spot incorrect number plates, and often look up the tax, MOT and insurance status of vehicles that he thought looked a little dodgy, and in some cases did find a few that had one or more of those missing.

On one afternoon at a fast-food restaurant, he noticed a black Audi A5 coming into the car park, and from his table inside he could see the driver, and (he assumed) his partner and two young children. But there was something about the car that piqued his interest, so he picked up his phone and checked the government website which quickly informed him that the vehicle had neither tax nor MOT. He then checked the AskMID website, to check if it was showing as insured. It wasn't. How on earth does someone drive their family around in a car with no tax, MOT or insurance? What happens if they're in an accident? His bloody children are in there, and they are driving about having fast food!! What is wrong with people? Adrian was incredulous. He abhorred this kind of thing and it was so much worse when kids got caught up in it. What else don't they think applies to them? No seatbelts perhaps, probably drives too fast, and God alone knows what state their tyres must be in. All these thoughts were still whirring around his head when they were walking into the restaurant and for a fleeting moment, Adrian toyed with the notion of talking to the driver, to ask how he could be so arrogant and inconsiderate. But common sense prevented him from doing anything, as it always did, so he just stewed in the corner and made a note of the car reg.

Over the years Adrian had done this countless times, but more recently he felt his dissatisfaction growing each time he saw the same transgressions being committed each day. He hadn't realised just how much it riled him, that even in his quiet, provincial town there were so many occurrences, so many people flaunting the rules, and potentially putting many others in danger or one form or another. One thing he was aware of was the growing list of car number plates he had, each one with either I, T, or M next to them, or a combination of all of them denoting which infringement they had associated with them. He was just glad it wasn't too obvious if a car passing him on the road was stolen, unless of course it was being driven so badly it could be that, drugs or drunk driving. Adrian knew that this had escalated since becoming a father nearly a decade ago, and his fear of something happening to his kids out there just got worse, from that terrifying drive back from the hospital with that tiny, precious package on board.

Seamus and Jim left Bina and the team to get on with the unenviable task of going through the boxes and getting to grips with the details of just how Reg had ended up in parts. Both men often felt superfluous in the path lab. While it was always good to be part of each step in the process, they were aware that they didn't really bring much to the party except a little distraction, as today had demonstrated.

"Come on Jim, let's grab a coffee on the way back. My treat," said Seamus as they walked out into the fresh air. On emerging into the sunlight from the building, Jim squinted and took a very deep breath, some of the colour finally returning to his face. It was finally getting cooler now after a summer that seemed to stretch on for months with seemingly unrelenting heat. Even the nights were hot, making what little sleep Seamus got next to impossible and largely uncomfortable. The drop in temperature was very welcome and a gentle introduction towards autumn, undoubtedly Seamus's favourite season. Jim was still very quiet. The whole episode in the lab had shaken him. It wasn't embarrassment at fainting, it was that he was overwhelmed by the events of the day and really needed a little more time to process it all. He was glad to not have to drive back and even more glad to have the hot cup of coffee in his hands, now shaking much less than they had been for the past hour.

Jim had moved into the Major Crimes Unit five years ago, just a year before Seamus came over from his city post, so they had been able to create a good working relationship, that they both had allowed to extend a little outside of the job. But while Jim was far more outgoing, and happier to blend work and social life, Seamus was much more guarded, and even after the best part of four years still turned down more invitations for an after-work drink than he accepted. In Seamus's mind he didn't really want to be a reason to keep family folks from getting home at a reasonable time and spending the evenings with those close to them, who they wouldn't have seen all day, rather than being with colleagues for more hours that was really necessary. He told himself this to justify the polite declines to the drinks or, in rare cases, a BBQ at a colleague's or a party here and there. Despite the alternative being just him in his quiet flat, he told himself he preferred it that way. He would much rather be alone than a spare.

Over the years Jim had managed to eke out some of the history, the odd question in the car, prising out little bits the way only a seasoned detective could, trying to get to know Seamus a little at a time without coming across as invasive. He'd learned enough to know that his colleague - and, he'd like to say, friend - was a deeply lonely person and just as unhappy. But the job was not only his life; it was his salvation too. His reason to get up each day. Jim couldn't help thinking that if he would just let himself go a bit, maybe good things might start to happen for him.

On one occasion when the two managed a reasonable discussion on the subject, Seamus revealed that part of the reason for the move was to try to find a balance. Also so he could prove to himself that there was more out there, and to gain some confidence that he could exist outside the job that had consumed every waking hour, it seemed, since he had joined. He had confided a lot to Jim that day - more than he had anyone else - and added that to the growing list of things that kept him awake for far too long. He didn't want to be a burden on anyone and didn't need any sympathy. But recently he had realised that what he did need was guidance and, more than that, a friend.

SIX

October 2019

Seamus thought he had been through the whole gamut of emotions over the past few weeks. He'd cried more than he thought possible, he was angry with her and himself, he felt his heart was broken beyond repair and knew his marriage was. She'd said some really hurtful things, which he had no reason to doubt were true since he knew he had been difficult to live with - he just hadn't realised how difficult or for how long. He certainly hadn't considered the extent of his attitude and the repercussions of it or just how deeply he had managed to cut into her feelings. He wasn't much of a drinker, so he didn't turn to alcohol to try to hide behind or attempt to alleviate the pain - he simply couldn't operate. Nothing could take him out of the darkness that surrounded him and no amount of coaxing would get him to leave the flat he had to move into, even though he hated being there, by himself. As the weeks had gone by, he went through the arguments, dissected them to try to find something to hold on to, some kindness amid the bitterness, but it wasn't there. His colleagues hadn't really seen this side of his deconstruction since their perspective was from the op and its aftermath, and his personal turmoil was hidden from view. There were moments when the absolute blackness got too much. His mind had wound him up to such an extent, he felt he had no choice but to escape, to get away from all of this for good and leave the pain behind forever.

He had come close, a rope around his neck on one desperate afternoon as he had stood on a bench sobbing his apologies to an empty shed. He'd stepped forward and felt the rope tighten around him, his weight suspended from the roof and a feeling of release starting to envelop him. But the rope came away from the roof and he crashed to the ground and he didn't feel relief that he was safe. He felt angry at himself for not doing this right. Like so many other things he had messed up, he couldn't even get this done properly. From that day he'd needed to always wear tops with a collar to hide the scars. The last time was when he found himself standing in the kitchen with a knife at his chest, pushing it into himself hoping to pierce his heart. The pressure kept increasing and all he felt was rage inside, hoping that soon everything would be quiet and he could sleep at last. It was the faces of his children that rushed into his mind and stopped the blade from getting any further. By then a fair amount of blood had soaked into his shirt, and he'd needed to patch himself up.

Timişoara, Romania - October 2019

Hiding was a lot harder than he'd thought it would be, even with his contacts, but then he wasn't sure how many of those he could trust now. It had been five months since the whole UK operation had been taken apart by the police and he had almost died. The police officer that had got between him and his escape route had somehow managed to disarm him of the knife he was going to use. He hadn't expected that and was off-guard when he felt it cut into his leg, right at his groin. He had tried to fight him off so he could make it to the waiting cars, but he was getting weaker by the moment and the police officer was strong and wouldn't let him go. It was then that things had got even more out of control. The door of the car opened and Kelmendi strode over, grabbing him by the hair and telling him he was a marked man, that he would never be able to escape his fate, taking a swing with a baseball bat at the police officer. Bariu somehow ended up between the two men, taking the full force of the blow.

Kelmendi looked over at the officer on the ground, covered in blood and motionless. Satisfied he wasn't going to get up, he turned his attention to the other man. Bariu had woken up while in the back of a car, not on the seats but in the boot, crumpled up and still bleeding, although now with a filthy rag as a makeshift tourniquet to stem the flow of what he was sure was arterial blood. After what felt like a lifetime, the car had stopped and he had been unceremoniously dumped at the side of the road, only to see the taillights disappear into the distance. Severely injured and with no idea where he was, he had needed to find shelter first then a phone to call Dushku. He needed to explain.

Dubrovnik, Croatia – present day

Any other day, the sun on his back would have felt good and made him relaxed and happy to be there. He would usually have been at this bar in good spirits, enjoying the company of friends and discussing the future. But not today. It had taken weeks to get here, off-grid with none of his usual support available to him, moving at night when he could and when he felt there wasn't anyone watching, vastly narrowing down the windows of opportunity. He was very much a marked man, just as Kelmendi had warned him he would be. Bariu had a new perspective on his approach to others over the years, the threats he had made, the punishments handed out to keep control over the flow of the product.

He lit a cigarette and took a long draw, exhaling the smoke slowly into the air around him, before draining the last of the water from the bottle in his still-shaking hand. He was tired, dirty and hungry. He hadn't eaten properly for weeks and had scrounged cigarettes from passers-by who clearly thought he was a vagrant, not recognising him as the infamous 'Shepherd' who had reigned over these cities for years, branching out by violently staking his claim, city by city, country by country, pushing out the product and enforcing the payments with venom. He was known for his lack of patience, and for his edict being absolute, and was well-regarded up the chain as one who always delivered. Until that day, when all the planning and all the evasion counted for nothing, and that was all that was left of the UK operation. Nothing. Bariu paced the cobbled streets on his way up to Pile Gate, the agreed rendezvous point. After nearly an hour moving from one secluded area to another, he noticed a black Range Rover with heavily tinted windows driving up to the edge of the square. There was something in the manner it was being driven that set him on edge, as though the driver were looking for something or someone. Bariu retreated into a shadowed alcove and watched as the car continued its slow cruise across the stone street. He didn't dare move and had unconsciously slowed his breathing as much as he could as though the driver would be able to hear him.

Just a few feet away, the car came to a stop. Bariu froze and tried to blend into the building he was hiding near. The engine stopped and the driver's door opened. Dushku stepped out into the late afternoon sun, dressed in a linen suit and casual shoes, his eyes masked by dark sunglasses. At well over six feet tall he was an impressive figure, his lean and muscular body not giving much indication of his 45 years, and raven black hair as full as it must have been in his younger days. He took out a pack of cigarettes from his inside jacket pocket and motioned towards where Bariu stood. "You look like an elephant in a- what is it your English friend would say… a freezer!" and a wide smile spread across his face. Even though Bariu was reasonably sure that there wasn't going to be an imminent threat to his life here, in such an historic spot, he wasn't taking any chances. He stuck to the wall and slowly moved towards his old friend and closer to the car. "We need to be somewhere," said Dushku as

Bariu was within reach, and opened a rear door for him to get in. Once he was safely inside, Dushku got into the driver's seat, started the engine and pulled away, towards the main road and to safety. The blacked-out windows were a relief to Bariu, hoping that he was completely invisible from outside, as he slid down a little farther in his seat. He was aware how dirty he was, that there was a rather unpleasant odour emitting from him and permeating the car, and he was starting to feel self-conscious for the first time in a long while. It was as though his old friend could read his thoughts via the rear-view mirror, as he offered a reassuring smile. "Don't worry. We have clothes for you and a shower, you will feel much better in no time," and Bariu began to relax a little, something he had not been able to do for months.

Back in the day those two were as close as brothers. They spent holidays together, so comfortable in each other's company, there was never a cross word said between any of them. They had both come from humble beginnings, one from the rural villages of Romania, the other Albania. Their lives became intertwined when they had met Kelmendi – Bariu had been working in Istanbul at the time, just low-level stuff for a local dealer, mainly enforcement work, making sure the supply chain understood its place and knew what the repercussions were if they stepped out of line. He'd met Dushku during a visit to a club where the owner, a lavishly-dressed man whose personality really seemed at odds to his chosen career, was being less than open about a recent shipment that had mysteriously disappeared a day after his team had received it. Bariu was there, as usual, to 'explain' to selected individuals that this wasn't the way business was conducted, and anyone who decided to become a little entrepreneurial would need to revisit the rules. He was the rules! It was Dushku's product that was missing, and there was a lot of it gone. The street value ran into the hundreds of thousands of dollars. All their transactions were in dollars - it kept things easier. But this was big news further up the chain and Dushku had been deeply concerned that things could go very badly for him if this wasn't dealt with, and fast. He had been given Bariu's name by a contact and made the call the night before. Bariu had arrived by lunchtime and was briefed of the situation, given the details of those whose indiscretions needed to be addressed and just how far Dushku was prepared for it to go. As far as Bariu felt was necessary to make the point, was the response.

Lessons learned, the evening had become a little more relaxed and the two men were about to go their separate ways, when a cavalcade of black vehicles had arrived at the club. Once they had come to a stop, Kelmendi got out of one of the middle cars. In his late fifties, he had an air of a businessman about him, well-dressed in a tailored suit, short, functional haircut given his receding hairline didn't offer many options, and subtle jewellery, nothing over the top but just enough to make the whole look work as someone affluent and professional. In any other situation he could have been a lawyer or accountant, but in that one, he was someone very different indeed.

Bariu remembered the meeting like it was yesterday. This was THE man, into everything, everywhere. Drugs were the tip of a very deep and broad iceberg and Kelmendi was right at the top. So to see him in person was extremely rare. He had layer upon layer of people between him and even some of the highest echelons of his world, so there must have been a serious reason for him to arrive that night. "So, you are the one they call The Shepherd?" he'd said to Bariu, eyes boring into him.

His whole life Bariu had been a fighter, a strong and fearless young man who wasn't afraid of anyone or anything, but the man that had stood in front of him that night was something very different. He was not only dangerous, but he was also powerful and that made for a very chilling experience. Bariu had simply nodded, rather than try to speak and let his nerves find him out. "Good, good. I have heard many stories about you and tonight, well, I wanted to see if they were true. And you have not disappointed me, young man - not at all." This had been delivered with a smile that seemed genuine, but a look in the man's eye that told of past deeds that even Bariu might have recoiled at.

While this exchange had been going on, Dushku had been keeping as quiet and inconspicuous as he could. This was his territory, his product, his business and Kelmendi would have known all that, yet there he was. It was not the time for a turf war and, if one had kicked off, there would have been little chance of Dushku making it out alive, even with Bariu. Kelmendi covered the ground between him and Dushku in three purposeful strides and was inches away from the other man's face. For many seconds he'd simply stared at him, ice in his expression through his near-black eyes. He considered his countryman and finally nodded slowly. "You may continue here," he had said, in a hoarse whisper, "but I'm taking him," motioning over his shoulder towards Bariu. He hadn't time to respond, to try to point out that they had only just met and actually had nothing to do with each other. Kelmendi's men had surrounded them both, guns had been drawn, and it was clear the conversation had come to an end.

Bariu was snapped out of his memory when the rear window of the Range Rover exploded into a thousand fragments, showering him with glass. "Qij!" shouted Dushku and snapped the car across the lanes of traffic while trying to see what had smashed the window. The bullet was lodged in the dashboard, just inches from his right arm. Another explosion of glass, this time the front windscreen, transformed into a mosaic of broken glass before Dushku pushed out a hole to see through. "What the fuck is happening?" screamed Bariu from the footwell in the back of the car. "Who is this?" It was all he could do to push words out staccato-fashion as the vehicle swung from side to side.

A screech of tyres and wild acceleration followed as the Range Rover picked up speed on a straight stretch of the road, then roared into a smaller side street with a sudden swerve that sent Bariu crashing into the door. Another huge swerve left, down a steep lane towards the coast, and Dushku was leaning on the accelerator, trying to squeeze as much power from the engine as he could. "Keep your head down!" shouted Dushku, as he forced the car through impossibly narrow gaps, losing both door mirrors in the process. "Just keep out of sight." No need to be told twice. Bariu glued himself to the floor, still covered in glass and bruises from being slammed about in the back. Dushku was glad it hadn't been raining as he gunned the car across cobbled streets, its tyres complaining at their treatment in shrieks. "When I tell you to, get out!" Dushku practically ordered him, as they rounded a bend in the road, flanked by buildings on either side. He brought the car almost to a standstill at a junction of three lanes. "NOW!"

Bariu didn't question or argue. He opened the door and leapt from the Range Rover and into the open door in front of him, and saw Dushku take off down one of the lanes. Seconds later a black Mercedes streamed past him, windows down and full of men - Kelmendi's men. An hour later, Bariu could hear a mobile phone ring. He was dazed, bleeding and bruised all over and hiding in the building he'd practically fallen into earlier. There it was again, really close. It took the third ring for him to realise the noise was coming from his pocket. He reached in and took out the phone - just some cheap type, no fancy screen, just buttons. He jabbed the green one. "Yes?"

"It's me, I'm OK, I lost them. We need to get away from here. Meet at the jetty at 2am." Dushku had lost them. He had managed to get the Mercedes so close to the back of the Range Rover that when he hit the brakes the tow bar wedged into the grille of the car behind, sticking them together. He had accelerated towards the nearest coastal road and aimed the car at the wall looming towards him at speed. At the very last second, he leapt from the vehicle and saw it smash through the wall, the Mercedes stuck to the tow bar, and both cars plummeted down to the Adriatic.

SEVEN

Jim licked the end of his right forefinger, then put his whole hand into the bag of crisps he had been noisily eating. He picked up the last of the crumbs, licked them off his dampened digit, before carefully folding the bag on its longest edge over and over until it was a thin strip of red. Then he tied it in a knot and put it in his jeans pocket. Seamus watched all this, raised an eyebrow then shook his head. "You are odd," he said. Jim smiled. "I like crisps. What can I say?"

There was no word from the lab yet but, to be fair, they hadn't had much time to really get to grips with any of it. Good as Bina and the team were, none of them were magicians. So, while they waited and Jim filled himself with ready salted crisps, the two of them did some digging on recent car thefts, those where Reg had been the offender. It was quite a list. in the past six months, Reg Wilson had helped himself to eleven cars across a small local area. Four were the same make and model, obviously easier to steal. Two were high-value cars using the owner's keys that he had stolen from the houses, and the other five were just random, it seemed - opportunistic. Jim got to work looking into the higher-value two. These may have been owned by people with a bit of clout to them, connections perhaps to unscrupulous types who may not think twice about carving up a person. A Jaguar F-Pace SUV and a Maserati Ghibli. Not cheap by any standard, but also not in Rolls Royce or Bentley leagues either. Jim was working through in his head what the level was in terms of the kind of person who could kill someone - or more likely have them killed - and the value of the car they drove. Was there a correlation there, or had he just seen too many films?

Right, Jag first, thought Jim, I wonder what the report has about the owner. He read the incident report. 52-year-old sales director - house was broken into in the early hours but nobody heard it. The keys were on the table in the hall - classic! Car was noticed missing at 6:45 when the owner looked out of the window after getting up. Vehicle contents included a set of Ping golf clubs (the report listed them all, with model numbers). Yeah right, Jim thought, I bet it was just a motley collection of old crap and he was angling for an upgrade. Must think we're all twats. Apparently the owner, a Mr Joyce, had left the clubs in the car to be prepared for an early start the following morning to play golf. Jim read on: pair of Footjoy golf shoes, Elton John Greatest Hits CD in the front - OK then! – a collection of change and the usual car detritus. Sales Director for- Jim read on. PVR Plastics. Never heard of them. Must have been doing a good job selling. Insurance checked out and a financial check on Mr Joyce didn't reveal any issues that would imply he'd organised it to make a claim - just unfortunate. Nothing here to suggest he was the kind of guy, or even knew the kind of person, that would be putting people into plastic tubs. Although, plastics, plastic tubs - he quickly looked up PVR Plastics to see what they made, but there were no tubs or anything even close on their website. Next one.

Jim really enjoyed this aspect of the job. He found people fascinating and sometimes had to really stop himself from getting a little too involved. Digging into backgrounds and finding links was great, but there had to be boundaries sometimes. This was an area that would often worry him, his ability to end up in rabbit warrens and lose the focus of the investigation a little. It would sometimes happen when he was being assessed within the job, as he wasn't really keen on that nor had been for the exams needed for each promotion he had worked so hard for. He would always feel the pang of doubt, a voice telling him that he wouldn't pass, that his efforts weren't enough and he would have to stay a PC. He'd had nightmares about it too, not just while working but at school and university too. His overriding fear that he wasn't any good, just a lanky ginger kid who wanted to be a copper - well, he was a copper-top!

Seamus's hand on his shoulder brought him back with a jolt. "Coffee?" he offered. "You look knackered - fancy a Twix as well?" Jim nodded. It had been four years ago that he and Seamus met when the latter had transferred to their station from some big city role. There wasn't much info about why, but one look at the guy when he walked into their briefing room within the first week spoke volumes. Seamus had looked weathered – yes, that was a fair description. There was something about him that suggested he had been in a pretty bad place recently, and as much as Jim thought that it was good he had an opportunity to get away from whatever it may have been, he couldn't help feeling a little aggrieved that the powers-that-be decided here was the right place. Was this station and this town so quiet and provincial that this guy could come here for an easy time? But that was before he got to know him, before he saw that Seamus was a man with unquestionable determination to get to the truth. He kept himself very much private, it was just about work for him, no small talk, no joking about, just an absolute focus on justice. His eyes belied a quiet certainty but also had a depth and intensity when he was on a case that showed he would stop at nothing.

Over the years, Jim had been able to move up into the MCU team, and it was Seamus who had been instrumental in making this happen. He'd seen something in the younger man that he admired, a sharpness and instinct that Seamus would be able to nurture, helping Jim move to the rank of DCI before he'd reached his fortieth birthday, something Jim was certain would never have been possible otherwise. The more they worked together, the more Jim could see the moments of darkness that would sometimes engulf his colleague, boss, mentor and - yes - friend. At first, he didn't pry as he really didn't feel confident in bringing up the subject and to be honest, wasn't sure how. But slowly Seamus would be more amenable and drop his guard, just enough so that Jim, using degrees of wit and intelligence, would be able to strike the right balance of each to coax out a bit at a time. What he hadn't really expected was that this worked both ways, as Seamus was the superior interrogator of the two and would easily bring the conversation around to Jim. It was clear, though, that each of them had taken and received something profound from the other, a bond that would never be broken and the knowledge that neither would hesitate to be there for the other.

It was with this in mind that Jim refocused on the task in hand. A coffee and a chocolate bar on the way, he switched to the Maserati's owner. Geoff Plank. Geoff Plank, a chartered accountant, works for one of the big firms in the city, clearly a bit of a show-off, but each to their own. Same as the Jag, Hanoi job, where the keys are stolen from the house, easier to get these cars with the keys, and hang on… yup, table in the hallway. Will these people ever learn? Geoff lives in Allerton Crescent, nice part of town that, big houses. Where was our Mr Joyce? OK, Priors Lane, miles away – no connection there then. Financial check shows he is- bugger me, massively in debt. What a shit accountant, thought Jim – I wouldn't trust him with my money, if I actually had any, that is. Let's have a dig about here. Jim spent some time looking over the financial checks. This guy was properly in the shit, debts coming out of his arse. He leaned back in the chair when Seamus came back bearing coffee and chocolate bars. No crisps, Jim noticed. "Guv, have a look at this – did you see this at the time?" Jim didn't call Seamus Guv very often, and Seamus noticed his use of the word and recognised he was 'in the zone'. "What's up?" he asked his DI. "The accountant - sorry, Chartered Accountant, that had the Maserati stolen, was past his balls in debt. Isn't that a major issue for Chartered Accountants? Don't they have to declare it?" "No, only if they have to take formal steps to deal with it," Seamus replied. "IVA, bankruptcy, that kind of thing, has to be declared to the ICAEW." Jim nodded sagely, giving a reasonable impression of someone that understood what they had just heard. "Individual Voluntary Agreement" said Seamus, not missing the subtle look on Jim's face "and Institute of Chartered Accountants for England and Wales." Jim smiled. "Am I that obvious?" he asked. "Maybe" said Seamus, with a grin. Jim dug a little deeper into Mr Geoff Plank. Where does his money go, how long has this been a problem, when did he get the car, when did he insure it and with whom? Are they any other things that look or feel out of place with him?

Hours seemed to pass in seconds, but Jim - even with the support of caffeine and chocolate - couldn't find anything that would constitute grounds for a visit. He did delve into his finances a little more though. An accountant who can't manage money, there must be something in that. But there really wasn't. No massive gambling addiction, no £1,000-a-day cocaine habit - just living way outside his means, and would no doubt be going for bankruptcy or similar. Jim was disheartened to some extent, although also a little relieved that he wasn't going to be face-to-face with someone who was OK to cut up a body. Not yet, anyway. "It's not these two," said Jim despondently. "What's next price-wise on the list of cars?"

The rest of the evening was spent looking over incident reports from the stolen cars, and every single one went nowhere. "Go home, Jim," Seamus called across the office. "No need for us both to be here this late." Jim nodded, but didn't feel it. The answer must be staring him in the face, but he just couldn't see it. Maybe he'd been staring too long at this, and he just needed some sleep and to come back fresh in the morning – and then it would most likely just appear there on the pages. Or maybe not.

"Aren't you getting a bit old for bedtime stories?" Adrian asked, when Sam presented him with a book to read. "Not when you're reading them, Daddy. I like the way you make everyone sound." It was true, thought Adrian - he was good at accents and giving voices to characters, and he really enjoyed reading the stories. This was a good one, as well. It was fortuitous timing actually, as Adrian needed to calm down after a particularly stressful day. He had been installing some equipment at Police HQ, and couldn't help overhearing some of the discussion at the custody desk which was right next to where he was working. Three people in a row had been brought in, petty thefts, driving whilst banned and drug offences – all had been there less than a week ago, all were familiar to the officers that brought them in, and one was almost on first-name terms with the custody sergeant.

He was so wound up by the end of the day that he drove a few miles further than necessary on the way home, just to try to shake it off. He was aware that these things were really getting to him, these little shits with no respect for anyone, wasting the police's time with their pathetic behaviour. He tried once more to put it out of his mind and concentrate on the story, but it just kept bubbling up to the surface. It wasn't long before Sam realised that his dad's heart just wasn't in it. "What's up, Daddy, why do you look so cross?" His innocent face looked at his father from his Paw Patrol duvet. "It's nothing, sweetheart - just some people out there can be really unpleasant, I saw a few very rude and inconsiderate people this afternoon and they have made me a bit angry. Let's carry on with the book, shall we?"

He could feel the frustration still, hearing these ignorant little pricks just goading the police, and the officers powerless to take what he felt was appropriate action. You couldn't just cuff them to a pole and leave them to think about it, no chance of a night stick to the balls either - just had to play the game and then wait for the CPS to decide that even with bodycam footage, car cams, fingerprints and a breath test, there was still 'insufficient evidence' and off they went again.

By the time Sam had fallen asleep and the rest of the family were in bed, Adrian couldn't relax. Surely there must be a better way to deal with these folks. There had to be something that could be done to get them to stop once and for all. Prison clearly wasn't the deterrent it was supposed to be - most of these kids came out with more nefarious skills than they went in with, longer-term visits and they had a better degree than he did, for Christ's sake. The punishment should fit the crime, he understood that, but when the crime is committed again and again by the same person, the punishment surely needs to align to that too, right? What about their victims, what about the impact on them, never mind protecting the rights of these arseholes, what about the rights of those whose houses had been broken into, whose security had been breached, their confidence shattered – what about them?

He finally fell into a fitful sleep, allowing his subconscious mind to carry on where he had left off, formulating a plan to help redress the balance.

EIGHT

Seamus felt his phone vibrate in his pocket and fumbled it out to check who was calling and whether he wanted to answer it. The lab's number was on the screen, so he decided he would. "Corrigan," he announced, and listened to the caller as the latest news came to him. It seems Reg had been alive when he was cut up, according to the results of their tests - the wounds were ante-mortem. The first thought Seamus had was how much of a mess that would have made - it would have left a lot of blood behind and perhaps a scene that would be hard to cover up. His next thought was about the ink, so he asked Henry, Bina's second in command, if the ink aging test results were back. "Oh, yes- give me a sec," and Seamus heard what sounded like the handset being placed on the bench and Henry whistling to himself as he went to fetch the report. Swabs of the ink used to leave a cryptic message had been taken and analysed, to see if the writing had been done at or around the same time as the body parts had been put into the plastic box it was written on.

The whistling got a little louder, then stopped as Henry picked up the phone again. "Let's see," he continued and sucked air over his bottom teeth. Seamus hated it when people did that - it just seemed to him to make what they would say next a bit disingenuous.

"CCA suggests it was a Sharpie, black ink and applied approximately 13 months ago, so unless our man has been frozen a while - and he hasn't - then those marks were already on the lid." Hmmm, that blew one theory out of the window, thought Seamus. "Are you absolutely sure that's what the chemical composition analysis says?" he asked and immediately felt bad for having done so. He hated it if someone questioned his experience and judgement, yet he'd just done it to Henry. "Sorry," he said quickly. "I mean, how certain are the results?" Henry audibly shrugged away the accidental insult. "Don't worry. Yes, the test is a very good one and the results are in the 90% range, so the events are not connected. Sorry if that's not what you needed to hear."

"Right, so we have someone chopping folks up, slinging them in old plastic boxes and leaving them at farms, and a bunch of recently stolen vehicles, none of which were owned by anyone remotely dangerous," said Detective Superintendent Bowler, when Seamus briefed her later. "I was kind of hoping for something local, and easy to wrap up, but now it's seeping out of our fingers. I can feel this turning messy," she said, looking Seamus in the eye. "I think it's time we brought in the press. I really don't do it to cause hysteria, but I think it's unavoidable," Bowler continued. "Maybe we can flush the sicko out if their handiwork is all over the TV." Seamus gave a thoughtful nod. "Certainly worth a try," he agreed.

The drawbacks to this approach were manifold, the first of which was having to speak to the press in the first place. Not his favourite part of the job. Seamus would much rather leave it to Bowler and the press office and stay out there getting actual work done, but he knew it was a necessary part of the process, so went to get himself prepared. On his way along the corridor something occurred to him - this would be an excellent opportunity for Jim to get some more experience in this area - so he made a slight detour and presented Jim with the good news. "Can't we draw straws or something?" Jim protested. "It's not that I'm not grateful, but I really don't need to get too much more experience, you know - too much of a good thing and all that." Seamus just smiled. "It will be great, you'll be great – just make sure you write down what you need to say, that way you won't waffle on and repeat yourself."

If Jim wasn't nervous about doing a press briefing before, he was now. "I don't waffle on, do I?" His question went unanswered, as Seamus had already disappeared and was halfway to his car. Bina was excellent as always, making sure he had what was needed for the conference. She had called Jim as soon as she was advised there would be a press update, made sure he had the salient facts at his disposal and said that she would be more than happy to accompany him - that is, if he wanted her to.

Jim had been single for a long time. His last relationship had faded away as she had become tired of his late nights and lack of attention, so she had eventually sought it elsewhere. He wasn't one for clubs, despite the comments that he'd love to go to them and party all night - the reality was somewhat different. The truth was, he didn't like crowds much, or music that was so loud that you had no chance of actually having a conversation with someone - and, well, he'd never pulled in a bar or club in his life. When it came down to it, Jim was pretty hopeless with relationships. He had no idea if he was being flirted at, or was it 'with' – just goes to show. His job made things even more complicated: not just the uncertain hours, the weekends that the odd case may have needed, but that he cared so much about it, he really had nothing much else to talk about. So if he was fortunate enough to find someone that wasn't ashamed to date a ginger bloke, the next hurdle was work. He was also rubbish at small talk, so much so that at family gatherings he would usually be the one in the room by himself, while others around him wittered on about any old crap. He met someone through a mutual friend some months back but the second date didn't happen. Jim had run through that first date a lot, analysing what he'd said and trying to determine what point in the evening it had gone wrong, but just put it down to his inability to get past his nerves, staring at his feet like he was back in the playground.

As Bina watched Jim get himself ready she couldn't help but admire him. She saw a dedicated, kind, considerate and sensitive man who was humble enough to still be self-conscious at times like this, and certainly worth some attention. Not to mention he had such a beautiful smile.

NINE

Adrian walked into the office that morning with the remnants of the previous night's thoughts still processing through his mind. So many offenders just doing the same thing, week in, week out – the penal system doing nothing to dissuade them from their relentless endeavours either. Those that get awarded a longer stay got some courses to do, nice opportunities to work out and some extra-curricular learning from some of the other 'guests' on better ways to carry out more reprehensible deeds, and maybe get away with them for a little longer. Let's face it, they're not going to suddenly decide to get a job in accounting or marketing, not when this is so much fun and they get free B&B every now and then. He'd been working on a little side project for a while now and felt that today was the day it needed to be implemented. Working within the police headquarters as a civilian IT contractor had been very enlightening for the past few years, seeing the comings and goings and helping some of the officers deal with issues on the system the company he had been working for had installed some time back. He'd since gone freelance to provide force-wide support since the company hadn't really developed their business model that far out.

Over the last year specifically he had been getting closer to how the data was used in the system, initially to provide better support should there be an issue, but as the months progressed his side project began to take shape in his mind. He could create something that would 'harvest' information on offenders, something that matched specific criteria. To get things started, he had talked with a number of officers about adding functionality to the system, for more focused searches to categorise offenders based on a series of conditions – such as how many arrests, similar crime patterns, locations, so they could create reports on these specifics should they need them; He did. The extra functions were added under the guise of business requirements, and even better, he'd been paid to add them. What his customer didn't know was that he had also created a route for him to access the system with different credentials. He already had remote access, so he could provide support from home if needed, but now he could connect as though he were in the HQ and have the same level of access as a senior officer, with a legitimate login ID as well.

Today was the day he decided to test it out. He connected to the system in the same way he always did, checked the log files from overnight, made sure there were no major issues to deal with, had a quick look over system messages and database logs – everything looked fine. Now he needed to get hold of one of the spare laptops that he had been using for testing and log in as his new user. It worked - so far, so good. On to the other PC now to check that the login couldn't be seen on the logs. Excellent, nothing there. Back to the laptop to do some searches – select offence – car theft. Select from offender list - the list on the screen showed the names of each person charged in the last twelve months for car theft, with the number of times they had appeared in custody next to their name. Adrian scrolled through the list until he found a few in double figures, then clicked on one.

James Miller, 23, car theft x 12, address 45B Winston Close, Penhill. There was a very clear photo of him too, and he was pretty easy to spot. Adrian took out his phone and took a picture of the screen, which was a lot less hassle than printing it. He checked how far that was from where he lived: about 15 miles and maybe 30 minutes in the car. He looked up a few more names, and took screenshots of each, making sure he could clearly see addresses and photos. It was very important that he knew where they lived and what they looked like, because he needed to be certain he was going to get hold of the right people. All he had to do now was work out what to do with this information.

Within an hour Adrian had a file of over 20 people, all repeat offenders, all costing the police money as they were so prolific, all of them clearly remorseless of the pain and suffering they caused their victims. It was definitely time that they learned something other than the soft arm of the law. Adrian spent the next few evenings at home looking over adverts on Facebook Marketplace and Gumtree for vans. He really wanted a black one with a sliding door and preferably no bulkhead between the front and back. It was looking like it would have to be a white one, but he was patient and not in any great hurry, so kept the search going, careful to delete his browsing history each time, just before closing his laptop. Over the past week he had taken a detour from the various locations he had been working at on his way home to prepare the other part of his plan. An old farm on the outskirts of town had caught his eye some months back - there were some old outbuildings and no house, no CCTV and no sign that anyone lived there or even worked there. It was perfect, remote enough that nobody would hear anything, close enough to not be obvious when a visit may be needed. Over a series of evenings and afternoons, Adrian had stopped in the main yard and waited to see if anyone would turn up, but nobody did. This was the place he had decided on his last visit. On one of the visits he had noticed a large pit that had been covered in tarpaulin to start with, but he had moved some out of the way to peer underneath. It must have been an old slurry pit or a hole dug out for such a purpose – about 20 feet deep and almost concave, like it had been dug so that nothing could get out. It was exactly what he had imagined – deep enough so it was practically impossible to climb out of. It was time to pay Mr Miller a visit.

TEN

"Well, like I told that woman a week back, the old boy that runs the fabric stall with the shoes and clothes like, he has all these new lads working the stalls for him. Nice lads mind, but they don't speak much English – makes it hard for the punters you know, they can't understand a bloody word each other are saying, but they get by, like. "Well, I got sort of talking to one of them just casual like, you know, where you from, been here long, that kind of bollocks, and he was telling me something about a load of them living in one room in old town, not getting paid or nothing, just having to work all hours, not just on the stalls either, doing all sorts. Then the gaffer starts walking over, and this lad turned whiter than a sheet and just stared, terrified like and stopped talking. The old boy says something to him in foreign, no idea what but the lad buggered off pretty sharpish, like."

"What did the 'gaffer' look like?" Jim asked, leaning across the desk. "Let me see. He was tall, like you chaps, slim and had black hair, well-dressed, like. He turned up in some fancy black car and got out the back, which I thought was a bit odd, like." Seamus opened his laptop that he took everywhere, and after a few clicks of the mouse and some typing, he turned the device round so Mr Elliott could see the screen, on which were six mugshots of people associated with Kelmendi. "Mr Elliott, do you recognise any of these people?" he asked, hoping the answer would be a firm no. "Yeah, those two are always hanging around, and that one there, he's the chap with the posh car," exclaimed Mr Elliott, with as much excitement as though he was going to crack the case on his own. Seamus took a minute to process what he'd just heard, and looked across the table at Jim, eyebrow slightly raised. "Thank you, Mr Elliott, that was very helpful". The other man grinned. "Just call me Bill, everyone does– like that bloke in the film. You know, the dancer." Jim's turn to raise an eyebrow now, as he looked over and the penny dropped. "Right, Billy Elliott – I see. Well, erm… Bill, you've been really helpful. If you would be kind enough to read over what we've captured from this conversation, and if you're happy with it, could you just sign the bottom of the page?" Jim flicked a look at Seamus, who by now was typing into his laptop and frowning. "Yep, all looks in order, like," exclaimed Bill, signing his name with a flourish at the bottom of the statement. "John, will you see Mr E… I mean, Bill, to reception and sign him out, please?" asked Jim to the sergeant. As soon as the room was clear Jim sat opposite Seamus, who raised his eyes from the screen.

"Fuck me, this is on our doorstep," Jim said, a look of genuine concern across his face. "Right here, people being trafficked and used as slaves." "Steady on, Jim," warned Seamus. "We don't know that for certain yet – although that statement does go a long way to substantiate some of the hearsay and other feedback we've had from the markets at least. We need to be really sure before taking this up a level, as it could turn into a major operation."

"Who were the folks on the laptop then? As soon as Wild Bill there ID'd them you looked like you'd seen a ghost." There was an air of inquisition in Jim's voice, as though he felt Seamus was holding out on him, and he looked worried. Seamus looked worried too. He knew that this was heading towards something significant and also knew the calibre of people that manage this sort of thing, very dangerous people who don't care who gets in their way. He wasn't sure he really wanted to go down that path again. "What's the latest from Bina on Reg?" Seamus asked. It had been a while since the last report and they weren't getting any closer to a suspect.

The press conference had done the job of flushing out the usual weirdos claiming to have been the murderer, or blaming it on a cheating ex. No leads at all and frankly Seamus really wasn't expecting any. This was not your run-of-the-mill murder, and he needed some time to process this revelation. He could do without Jim asking him things he really wasn't sure he wanted to answer. Jim's face lit up, which Seamus noticed and would usually have made a joke about it being a sick person who was that excited to go to the morgue. But he knew - well certainly hoped - that something was warming up between Jim and Bina, so he just nodded as Jim stood up to leave. "Ring me if there's anything interesting," he said instead and turned his attention back to his laptop.

It had been some time since Seamus had opened the file on Kelmendi, but the conversation with Bill had got him thinking. The guy is into everything so it's possible. The file was expansive, as was the reach of the man and his empire. As Seamus already knew he controlled most of the serious drug markets across Europe and had become a key player in providing weapons to the highest bidders. Seamus had his suspicions about Kelmendi's involvement with people trafficking, he was never able to prove it. Maybe this was that opportunity, but there was no way he was going near him by himself. It was time to make a few calls. "Jim's in reception, Bina," called Roger from the other side of the room, and despite herself she could feel the colour making its way up to her cheeks and the heat start to build. Get a grip, woman she ordered herself as she walked, as calmly as she could manage, towards reception. He was sat on one of the sofas, dressed in faded jeans and one of his floral shirts, slightly unshaven as always and deep in concentration on something on his phone.

The stark light of the lab offices made both look much paler than they were, as Bina moved over to the computer monitor to pull up the notes on Reg to give Jim an update. "To be honest, Jim, we're not much further forward than we were the other day, except…" and she trailed off a bit while scanning the screen. "This!" she announced. Jim went over to where she stood and looked at what she was pointing at on the screen. "The striations we can see here," Bina pointed at some marks on the x-ray images on the screen, "show that the cuts were made by something flat and v-shaped, so not a saw as that would leave more of a 'u' shape on the bone. This was very sharp as there was no evidence of multiple attempts, just what appears to be a single strike on each removed limb." Jim stroked his chin thoughtfully while looking at the images on the screen. "What are you thinking - an axe or something like that?" he finally asked. "Something like that," agreed Bina, and went on. "It's not a traditional shape for an axe we would think of, the head of those widens out quite quickly, so the wound and the bone would have signs of almost being cleaved apart. This is much narrower, neater even, than that." "A sword?" said Jim, sort of thinking out loud while looking at the images with his head tilted to see the angle and shape of the marks more clearly. "It's unlikely," said Bina kindly, "mostly because a sword may well be a thinner blade. "We're somewhere in the middle – I know that really isn't helpful, but like I said, we haven't got much further."

She looked apologetically at Jim, her dark eyes locked with his blue eyes where they both lingered for a few seconds before she looked back at the screen, tapped a few keys and brought up another image. "Have a look at this," she said, and moved slightly to the side so Jim could get a better view of the screen. "What am I looking at?" he asked, squinting slightly at the image. "This is the base of his skull, there are clear signs of blunt force trauma here," and she pointed at part of the screen where, once she had said it, Jim could clearly see the cracks consistent with such an injury. "Our current theory is that Reg was incapacitated by this blow to the back of the head, and the rest of this was done while he was on the ground and, hopefully, unconscious." Jim remembered the earlier report info stating that the evidence supported Reg having been dismembered ante-mortem. "So he gets knocked out, or at least down with this initial blow, assumingly to make it easier to do the rest of the work without him trying to run off, and then-" Now it was Jim's turn to trail off. Bina nodded. "That's our theory. He gets hit by something blunt with enough force to stop him moving and that also explains why there are no defensive injuries against whatever was used to execute him." Jim looked at her with a frown. "Say that again," he said quietly, with a questioning tone in his voice. "Which bit, knocked down, no defensive wounds?" Bina offered. "No – 'used to execute him,'" said Jim slowly and thoughtfully and pulled his phone out of his pocket. A few seconds later he turned the screen to Bina, and she found herself looking at a potential weapon. An executioner's axe.

Seamus sat in the seat opposite DCI Bowler while she read his update, her frown deepening with every word. She finally sat down, put the report onto her desk and picked up her now tepid coffee, took a slug and winced. "I have no idea how people can drink cold coffee, it's disgusting." "So, what are your instincts on this, Seamus?" she asked, locking her eyes on his, to try to understand his non-verbal cues. She was very aware of his history and the mental scars it had clearly left behind, but also knew that it had provided him with experience with these sorts of people - experience that not many had. "Well," said Seamus slowly, as he formulated his response in his head before letting anything out. "It certainly opens up the issues around the market trader's comments, and when we interviewed Mr Elliott, he was pretty convinced these guys were being taken advantage of. But it's still a bit of a leap from there to trafficking people and slavery, although…" and he trailed off. "Although what?" asked Bowler. "Although Bill identified three of Kelmendi's group from the photos I showed him, so it makes a clear connection between him and these guys on the market. And, thinking aloud, it is a reasonable front – get them over here, give them somewhere to live, albeit in a single room, but they're not being charged rent, make them work to get more control over them, and then – dunno, move them onto something bigger?" Seamus rubbed a few days' worth of stubble as he considered the wider implications of this.

Kelmendi was dangerous but was too far up the chain to be attending a market in person, so he had sent one of the area reps, as Seamus referred to them. Jozef Bardhi was probably third in command, and the intelligence on him suggested he was adept at handling difficult situations on Kelmendi's behalf. Interpol were very aware of his 'skillset', if you could call it that, but had yet to gather enough evidence to arrest him. He was the one Bill had identified as getting out of the car, a black Range Rover. The other two, Parli Morina and Vasil Abrashi, were foot soldiers, making sure those on the ground did as they were told and reporting back up the food chain. Either were capable of extreme violence, but neither had been linked to anything here in the UK but again were prevalent on the Interpol watch list. It was too much of a coincidence, even though Seamus didn't believe in them. "Guv, this is potentially huge, and as Jim said earlier when we finished the interview, it's on our doorstep. These guys know that place backwards, so putting someone into the market to watch would be too obvious, we would need to come up with something much more subtle".

Bowler looked over at him. "You read my mind," she said with a thin smile. "So, how subtle and what though? This lot are probably everywhere, so if they are that aware of the area, any change is likely to be reported and – well, who knows what may happen?" It was her turn to rub her face in thought, and her hand moved up to her temples and she began to absentmindedly massage them.

After a few seconds, she looked up at Seamus. "Right, come on – I need a proper coffee, and we need some fresh air." She grabbed her car keys off the desk and stood up, gesturing to the door, Seamus almost tripping over his chair in his haste to have a coffee bought by the boss.

ELEVEN

Bariu sat leaning against the wall, still shaking from the events of the last hour. There really was nowhere to hide, Kelmendi had warned him and came good on his promise. Dushku had managed to help him escape this time, but how many more times would there be? How many ways are there to escape death? Bariu had delivered death to many people, his being the last face they saw, and he had done so under the orders of his paymaster. His conscience was beginning to catch up with him as he sat there, bruised and bleeding and, yes - scared. He was pulled from his reverie by the phone in his pocket and its shrill ring. He fumbled it out with cold hands and stabbed at the button. "Yes?" he almost whispered, looking around furtively to check if he was alone. "Don't worry, nobody but me has this number," came Dushku's reassuring voice. Bariu relaxed a little, hearing his friend's voice. "Now listen, we need to get you away from here, somewhere he won't be looking for you. Are you able to get to the jetty like we said?" Bariu looked around again before answering. "Yes, yes – I can get there, but where can I go? He is everywhere." "Leave that to me," said Dushku. "Just make sure you get to the jetty for 2am." The line went dead. Bariu looked down at his tattered and bloodstained clothes. There was no way he would be able to be inconspicuous looking like this, so he needed to choose his route carefully. Dushku called the other number on his phone. "I said make it LOOK convincing, you didn't have to do that – those cars are expensive," barked Jozef. "I had to make it realistic - that's what he said," replied Dushku. "And he will be at the meeting point for 2am. You can pay me on collection." "Fine, just try not to damage anything else, he wants him alive so he can kill him himself." Jozef ended the call and Dushku let out a long breath and shook his head. I hope you know who you are dealing with, he said to himself.

If Bariu had learned anything in all the years he had been doing this, it was to never trust another living soul. He slowly got up and considered his route to the jetty. There was plenty of time until 2am, yet there was much to do. Maybe it would just be Dushku, maybe he really was trying to help, but there was always a niggling doubt. Call it an occupational hazard. The jetty was overlooked by many buildings, and any one of these could hide a sniper, too many options for lookout posts, minimising where he would be able to move unseen. Bariu thought about the location of the meet, which was clever – public, yet plenty of places for a decent ambush. He could be jumped on from any number of side-streets on the way there, and even if he made it to the jetty he was a sitting duck. This must be a setup, it would be if he were orchestrating it - so why not? He needed a car. There was no chance of him making the journey without one, and it would also keep him disguised for a little longer, while he scoped out the overall location. Some skills never leave you, he thought as he drove the borrowed car towards the coast, taking in as much detail as he could. He skirted the town first, checking side streets and making mental notes of where the taller buildings were in relation to the jetty. Where would make a good place to take aim from? Two more circuits of the main routes leading to and from the water, out towards the road from the highway. 00:43.

The jetty had been a landing stage for many years, used by Kelmendi's men to bring product onshore, as well as removing unwanted debris. He had been here many times before, so was well aware of how the cars would get there - but more importantly, where certain things were stored. Moments later he stopped outside a plain house on a nondescript road on the edge of the town, and slowly and painfully got out of the car. The house was an investment he had made years back, when he was in and out of the area regularly, and needed somewhere he could go when he needed to be alone. He had never taken anyone there, never mentioned it, and always made certain that he was not followed when going to the house.

The key was exactly where he had left it on his last visit, and with a furtive glance around him, he slid it into the lock and opened the door. Aside from the musty odour, it was exactly how he remembered. Sparse furnishings in each room, shutters at the windows, paint peeling from every surface. He was home. Hobbling up the stairs, he felt safer than he had for months. There was nothing he had seen in the quick search of the rooms that was out of place, no sign that anyone had been here, other than him. He made it to the bedroom and lowered himself onto the old mattrass, which creaked in response. The room was dark and empty except for the bed and a small table. Wallpaper peeled away revealing tired plaster, cracked over time and with the humidity outside. Bariu leant forward, his elbows on his knees, let out a long sigh and closed his eyes. He knew the next few hours would decide his fate and he would have to bring all his skills and experience to the fore. To do that, he needed some rest. 01:07.

Years of conditioning meant he knew when to wake, and twenty minutes had done the trick, and it was all he was going to get for now. Time to go to work. In the bathroom, there was a tall cupboard in the corner. Bariu opened the door, then slid the rear panel away to reveal an armoury. He pulled out a backpack, and began to load it with clips of ammunition, two Sig Sauer pistols and a box of hollow-point bullets. He closed the bag and slung it over his shoulder, then reached into the cupboard and removed a large, narrow black case. Walking into the bedroom, he placed the case onto the bed and opened it. Inside was a high-powered sniper rifle, one he had used many times before in the service of the man who was now hunting him. He took it out, inspected it end-to-end and made sure it was clean and clear of any dust and reassembled it. Then he checked the ammo, 20mm calibre rounds that could bring an elephant down. Everything seems to be in order. It was time to go and see what, or rather who Dushku had brought with him. 01:31.

"Check all the alleys again, I don't want him suddenly appearing, you know who he is, right?" Dushku was on the phone, making sure the six people Jozef had sent along were positioned well, and would be able to disable Bariu on sight. He knew very well how dangerous the man was, why he had been called 'The Shepherd', and also how indebted he had been to him, many years back. But there was no time for sentimentality now. His family was at risk if he didn't bring him in, and he had no desire to end up like that English guy.

Bariu could spot them a mile off. He was just under a mile from the jetty using his sniper scope to assess the situation before deciding his next move. The rifle was loaded, cocked and ready with the ten-inch suppressor attached - a bit of extra distance on the shot, and a bit less noise too. He spotted Petric first, sauntering the way he always did, hands in his pocket with the arrogant air he had about him, like he was some hot shot hitman, and untouchable. It was clear there would be a party waiting for him at the jetty, so it was time to thin out the numbers a little. 01:49.

The shot couldn't be heard from the street, but the impact was obvious. Petric's head exploded like a ripe melon being struck by a sledgehammer. He dropped where he had been standing, a lifeless husk. Casper was next to come into view. His stupid white shoes, why did he always have to wear them? Bariu leaned back to stabilise himself as he took aim, the young man in his sight making it very clear he was armed and was not to be approached. He waited until he had stopped at the end of the alley he had been walking along and stooped into a deep porch to light a cigarette. Casper didn't have a chance to put the cigarette to his lips before Bariu's bullet tore through him. Four left. 01:53.

Lukaj and Niziri were side by side, smoking and goading each other by the look of things. They always seemed to have to have some kind of competition of who could inflict the most damage on someone, while keeping them alive. Kids! Still fooling around, Niziri pointed at Lukaj's feet. Bariu watched Lukaj bend down and took the opportunity to remove Niziri from the equation, and when Lukaj stood up again, just as he picked his phone from his pocket, he too joined his friend. 01:56.

Time to get a little closer and make a call. Bariu called Dushku on the phone he had been given, and made a concerted effort to sound as uncomfortable and in pain as he could. "I'm nearly there, please wait for me. My leg has been hurt a lot and it's hard to walk," he croaked down the phone. It seemed to have the desired effect. "Don't rush, take the time you need, we have to make sure you are safe, my friend - then we can get out of here." Dushku ended the call and took a deep breath, nodded and smiled. His quarry was on the way, injured and helpless.

At the bottom of the hill, Bariu spotted Gorja waiting by a car and talking to the driver. He had a pistol in his hand, another in a holster strapped under his left arm. Looking across the street Bariu could see the driver more clearly too. Shehu - what the hell was he doing here? He was just a kid, he was the guy they used to tease about his lack of a beard. FUCK!!!! Gorja was easy, he was an arsehole, everyone hated him and it was a surprise he hadn't been killed long before now. But Shehu – why did he have to be here? There was no way he could let him go, Jozef, Dushku or even Kelmendi would kill him on the spot for being a failure. It had to be done now. Bariu got into a car down the road, took out one of the pistols, attached a silencer, then got the car started. He put the auto gearbox into drive, used his scarf to keep the steering wheel steady, and climbed into the back seat.

As the car moved slowly along the road, he opened the back window. The two men were still talking when the car started to close in on them, Gorja looked over and pulled his gun up a little, more as a show of dominance than aiming at anything. The two shots from the back were almost silent, each hitting their mark and dropping the target. Gorja fell to the floor, and Shehu slumped sideways into the passenger seat.

02:02.

Dushku looked impatient by the time Bariu arrived. He had parked the car a street away, ready for if he needed it, and walked the last few metres to emphasise his limp. The men greeted each other like old friends, a weary traveller being welcomed by a hotelier could have been the scene. But not this morning on the jetty.

Bariu took a step back and assessed the man in front of him, his head slightly to one side. "What is it, old friend?" Dushku said, with a strained smile. But his eyes gave him away. Even though he must have been trying hard to keep any emotion at bay, Bariu saw it, for the fleeting moment before Dushku could control it. Pure fear.

TWELVE

The van moved slowly along the residential streets, the driver clearly looking for something, or someone. It had gone past Winston Close three times, but nobody had noticed. There was always some van or other around here. Adrian saw him walking along Penhill Road from the chip shop, bundle of paper in his hand, feeding chips into himself like they were about to be stolen at any moment. His heart quickened and sweat started to appear on his forehead – there he is, Miller, in the flesh. He stopped the van just metres ahead, and climbed into the back, pulling the balaclava he had brought over his head and putting gloves on. He grabbed a baseball bat and as quietly as he could he slid open the side door of the van.

James had no chance to react, Adrian rounded on him from behind and with a decisive blow, had knocked him out cold. He put a hessian sack over his head and used thick cable ties to bind his hands and feet. He did not need him getting mobile during the journey. Adrian's hands were shaking when he got back into the driver's seat and started the engine. He had him, he had James bloody tricksy little tosser Miller in the back of his van. He kept an eye on his speed and stuck to the route he had memorised - no obvious traffic cameras to be seen, or more importantly to be seen by. After fifteen minutes he arrived at the site of the old farm on Manor Hill, turned off the lights and drove towards the old slurry pit. It was better than he remembered: deep enough to be as good as impossible to climb out of, but not too deep to cause death by falling in.

With James unconscious there was a good chance that he wouldn't be too badly hurt on landing as he wouldn't tense up. Adrian hauled his first student out of the back of the van. "Today, you will learn that your lifestyle has consequences, and this is the last time you waste police time or hurt another person." Somewhat unceremoniously Adrian pushed James over the lip of the pit and heard a dull thud as he landed. He waited for a few minutes and heard a faint cry. "What the fuck is going on? - where am I?" There was an edge to the voice, but Adrian was pleased that the lad was awake, so got into the van and drove off. By the time he reached home, Adrian had collected a takeaway. He breezed through the front door, a little more than his usual happy self.

Jim kicked away a stone from the path in front of him as he walked back towards his car, two coffees in hand and a bag of pastries under his arm. Seamus had called him in early to go over some of the details of Bill's update the previous day, and he had sounded like he really needed some help. The conversation with Bowler had managed to get them both concerned. The potential of where this could lead was pretty terrifying, and neither really wanted to accept that bit was happening. Bowler had had to summarise it for her superiors, and Seamus had to work out how to brief the rest of the team without causing mass panic. This kind of thing just didn't happen around here. On arrival at the office Jim struggled with the door until one of the uniformed sergeants came to assist. "Cheers mate," said Jim, and gave him a sincere smile. He made it to the office where Seamus was waiting, the rest of the team already assembled and looking somewhat bemused and expectant at the same time.

"Take a seat, Jim," said Seamus as Jim hovered at the door. As he passed, he handed his boss a coffee and pulled up a chair.

"Right, everyone is here, so let's get started," said Seamus, looking at the faces of his team and ordering his thoughts. It didn't matter how many times he did team briefings, he was never comfortable standing in front of everyone like this and today was no exception. "Some of you may be aware of the investigation into concerns raised at the market, that there may be illegal immigrants working there. Well, Jim and I met with the prime informant yesterday and in the course of the interview he identified a number of members of an international OCG involved in drugs, weapons and now, it seems, people-trafficking too. If what Mr Elliott has told us is true, and we have no reason to doubt him, then we could be dealing with some extremely dangerous people in our area, so this morning we need to make sure we all know what we could be facing." Seamus sat on the edge of the nearest desk, looking less than positive and nodded to Phil Graham, a representative from the Met, who had been seconded to his team.

Phil walked to the front of the room with a huge folder under his arm and stopped at the desk next to the one Seamus was perched on. He cleared his throat and set the folder down. He opened a small bag he had in his other hand and took out some small colourful magnets. As he took a page out of the folder, he attached it to the wall board with a magnet, and in no time had created quite the collage of faces. Once he had put the last page up, he turned and addressed the room. "These people," he began, his voice wavering a little in the limelight he wasn't used to, "are all part of a known Organised Crime Group, well-known across Europe for drug trafficking in large quantities, involved in arms trafficking too. A pretty nasty and very well connected OGC, lots of fingers in lots of legitimate pies keeping the bulk of their money clean and keeping them a step away from us and Interpol for years."

Phil took a sip of water from a bottle Jim brought over for him and nodded his thanks. "The guy here" Phil pointed at a good-looking man, late thirties and olive-skinned. "This is Jozef, he is the guy on the ground, the link between many of the interests they manage and the guy in charge of it all. He is ex-military and tough as they come, takes no prisoners and seems to have a death toll as long as your arm. He is also a formidable business mind, managing the operations day to day. Once in a Thai prison but fought his way out and is by no means to be underestimated."

Another swig of water and a deep breath. "This is Niziri Kroitz, a weapon on legs – background data on him is limited, but he appears to have worked his way up the ranks, dealing with any obstacles put in front of him. He was last seen in Romania, leading out a group of local top-tier dealers who decided to try to renegotiate their rates. None of them were ever seen again. Over here-" Phil trailed off when he pointed at Lukaj. He hesitated and drew in a long breath and let it out slowly. "Lukaj Bedri came to our attention a few years ago, but wasn't anything to do with this group at the time. He has since been recruited as negotiator, by which we mean he was sent in to get the answers the boss is expecting, by any means necessary. Because of this, he seems to have elevated status in the OCG and this has afforded him a degree of protection. He can be seen swaggering about one of the many clubs the group owns, and is a flashy bastard, but slippery as an eel. He is responsible for the death of four of our colleagues from the Flying Squad two years ago, so there is a special reason for us to find him."

Seamus stood up, partly to give Phil a rest but also as his backside was going numb. He took a spot next to Phil. "These three are important for us to focus on first, as they were the ones identified by Mr Elliott yesterday." "What we need to do is keep our eyes peeled but maintain a safe distance. I don't want anyone getting caught up with these people directly, as there may be repercussions that none of us want. Let me reiterate, these are extremely dangerous and very well-connected people who could have you followed, they could have your family followed. It really doesn't bear thinking about."

Phil stood and watched Seamus as he delivered this message and saw the fear creep up within him - not fear of the unknown but that which can only come from experiencing this kind of terror first-hand. Seamus had been a target because of his links to Bariu, and having been running the investigation that created the bulk of the file on the desk in front of them both. What Phil knew was the private impact this had on Seamus, the destruction of his marriage and the longer-term mental health issues he had to deal with. Phil also had some of his own demons to deal with. This had been a long game for him too, with its own personal tolls. Leading the counterterrorism and intelligence units, having invested years of his life in the pursuit of these kinds of people to the detriment of his personal needs, he was very well aware of how deep this went.

The two men exchanged glances as they reviewed the file contents and prepared themselves for the next part of the briefing. This was the difficult part – the photos of the kind of equipment that this group had been bringing into the country and distributing amongst some of the less trustworthy types of society.

Seamus turned on the large screen on the wall and fired up the laptop.

THIRTEEN

When Dushku woke up he had no idea where he was but was aware of the acute pain throbbing in his head, the tight bindings on his wrists and ankles and the dull ache in his lower back. Bariu sat opposite him, cigarette in hand, and watching Dushku come to. "Good morning, did you enjoy your rest?" he asked. The man in the chair tried to stretch as much as he could, given the restraints attached to him, and looked up to meet the eyes of his captor. "What do you want, why are you doing this? I thought we were friends – I saved you!" Dushku almost spat out. Bariu just looked at him, with cold impassive eyes.

"There is a difference," he began, "between saving someone and keeping them for later. You know what I mean - making sure that nobody else does anything to them until you have been able to deal with them." "So, now I have to ask you, what did you want to do with me, what was it you needed to keep me safe for, and what was it you… saved me for?" Dushku shuffled as much as he could in the chair he was attached to. As much as he tried, he couldn't keep up the façade much longer. The pain was getting worse - he couldn't check to see the extent of his injury but could feel the warm trickle of blood continuing to run down the back of his neck. It had been like that for as long as he had been conscious, so he had no idea how long it had been going while he had been out. Perhaps it was an appropriate opportunity to come clean. He had a feeling time was running out, and maybe he owed it to his old friend. He cleared his throat. "He wants you gone. But he wants to do it face-to-face, he doesn't want anyone else to have the pleasure. Those were his words." There was no pretence there, Bariu realised, the usual air of calculated response was gone and this was real. Dushku was telling the truth, for once. But this was no time to be sentimental based on old times - he had already shown his hand in that respect. It was time to get some answers and formulate the next step. Kelmendi was behind all of this, and it was now time to put this to rest.

"What the f-" was all that Rob Marshall managed before he felt the pain of the baseball bat hitting the side of his head and dropping him to the ground. Adrian grabbed his wrists and pulled him into the van, struggling a little as Rob was a pretty heavy guy. He managed to get him in, covered his head in one of the hessian sacks he had found, and quickly bound his arms and legs together. He wasn't going to take any chances with this one. In no time he was behind the wheel and making his way to the derelict farm, another repeat offender in the back ready to join his first… victim? No, not victim, more student. Yes, that was more accurate, as they were there to learn that their way of life wasn't appropriate and that their time of being a burden to the taxpayer was over. As Adrian rounded the last bend, he could hear Rob stirring in the back of the van and became slightly unsettled. He'd left the baseball bat in the back, another lesson to learn, but didn't really relish getting into a fight as there was no way he would be victorious, such was the difference in size. He pulled into the yard and backed up to the edge of the pit. The idea going through his mind was he could open the rear doors, get behind the guy and just push him out. With the ties and the bag, he wouldn't see him coming which should buy him the time he needed to deliver him.

The noise was more guttural than angry, so Adrian took the opportunity to make his move since it was clear Rob wasn't quite recovered yet. He grabbed at his legs and in one swift motion that surprised him, he practically slung the man out of the van and watched him slide into the pit. Rob landed with a resounding thud onto the ground, and James stood there for a moment before shouting up, "Oi, what the fuck! Who are you? What is this?" He walked over to the latest arrival, helped him to sit up and eased the bag from his head. The other man was still somewhat stunned from both the blow to the head and the fall and was struggling still to make any sense of his current situation. Finally, he managed, "Who are you, where is this place?" His fellow offender looked up to where Adrian had been standing and realised he had gone in the time it had taken him to welcome his new acquaintance. "I have no idea, mate. I've been here since yesterday and haven't got a clue what's going on. I've tried to climb out, but the sides of this place are like fucking slime and you can't get any grip. And it stinks of shit too, everywhere. I don't know what this place is, but I'm fucked if I'm going to be stuck here much longer." The new arrival surveyed his surroundings through narrowed eyes, his head and body still throbbing with pain and mentally swimming with a hundred thoughts about how he had got here.

Adrian moved the baseball bat to the passenger side of the front of the van and made sure the cable ties and sacks were in the front too. He needed to be sure that should the next one put up any resistance he would be prepared. He left the van in the shed at the side of one of the old buildings and got in his car he had left along the track, still on tarmac so it wouldn't pick up any mud. He'd seen too many of these forensics series to fall for that.

Before getting into the house, he caught a glimpse of his reflection in the window of his front door. He was smiling. This was working out just as he had hoped it would. Two down… who knows how many more to go?

FOURTEEN

Ten days earlier

"Yeah, black, black leather, all the gear mate and it was just sat there on the side of the road, engine running, keys in – I mean, you can't pass that up can you? Yes mate, Velar, all the goodies, 70-plate - you'll like it!" It was a gift he thought. You don't spend half of your life stealing cars then walk away from one like this. It was going to be a big payday when this was shifted, but for now he was just going to enjoy it for a little while longer.

"Boss, one of the cars is gone." Pavel relayed the message on the phone to Jozef once he had realised his car had gone missing. He listened intently as all he could hear was breathing. "Track it and bring it back, do what you like to whoever is driving it," came the instruction, and the line went dead. Pavel opened the app on his phone and put in the registration number of the Range Rover, and after a few seconds its location appeared, moving along the map. He motioned to the others to get into the remaining cars that had been around the corner and locked. "Follow this," he said and showed the phone to the driver of the first car as he climbed into the passenger seat. It didn't take long to find it. Whoever was driving was in no hurry and wasn't doing anything to attract any unwanted attention. They were in the middle of nowhere so no ANPR anywhere and not many houses, and there would be fewer by the time the other two cars caught up. On the map there was a small junction up ahead, so they chose this as the best place to stop him. When they arrived, it was the entrance to an old farm, with a wide sweeping yard - the ideal location to cut him off. The lead car overtook and cut across the path of the Range Rover, forcing it to a stop, the other coming in close behind to block any attempt at escape. The thief froze. Out of the cars came six men: two were clearly armed and not hiding the fact, as their pistols were in their hands, pointing at him – they were shouting something, but he couldn't understand it. In a blur, the door was pulled open by someone he hadn't seen - they must have come from the car behind - and he was yanked out and thrown to the ground. He didn't really have time to consider if it was a good or bad thing that he never wore a seatbelt.

Face down in the dry ground, his wrists were bound together and his ankles too, then he was hauled onto his feet by two of the men and was standing face-to-face with a giant of a man, who appeared to be mostly beard and muscles.

"Did you enjoy my car?" he asked, with a very thick accent that was hard to place - was it Scandinavian? "I, it was, erm – no, sorry," he stammered out with dust still in his mouth, a headache starting to creep across his skull. "Right, good. I suppose I should not leave it running, that was wrong." The beard was nodding sagely, looking almost apologetic. "Listen mate, I'm really sorry – look, you've got it back, I'm miles from home so you know, if you all just want to go, you can leave me here and we can just forget about it all, yeah?"

The bearded giant slowly lifted his head, as though contemplating this offer. "No," he said, and with a single punch, knocked the other man to the ground.

From the back of the Range Rover, one of the men retrieved some plastic boxes while the beard pulled out a large antique Labrus axe. "Open them and put them on the ground," he growled, then in one swing, brought the axe down on the man he had just knocked out, removing his feet. As he worked his way along the body, roughly measuring his axe cuts to coincide with the width of the boxes, he took a pair of bolt cutters out of the boot and walked back to what was left of the body, then slowly bent down and cut off the man's thumbs. One of the others looked over at this, as if this one action was the worst thing he had seen that day and raised an eyebrow. "For my dog," came the cold response.

A matter of minutes later, the car thief had been cut up and placed into the various plastic boxes. The axe head had been wiped on the torso and put back into the boot of the Range Rover. "Bastard stole my favourite axe as well. I got it while doing some work in Crete many years ago," muttered the bearded man, looking at his prized possession with fondness. "Put him in the car - we will take him to Jozef, then find his family and show them."

Two of the other men were tasked with loading the boxes up, but as they lifted the first box, they spotted a van on the far horizon, heading their way. "Leave him here, let's go!" ordered the man, and everyone climbed into the nearest vehicle and sped away from Sykes Farm, leaving Reg Wilson behind. From the car, he made the call. "Yes boss, we have the car back. The driver has been dealt with." "Good, now enough games and timewasting - get back to town. We need the product moving, there is too much attention. And if you get time, you need to talk to Alma about what to do on the market, the product has been talking it seems and needs to be silenced".

The cars made their way back along the winding country lanes, away from the farm and back towards the house on the edge of the town centre where the most recent shipment had arrived and now needed to be moved. Esad sat in the passenger seat, stroking his beard thoughtfully. Drugs and weapons were much easier to move than people - one or two was OK, but eleven was going to be tricky. He was still thinking as they pulled into town and drove past a minibus parked outside the house. Great, that would make things simpler, he considered as he looked it over while enjoying a cigarette. He got out of the car and strode over to Alexei who was walking up to the house and grabbed his elbow. "Make sure nobody tries anything stupid; we don't need to lose any of the product like we nearly lost a car today. Tell them all, tell them don't be foolish when they come out to the bus or there will be consequences." The thin young man nodded furiously, clearly showing he had just topped himself up on cocaine. Esad hated that and would see to it after the move that Alexei was sent to a new location - as far away from him as possible. He couldn't stand these coke heads.

"Alexei, get this product out now, we will deal with those at the market later. Just keep them here and make sure they stay where they should be, do you understand?" Esad walked away, shaking his head in frustration at having to be stuck here babysitting the product on the market stalls and not doing anything interesting. Mind you, that was a nice and welcome distraction earlier, so it wasn't a completely wasted day. He walked into the house and to the back room he and his dog occupied, reached into his pocket, pulled out a plastic bag and emptied its contents onto the floor.

"There you go - a snack for you."

FIFTEEN

Present day

"People trafficking and slavery, at the local market?" DCI Bowler was standing next to her desk, almost shouting this towards Seamus and Jim who had just delivered their report following the briefing with the team. "What the hell is going on? Do these arseholes think it's OK to bring that kind of thing HERE?!" By now she was purple with rage, not directed at her officers but at the sheer audacity of this OCG and what they had been doing right under their noses. "I mean, actual people." She was incredulous. "Drugs are bad enough, getting to know the same OCG are moving weapons about the place, that's pretty shitty to have to deal with, but people trafficking – Jesus!" "We need the Chief Super in here, hang on," and with that she picked up the phone and called her superior. "Sir, we need you – something very urgent we need to discuss. Could you spare us some time in my office please? - OK, thank you, Sir." "He'll be right down," said Bowler, a very stern and concerned look on her face, and she finally sat.

Less than five minutes later, Chief Superintendent Jackson knocked and entered the office. All three stood up. "No need, take your seats," he said cordially. "Dawn, what's got you so excited?" DCI Bowler looked over at Seamus and nodded her approval for him to explain. "Well, Sir – if I may," he began, and Jackson gave a small nod. As Seamus presented the background, Chief Superintendent Jackson went from standing straight up and periodically frowning, to sitting on the edge of Bowler's desk with an ashen look on his face. "And you're sure this is going on, Seamus?" he asked when Corrigan had finished. "Yes Sir, all the intel we have gathered and the file we have from the Met are pretty conclusive. Add to these the interviews with the market workers and it's painting a worrying picture about what's happening and who is behind it all."

Jackson looked Seamus directly in the eye. "Are you sure you want to stick with this, Seamus? He's part of the reason you're here." Seamus looked at the floor, then took a moment, swallowed and looked back at the man. "Sir, he has to be stopped, and I have more experience with him, his group and their operations than most people on the force - certainly anyone here. I want to be part of this, whatever it will be, to be there when we close Kelmendi down for good." Jackson seemed to mull this over for a minute or so, keeping his gaze on Seamus, maybe trying to ease out a change of heart and testing his resolve a little. He stood up from the edge of the desk. "Right!" he announced, clearly having found his assertiveness after hearing the full briefing. "Set up a task force, I need you Dawn to lead. Seamus and Jim – give me what you need and fuck the budgets. This bastard has been here too long, it's time we put him away." And with that he left the office, leaving the three of them staring at the door.

"Well, you heard the man" said Bowler – still processing the latest chapter in a day of strange updates. "Get on with your wish lists, and let's send this OCG down."

"What have you got him for this time, what's he meant to have done now? This is harassment!" came the shouts down the phone at Swindon Central Police Station to a very confused operator. "I'm sorry, Madam - could you please tell me who you are referring to, then I may be able to try and help you," came the courteous reply. "Don't give me that shit, you know who I mean. You lot 'ave pinned some shit or other on him and chucked him in a cell again for your quotas!" Those last words were practically spat out. The police call operator looked at the mug on her desk that she had bought herself last year, mainly to cheer herself up during calls like this one where it really didn't matter what she said, she was never going to diffuse the onslaught of vitriol. 'Shit Circus Ringmaster' it proudly displayed, alongside a cartoon of a Big Top filled with people. "Madam, I really need a name so I can check with the custody desk to see who has been brought in, and take it from there," she said, far more calmly than even she expected.

"Fuck's sakes, I'm Sandra Marshall, it's Rob – where the

fuck is he and what have you arseholes done with him this time? I know you've got him, you always pin something on him, you must think I've gone soft in the 'ead or something. Just let him go, he needs to look after me."

"Just give me a moment please, Mrs Marshall, while I check with the custody sergeant to see who is here." She put her caller on hold and took a deep breath.

Join the police, they said - make a difference, they said. If only! Less than a minute later, after the custody sergeant had advised her on everyone that had been booked in, she went back to the now seething Mrs Marshall. "Hello, Mrs Marshall – thanks for your patience – we've checked the logs from the last 24 hours and Rob isn't here. He hasn't been booked in or even on a list to look out for. Is there anything else I can-" and she was rudely interrupted. "Well where the fuck is he, then?" Sandra Marshall barked down the phone. "You lot have probably bundled him into a car and he's on his way there." There was a slight change of tone, almost desperation, that the operator picked up on – she had been doing this job for a while, and this was one of the many skills she had been selected for. "Mrs Marshall, when did you last see Rob?" "He didn't come home for the last two nights," Sandra said. The volume had come right down and she was now sounding more concerned than angry.

"OK - let me get some details from you and I'll pass them to our team." "They won't bother, as he's always in trouble," she snapped back at this, her tone back to being aggressive. It was very clear she was not a fan of the police. "Mrs Marshall, I can assure you our team takes every report of a missing person very seriously. It doesn't matter who they are, criminal record or otherwise. We will do our best for everyone. Now, let's start with some basics. What was he wearing, do you remember?"

Sandra Marshall described in as much detail as she could recall, since Rob was always in and out of the house but generally wore the same kind of things: jeans and a t-shirt with some logo or other emblazoned across the front. Always trainers. "Did he say where he was going when you last saw him?" She knew it was a long shot, as Rob's history with her colleagues was now on the screen in front of her, and it was a long list of anti-social behaviour and petty crimes - and there was a fair chance that even if he had told his mother where he was going, it may have been a lie.

"Just out with his mates, was all he ever told me." Sandra's voice had lost all the venom and was that of a mother concerned for the welfare of her child. Irrespective of their relationship and his often scant regard for her feelings, he was still her little boy under it all, and she didn't know where he was.

"Thank you, Sandra. I know this is difficult but the more we can find out now, the better prepared the team are when looking for him. Could you please let me have his phone number?" If nothing else, she could start that process just by calling it to see what happened, then if that didn't work passing it over to the tech team to see if they could find it.

"I've tried calling him, it just goes straight to voicemail

each time – and sometimes I know he doesn't answer, but it still rings for a while, so that's when I thought something was wrong. He always calls back."

One less thing then - straight to the tech team with the number.

"OK, Sandra – I'm passing all this to our missing persons team right now, and the phone number to the tech team to see if they can track it and pass them your details too. They'll come to see you later today."

SIXTEEN

Adrian sat at his desk looking over his list. Two names had a small mark next to them that made him smile involuntarily, the next two below them were well into the twenties in terms of their arrest records – theft, burglary, car theft, assault. Just a constant drain on police resources as well as a regular local menace. It was about time they were dealt with too. His approach had been better the second time around, so this evening's plan was along similar lines. Make sure his target was effectively subdued, tie wraps were in the front of the van now, so much easier to grab them than before, same for the bags. Just two hours to go before he would go and find Sean Hicklin – phone details already in the system so he was already being tracked. His photo showed a rather sickly-looking individual, so perhaps this one wouldn't put up much of a fight, but he wasn't taking any chances.

He looked over the names one more time before hiding

the list in the laptop folder and moving to his actual work list. It was certainly time for a coffee and a walk about to stretch his legs as the evening ahead could be long. He called Lisa to tell her he was going to be late home, due to some complicated IT problems that he was certain she wouldn't question. There was absolutely no way he could tell her about this, however excited he was about the plans and how he had progressed so far.

One final check, again, that the number plate on the van didn't come back to him but to his patsy, selected based on his recent expiration. Adrian had been looking out for potential candidates and this poor gentleman was an opportune intervention. He'd been living on his own up till then, so nobody around to open the post from the DVLA. Right then - just a few more things to do in view of his colleagues before heading out to 'that data centre' again to 'fix this annoying problem'. The nerves had already started.

After making enough of a scene and shouting at his laptop for a few minutes in mock annoyance, he grabbed his car keys and left the building. It was still quite light outside, so he needed to kill some time before heading to Covingham to rid the residents there of this pain in the hole. He had a pang of guilt, but it was more to do with whether or not he ought to throw some food and water down for them – probably a reasonable thing to do and would use up a bit of time. He checked the laptop again for the location he was aiming for, made a mental note of distance and an approximation of time and headed off to the Spar shop on the way into Swindon. Just some cheap cakes and water would do it, just enough to stop them from expiring but not enough to build up any decent energy levels.

On entering the shop Adrian was careful to keep the brim of his unbadged baseball cap over his eyes, as well as hope it was obscuring as much of his face as possible from the cameras that were positioned seemingly everywhere. Dull clothes that he had 'borrowed' from a Salvation Army clothing bank, thanks to whoever was too lazy to put them into the steel receptacle. Cash was of course used for the purchases – two 2-litre bottles of still water and two packets of own-brand cakes. He had parked around the corner from the shop, away from the onsite CCTV so he couldn't be tracked back to the van, and he looked pretty unkempt so could have passed for someone living in the nearby hostel.

He drove the 20 minutes to Covingham and parked up just two streets away from Sean's house. Given his usual route and lack of imagination, it was a certainty that he would be coming along within the next few minutes, but to make sure Adrian opened his laptop and the tracking app. It wasn't a long wait until the indicator on the screen advised of the approach of his next target.

Sean Hicklin had been in the pub all afternoon, as usual. Talking rubbish with his mates, goading the non-regulars who dared enter 'his' pub and affecting his usual swagger between the bar, his table and the toilet. King of all he surveyed, a rather pathetic fish in a shallow and muddy pond. The more mature regulars had long since learned to ignore him, his mouth and the near constant stream of obscenities that flowed from it. Unknown to Sean, he was seen as the village idiot here – all mouth and petty crime to try to make him seem as though he was tough and worth thinking about. In reality though, there were many here who had seen, and indeed carried out many more devious and destructive acts. To them, he was just sport, so easy to wind up and even easier to put down – if nothing else, it kept a handful of people busy.

Adrian pulled up at the side of the road between the pub and Sean's house, slipped the cap off and put the balaclava on. He'd forgotten how itchy it was but had to put up with it. He grabbed a handful of zip ties and shoved them into his jacket pocket, and grabbed the rounders bat he had chosen in favour of the baseball bat – it was shorter, easier to hide and store - and, more importantly, wield. He got out and opened the back doors just enough so they would be easier to access when he needed to. He could see people on the other side of the road, quite a distance away in the fading light and hoped he hadn't been spotted – it didn't seem so, as they were very much engrossed in their conversation. And there he was.

Swaying slightly from his obvious intoxication, he looked so young and yet his features lent themselves to someone who had spent their life so far in a state of anger and almost contempt. It was time to deal with him. As Sean passed the van, Adrian walked around it so he was directly behind him. After taking a few quick and quiet steps, he raised the bat and brought it down on the nexus of Sean's neck and shoulder. There was a loud crack as the wooden bat hit Sean, and instead of him dropping to the ground as Adrian had expected, he swung around to look at his assailant. "What the fuck are you doing?" he stuttered out, clearly in pain from the strike to his neck and in shock at being face-to-face with a balaclava-wearing person. Taking no chances, the heel of Adrian's hand connected with Sean's chin and sent him crashing to the ground. He grabbed a sack and struggled a little to cover Sean's head, then pulled him into the van with its waiting rear doors open. Once in, he bound Sean's wrists and ankles and rooted about on his person for his phone. It wasn't hard to find, so with a smack from a hammer, the screen was smashed and, like the first two, he dropped it down the nearest drain. No chance of it being any use in tracking him now. Adrian closed the van doors as casually as he could so as not to draw any attention, then climbed into the driver's seat. On the way out towards the farm there was no sound from the back. Adrian thought that this was probably a good sign, but there was a niggling doubt. Had that strike to the chin just knocked him out, or had it… no, it wasn't that hard… can't have been.

It was a long drive to the farm with the same thought going round and round in his mind, but he couldn't pull over in case anything happened – who knows, he could be awake and waiting to ambush him. He finally pulled up at the old farm and drove over to the pit. As he got out, he could hear the other two shouting, they had clearly heard the van and were trying to attract attention - little did they know who had arrived. Adrian pulled the balaclava back on and got out, then walked slowly to the back of the van and carefully opened the doors, making sure one was between him and his cargo. Sean lay there, motionless in pretty much the same position he had been unceremoniously left in. Adrian was still wary: even though the other man's wrists and ankles were bound, he didn't really trust him. He checked to see if he had anything in his hands – nothing – so crept closer to check his pulse. Thank fuck for that – it was there. He hadn't killed him. It was one thing to knock people out and take them out here, but there was no way he would handle it if he had actually killed someone. Adrian slid the unconscious man to the edge of the floor of the van and carefully moved him to the ground. Dragging him with a hold under his armpits, he got him to the edge of the now pitch-dark pit and let him go.

"Let us out, you wanker!" came the shouts from the dark as their latest guest arrived in a heap. "Oi, you can't leave us here – who are you? What's this about?"

Adrian retrieved the water and cakes from the van, used some spray cleaner and a rag to wipe off any fingerprints and put them into a bag and dropped them down.

This small act seemed to give him a sense of wellbeing, knowing that he wasn't likely to leave them to starve or die of dehydration. He got back into the van and drove sensibly back to the road near where his car was. He was close enough to a data centre to make his alibi check out, and since he had left his phone in his car there would be no doubt as to where he had spent the evening.

The other two men sat Sean up, as he was still unconscious and had landed just next to them. They had developed a kind of camaraderie over the last 24 hours and with another person having dropped in on them, they felt compelled to help.

Neither had been able to work out why they, specifically, had been dropped into a disused slurry pit in the middle of nowhere.

SEVENTEEN

Adrian reviewed his list and checked off the seventh repeat offender he had managed to remove from society and deposit into the pit. His original trepidation at the start had been replaced by a growing sense of accomplishment. More timewasters out of the way, less time spent by the police having to constantly deal with them. He looked at the next name on the list while in the van and parked up at the side of the estate, double checking that all the equipment he needed was readily available to him. He had learned over the past week and each 'collection' what had to be to hand and what was OK to be in the back of the van. He had the feeling that tonight was going to be a breeze. Gary Walmley was not known for violence - his photo on file suggested a slight build and meek appearance so should be relatively straightforward - even so, no reason to drop any guard or change the approach. Adrian had learned to treat all as potential threats and assume they could all overpower him. He drove 50 yards down the road and waited, door slightly open with his recent acquisition, a police issue baton, in his hand. Gary practically fell out of the pub and turned back to someone he was clearly still having an argument with inside, making sure he had the last word before leaving. "Aye, and yous can shove it up your arse, ya fat tossbag," he yelled over his shoulder into the pub, then steeled himself for the walk home.

As he approached the van, Adrian pulled on his gloves and balaclava and waited for him to walk by. Adrian opened the door and as quietly as he could, slid the side door open, grabbed a sack and walked up behind Gary. He pulled the bag up and got ready with the baton and went for a strike to the neck. The baton struck the right place, but Gary simply turned around and stared at Adrian, an incredulous look on his face. "What're you doing, pal?" he said quite softly, clearly stunned with the blow he had just received.

He steadied himself, took a step back and swung a punch out of nowhere, hitting Adrian square on the nose, breaking it instantly. Pain radiated through Adrian's head as blood poured from his nose, soaking the balaclava and making breathing difficult. Gary was taking another swing, but Adrian was ready this time and blocked the incoming punch and with a swift strike of the heel of his hand to Gary's chin, and he dropped his would be assailant ground. Adrian quickly slipped the sack over Gary's head, bound his wrists and ankles and pulled him into the van. He shut the door, got into the driver's seat and left the scene. His head was pounding. The balaclava had soaked up a lot of blood and breathing was still a challenge with it on, but Adrian knew it had to stay there until he had finished the job, so he made a direct route to the farm.

"Police emergency, how can I help?" the operator said when the call came in. "Hi, yeah – erm, I was outside the Deers just now and there was a bloke in a mask or something having a fight, then I think chucked the other bloke into a van and drove off down Durrington Walk." "OK, did you see the van clearly or see the number plate?" "Yeah, little white one, the bloke who was driving got punched in the face then punched the other bloke back. Knocked him out and just sort of pushed him into the van and sped off."

The caller provided the number plate details and the police operator passed everything over to response officers to follow up. PC Gibbons carried out the number plate check on the Police National Computer, checked the address and started a file on the registered owner of the van. He updated his sergeant on the name and address and was given authorisation to attend the registered address in South Marsden.

On arrival it was clear to PC Gibbons that the house had not been cared for or maintained in a long time. The garden was very overgrown, two of the windows were broken and paint was peeling from every surface. After a cursory look around the property, he found a way in, tentatively entered the house and quietly searched, all the while listening out in case there was someone there.

After a few minutes he called it in. "Nobody at the address. Can you check the details of the registered owner again, please? Have you got another address, date of birth, that kind of thing?" The operator carried out another check on the PNC. "No other address, and the DOB comes back as 11.02.1944." PC Gibbons was getting the distinct feeling there was something wrong here. "Could you check when the vehicle was registered, please?" "Yes, yes – vehicle registered 14th September this year." Just six weeks ago, but this house looked like it had been neglected for years. This needs more attention, thought PC Gibbons, and asked for the duty sergeant to be informed.

The three others already in the pit received the latest occupant as he slid and bounced down the side and landed in a pile of limp limbs. Sean, now one of the group who had been planning how to get out, went over and helped remove the sack from the latest arrival.

Adrian finally removed his balaclava and looked at his swollen face in the mirror, wincing as he touched the sides and could see the bruising already coming up. This was going to take some explaining when he made it home. He did his best to clean up the dried blood from around his face, and realised his t-shirt was also covered. Shit! - that little bastard. He cursed Gary for having been able to get a punch in first and potentially causing him to have to come up with a story for when he got home later.

It was then he got a feeling of unease that during the time it took for the little scuffle to have taken place, he may have been seen getting the lad into the van. This sort of hassle he really didn't need. All the planning could be undone due to this little prick and his inebriation-fuelled ability to withstand the blow from the baton. He stopped at a supermarket on the way back and got some baby wipes to get a better clean-up, as well as some pain relief. His head was killing him now. It was late when he got back home, and Lisa was still up, waiting for him in the kitchen with a glass of wine in her hand. She looked at him, the obvious bruising around what was clearly a broken nose and eyes getting blacker by the minute.

"Hi - sorry I'm a little later than planned. I had a bit of an accident at work, walked straight into a glazed door that I could have sworn was open and - well, it wasn't!" Adrian sort of grinned while pointing at his face. She looked impassively at him, no sign of emotion or concern on her face at all. How long had she been drinking and how much had she had? Adrian was trying to think as fast as his sore head would allow him. Had he left anything in the house that may be able to make her suspicious? Can't have - it's all in the van and miles away. What else? Maybe it was her family, or work or… he really didn't know. Lisa was still silent, just looking at him and occasionally sipping her wine, but letting nothing slip about what was on her mind. Her husband coming home late with a broken nose, after a few weeks of strange behaviour and late nights and always looking like he had just got changed. Women notice these things, she thought to herself, and he won't have even considered how obvious it all is.

She placed the glass on the worktop and looked him dead in the eye. "Who did that to you? Was it worth it, to get a broken nose from the husband? Am I not enough for you?" There was still no emotion in her voice, nothing for him to work on - she was just staring at him. At least, though, he didn't have to lie to her about any affair, which was clearly going to make it easier for him to talk his way out of this.

"There really isn't anyone else, Lisa, I absolutely promise you. It's just work that is keeping me out more as we move to a new system and this," he pointed to his face, "like I said, I just walked into a door that I could have sworn was open and I ended up on my arse in the middle of the corridor. I swear to you, that's all there is happening."

"Whatever you say." She sniffed, picked up the wine again and took a long drink. "You can sleep in the spare room tonight, I'm off to bed and I don't want you with me." With that she gently placed the glass down, stood up and walked out of the kitchen, leaving Adrian at a loss for words. He judged the situation well enough not to push it or argue – she would calm down tomorrow and this would all be sorted.

His thoughts went to the incident on the street and whether he had been seen, since that was far more concerning since he had handled Lisa's jealousy before. Besides, a night alone would do him some good, spread out a bit in bed and be able to toss and turn as much as he needed. Although throughout the night he was plagued with the increasing worry that he may have been witnessed. Even so, he thought, he had the balaclava, the van is registered to that dead guy whose details he had been so careful to find and set up - no way the trail could make it back to him.

EIGHTEEN

PC Gibbons was like a dog with a bone after the visit to the old, tumbled down house that was alleged to be the residence of the owner of the van spotted on Durrington Lane, bundling someone into the back. An eighty-year-old registering a van seemed just as odd so it was time to hand it over to CID, but he wasn't quite ready to do that just yet. Gibbons started to do some more digging into the driving licence on file – it was cancelled three years ago after DVLA received notification of his death. That makes sense with the state of the house, so how is a van registered to that address in the last few months against a name of someone that the DVLA has been advised is dead? He decided to go upstairs and share this with CID. Something dodgy was going on here, and the sighting of someone being pushed into the van was now something that needed serious attention.

DC Burridge was at her desk when he got upstairs, the

file in his hands now slightly bigger with the extra information he had gathered. "Hi, DC Burridge, you need to see this – I think we have a potential kidnap here." She looked up at him from her screen, an eyebrow raised. "Go on – what have you got?"

They sat together while going over the information and then created a plan for getting more evidence. The next job needed to be a trawl through local CCTV and a door knock with anyone with an obvious camera that looks over the roads. Then check ANPR for the van in the vicinity of Durrington Lane before and after the sighting. This was now a major issue and had been escalated within CID. Now both needed to check any missing persons reports in the last 24 hours and get a team together.

Jim and Seamus were enjoying a quiet moment with a coffee and a non-work catch up following the weekend, Jim regaling Seamus with tales of a stag do in town and copious beverages consumed. "And I'm still here this morning but yesterday, honestly Seamus, I was a wreck – I'm just getting too old for this drinking lark. Some of the others were really going for it though. I gave up at 2am and got an Uber home." Seamus smiled while remembering similar nights out in the past and having got to that point some time back - just calling it a night, or a morning in many cases, and going home to limit the inevitable damage to the next day. "Sir! Do you have a few minutes, I think you need to be aware of this." DC Burridge was nearly running towards them both with a file in her hand, almost waving it.

"Let's have a look," said Seamus to the incoming DC. They found a room and she placed the file on the table in front of them all while giving them a summary of where things were, starting with the headline of a potential kidnap. The affray on the side of the road wouldn't go anywhere near Seamus or his team, nor the issue on the address coming back as it did, even following the visit to the property – but the potential kidnap was exactly the thing that MCU were very interested in. The three of them went over the details of the vehicle, the registered owner and the DVLA information of his death, the information on the derelict house and the photos that had since been taken showing the state of it. Then the ANPR and CCTV work that was under way, and the progress so far. The small team had been busy and collected a lot of data already: the vehicle purchase record, insurance payment details and more information on the alleged owner, based on his death certificate. The insurance had come back to the house too and on investigation there were letters from the insurance company on the floor when PC Gibbons had visited. These were also on the table. The payment had come from the same address and name as the deceased owner of the house. So now they were looking at fraud and identity left to add to whoever was behind this – documents from the same bank were on the table too, so it was clear that the whole thing had been planned meticulously and very well thought-through. Had it not been for the witness, this would never have been discovered. Now things had escalated with the abduction, or alleged abduction at this stage, the small team needed to get to the bottom of this.

"Right, let's see where we are – we know the insurance has been paid for from an account set up in the deceased's name and using their address, so obviously whoever did it is aware of the status of the address and its former occupant. They knew they could collect post from the property, so they must be reasonably local to be able to visit as needed. All documents are in the name of the deceased including the registration for the van, which we have to assume has been collected too. Where have you got to with CCTV and ANPR data?" DC Burridge was fully prepared for this. "Well Sir, we have found three properties on and near Durrington Lane with CCTV that covers some of the road, although one didn't have any video saved, but the other two show the van arrive and the driver get out and open the side door. Driver is approximately 6 ft, slim build but all in black including a balaclava and gloves, so no idea of ethnicity, hair colour or anything like that. They appear to be getting prepared to abduct the IP, then wait for them to pass and hit them with what appears to be a baton." The DC opened her laptop to show the footage gathered, and it was as she had described - the moment the baton was used and the retaliatory punch.

"Have we checked hospital entries? That looked like quite a punch." This was met with a scribbled note from Burridge and a further update on what ANPR had shown. "We can see the vehicle enter the area from the north-west of the town and we've tracked it back from Blunsdon Way, but there are so few cameras out there, that's where it stops. When it leaves, it follows the same route out towards Blunsdon, then into country lanes and out of sight of ANPR. We are trying to find older data to see if we can spot it anywhere else, but it's still a little early to see if it's going to yield any results." "What do we know about the IP - where did they come from and why them?" It was Jim this time who had been quietly taking in all the information and the focus on the van. "Anything coming into the phones about people not getting home when expected?" DC Burridge looked across the table and nodded. "Yes, Sir - we have footage from the pub and nearby houses and can see the IP coming out of The Deers Leap - he appears to be having a conversation with parties inside as he leaves. We've spoken to the landlord and the IP is well-known at the pub. He is Gary Walmley, 26 and from Penhill, known to us, burglary, TWOK etc. Just low-level stuff but a consistent offender. We are considering any number of these as motives and looking at recent victims to see if there is a connection." Both Seamus and Jim smiled. This is clearly a DC going places seemed to be the unsaid comment between them. "So, we have a person in a van registered and insured under the name and address of a dead man, driven by someone who potentially knows where ANPR cameras are, so their route in and out of town stays out of sight. Clearly taken time to organise this, planned out the vehicle, the route, timings and location of the IP. This Walmley bloke must have really pissed them off to have gone to this much trouble to grab them."

The team went over the rest of the data gathered from the past few hours to try to build more of a picture of who had taken Gary Walmley off the street and why. There had been a lot of work involved for just some small-time stuff, so perhaps there was something more personal going on. "OK, let's find the last few victims of this Walmley guy and get uniform over for a chat with each, see if any of them know our deceased too. Seems quite the leap from nicking stuff to getting lamped in the head and stuffed into a van," Jim surmised to the room.

This is going to be a long day, thought Seamus as he surveyed the table full of information that had been gathered already. DC Burridge handed over the documents that had been gathered and gently guided PC Gibbons to stand in front of her. "Sir, I think PC Gibbons should drive this as he had compiled most of this and carried out the initial investigation." Jim agreed and Gibbons was asked to join them, since he had been onsite at the property and was the one who had initially connected the dots from the call into dispatch earlier and brought it to the attention of CID. Seamus could see the guy was buzzing with energy and excitement about getting to the bottom of what was going on, so decided to have a more detailed conversation with him and see what he was made of.

Seamus was impressed with the approach taken and protection of evidence as Gibbons uncovered more details and handed them over, with clear summaries of each stage. This was someone who would make an excellent detective, so Seamus felt it would be mutually beneficial to try and second him to MCU for this investigation, to see how he fared. He would make the call as soon as Gibbons left the room.

"Oh, Sir – one more thing." Gibbons stuck his head back through the door. "When I checked on PNC about the IP, the record had recently been accessed but no notes added, which I thought was odd." "Usually if a record had been accessed there would be a note added as to why, since it should relate to an investigation or reference to an associate, but there was nothing. What was even more odd is that it was accessed by someone in IT - not an officer."

Now that was interesting. Seamus nodded, thanked the PC and picked up his phone. "Jim, ask one of the team to follow this up - PC Gibbons has something you may want to look into. Bright lad, that one."

NINETEEN

Jim listened and took his usual flurry of notes, incomprehensible to anyone other than him, or maybe a pharmacist. Gary Walmley and recent complaints or bookings made that involved him or mentioned him. Who has been accessing records on the system that isn't connected to an investigation? Jim's mind went down the obvious rabbit hole.

"PC Gibbons," called Jim as he walked into the main part of the building, away from the relative comfort of the MCU. A rather smart-looking young officer almost bolted to attention at the sound of his name. "Yes, Sir!" he announced as he stood. "Relax, no need to stand on ceremony for me. Have you got a minute?" Jim walked over, assessed the room and noticed there were a few concerned faces looking in his direction. They found a room along the corridor and Jim gestured for the young PC to take a seat. "You mentioned to DCI Corrigan that someone had accessed the record of Gary Walmley, but they weren't an officer - is that correct?" Jim asked in as casual a tone as he could muster. "Yes, Sir – that's correct. Access to the file was made by someone in IT, Sir." "Any idea why that would happen - I mean, is it common to have records accessed by IT staff?" Jim was watching PC Gibbons' face as he asked the question, noticing his reaction and how he was clearly processing the information while working out where this might be going. Jim realised a little encouragement may be needed. "DCI Corrigan mentioned to me that you have some pretty sharp instincts and were possibly on to something, so I just want to hear you out, let the theory play out and see where it may take us. Is that OK?"

With this, Gibbons seemed to visibly relax. He wasn't in any trouble and this could really be something useful. "Well Sir – I've not seen any other instance of a record having been accessed by anyone other than an officer before which is why I mentioned it, it just seemed odd. So, and I hope you don't mind me having done this, Sir, but I checked to see how many other records had been accessed by the same ID. It's more than thirty Sir, all local people and all of them with reasonable repeats based on small time stuff – few cars, burglary etc. - every one of them pretty well known to us and regularly in custody." Jim couldn't help but smile. "Of course I don't mind, that's excellent work – I'm really impressed. So, any idea who this IT person is?" Gibbons allowed a smile too and relaxed a little more in the senior officer's presence – maybe this was the break he had been looking for. "Well Sir – the name that comes back is Martin Collins, but I asked HR if they had a file for him and they haven't heard of the name. That isn't as strange as it may sound since our system is supported by an outside company, so he could be an employee of theirs. "So, I looked them up on Companies House, can't find the name there, but again – not a big surprise if they are just an employee instead of a director or shareholder. Then I looked at the website for the company, and it doesn't list their employees. But I have a name from Companies House for the MD, an Adrian Burch. He also has an ID on the system but no evidence of ever accessing any records. My feeling is we need to contact him and ask him about Martin Collins." Jim sat back in the chair, looked at Gibbons for a second or two, and slowly nodded. "Fancy a secondment, PC Gibbons?" he asked, knowing Seamus was already sorting this out in the background.

An hour later, Jim, Gibbons, Seamus and Adrian Burch were sitting around a table in one of the interview rooms. A file had been created and bulked up to make it look more concerning – a bulging folder always looked more imposing than a thin one. During the preceding hour, Jim and Gibbons had gone over all the records that had been accessed by Martin Collins and noted who each of the people were, their list of offences and addresses, and cross-referenced each name back to the PNC to see whether there was anything recent. Four names stuck out – Gary Walmley, James Miller, Sean Hicklin and Rob Marshall. None of these four had been seen for a few days. Gary had been bundled into a van, Rob's mum had reported him missing, and the others had missed curfew which was unlike them.

"Thank you, Mr Burch, for coming at such short notice

- we really do appreciate it," said Seamus, starting as gently as he could given the document in front of him. "I'm happy to help any way I can. Your officer mentioned a member of the application support team on the phone - what's happened to them?" Adrian managed to sound very plausible, given he knew very well that Martin Collins didn't exist - certainly not as an actual person, just a 'virtual' employee of his. Seamus gave a thin smile in recognition of the offer. "Thanks, now we need to understand a few things and hope you can assist. Over the course of the last few weeks, an individual that appears to work for your support company has been accessing records on the Police National Computer in two locations from our force area. Firstly, it's important for us to ascertain why this is, but we are concerned that someone that is not a Police Officer has access to such files. Given your company maintains our local systems, we needed to check with you if this is something you are aware of, or could explain how it could occur?"

Adrian didn't even flinch and showed no outward signs of discomfort or concern. He had read the room on arrival: two clearly senior detectives and a younger officer, probably learning the job which was a little incongruous to the scenario – why have these two heavy hitters and a rookie? Maybe there was more to it, maybe they knew more about the people he had been looking at. No, this was an employee doing things they shouldn't and as the boss, he had to assure them that steps would be taken. Besides, he already had his list so there was no need to delve into the systems anymore, he could legitimately tell them that Martin would be fired for misconduct, and this would not be repeated. There -

done!

“Gentlemen, I’m very concerned about this too – our staff should not have access to records on the PNC, we just maintain the systems used to provide it. We have no mechanism to do that, so I’m very confused as to how one of our team has been able to do that. From our perspective, and yours too obviously, this is a significant breach and will be immediately dealt with – I will ensure that Martin is dismissed today. You have my word that this will not be repeated, and in the meantime I will personally look through our logs to see how this has happened.”

All through this monologue Seamus watched Adrian - his mannerisms, movements, eye contact, tone of voice. He had participated in a lot of interviews in his career and come up against some impressive liars, and this guy was hiding something. He was just too composed - practiced, almost. Nobody who has a relationship with the force and access to systems is that calm when presented with a potential breach. There would be a level of concern that would show in their eyes, as they processed the potential damage for both parties. His swift and decisive action had been presented ahead of investigation into the allegation, too – a little convenient perhaps. “Thank you, Mr Burch. It’s certainly comforting to hear that such action will be taken, and so quickly too – that is good to hear. You understand, of course, that we will need to speak with Mr Collins as well, since this is a breach of confidential data protection laws. And while my understanding of GDPR may not be quite as in-depth as yours, while you may be named under your company’s policy on data protection, Mr Collins is the party that has, in our opinion, unlawfully accessed privileged information. So we'll need to convene a meeting with yourself and Mr Collins within the next forty-eight hours in order to fully understand the impact and implications of this."

There it is, thought Seamus – that reaction, fear mixed with desperation as to how to play the next move. However good he may have been with his pre-rehearsed story, he wasn't expecting that. Let's just see what happens next. "There is another aspect to this that may or may not be linked to Mr Collins," Time to play some more cards. "Four of the people whose records had been accessed are missing." Seamus watched as Adrian joined some dots. "Missing?" said Adrian with eyebrows raised. "And do you believe that Martin is involved in that?" Seamus was impressed that Adrian was able to maintain such composure, as he was certain something was going on. "That remains to be seen but is certainly a credible line of enquiry given the list of records accessed. It may be a coincidence – but I'm not much of a believer in those."

Those last words hung in the air for a few very long seconds, and Adrian felt a bead of sweat roll down his back.

TWENTY

Bariu picked at his fingernails as he contemplated what to do next. Dushku had been a good friend, once. Sentimentality had never been one of Bariu's strong points even when it related to someone he had known this long. Betrayal was very hard to get past – more so when his life had been put in danger - but that said, there had been ample opportunities Dushku could have taken to get rid of him and the reason that he had to keep him for Kelmendi was what really tipped the balance, not in his favour. He looked across the room at the lifeless body slumped on the chair, still restrained, and gave a deep sigh. He stood slowly and stretched – it had already been a long day and he was tired. Kelmendi would be out there somewhere waiting for Dushku to update him on his progress in bringing Bariu to the pre-arranged location, where he would most likely have been drugged and stuffed into a vehicle to be taken somewhere quiet. At least his old friend had shared that before his demise.

Bariu knew the location well enough and how easy it was to get in and out relatively unseen. That goes for all parties, though he thought while lighting a cigarette and staring out of the window. Kelmendi would have people all over the place from at least two hours before the agreed meeting time, covering all routes in and out and trying to blend into crowds and doorways. And they would all be very well-armed too, something he was not. Kelmendi himself wouldn't be there, so one of the team would need to be retained and encouraged to provide the location details of the handover point - even then there was no guarantee that Kelmendi would be there in person. He finished his cigarette and nodded to himself. He needed to watch for vehicles. Find one where the driver stayed behind the wheel while all the others were empty, and the driver would be waiting for instructions on where to go next. It was time to move – there were four hours to go.

Following a dusty taxi ride out of town towards Komolac and the marina there, it was an obvious place when Bariu thought about it. Plenty of places to hide, nestled in a valley, so a lot of aerial cover for snipers and good routes in and out. A lot of people drinking, messing about with boats or playing tennis… but not many tourists as they have cameras out all the time. He had to admit it was a good spot and well-selected, even so he had to formulate a plan and fast. He sat in the sun sipping from a bottle of water looking over the marina and the many people talking, minding their own business. In one of the car parks near the waterfront there were vehicles from all over the place: Hungary, Germany, France, Netherlands, UK – clever – they could turn up with foreign plates and nobody would blink an eye. And most were pretty new and expensive too – just right for Kelmendi's lot who were a bit showy when it came to cars. He went to the shop over the river and bought five phones: all had cameras and were cheap enough. As he made his way to the main routes he set each phone up and connected the camera to an app and then to the same app on his phone. Cheap and easy CCTV. He adjusted the settings so they wouldn't sleep, and within an hour had the four major routes covered and four boxes on his app streaming live images to him. While walking around it was clear that the area didn't have many cameras.

Bariu knew how easy it could be to hack into these systems and keep a watchful eye on the area – he'd done it enough times himself. One of the cars came in from Jadranska while the other two came the same way he had done, through the hills from the coast. They had tried to be inconspicuous but failed - their penchant for luxury cars gave them away. He made a note of the licence plates for all three, snapped the phone and threw it in the nearest water. He went for the car that had come by itself, since it was most likely to be the one used to transport him out and waited from his vantage point, watching four men exit and leaving the driver behind. The driver wouldn't be armed, nor would he know where he needed to go, as it would be programmed into the sat nav already and he would just follow the instructions. No need to do anything other than get him out of the car, check the sat nav and leave.

Bariu had taken the opportunity to let himself into the local tennis club and borrow some clothes and a racquet, and was doing a good job of blending in. He managed to walk unnoticed along the car park and right past the car. He circled back, opened the front passenger door and struck the driver in the temple with the end of the tennis racquet handle, knocking him out instantly. He leant over and checked the sat nav – noting the last few destinations and the one programmed. Closing the door and looking around, Bariu walked back to the clubhouse to replace the tennis kit with something more suitable. Walking through the changing rooms, he heard showers running and headed in that direction. Laid out on a sports bag were clothes - a little large for him, but they would do – and after a short search, car keys.

Back out in the sunlight he squinted while looking across the parked cars to see which one had its lights flashing when he pressed the button on the key fob. An old Peugeot with French plates – perfect!

He checked the rear-view mirror as he eased his way out of Komolac and relaxed only after he had covered ten miles heading north. It was going to be any time now that news would reach Kelmendi that his team hadn't found their target, and the driver wouldn't have any idea what had happened. Next stop would be the UK, as he had someone he needed to meet.

TWENTY-ONE

Bina picked up her mug of tea and just stared at it for her thoughts not on the moment at all. The whole thing with the victim being cut up, and clearly ante-mortem too, had been the worst case she had worked on to date. Not to say she hadn't seen some truly awful things that people had done to others. Taking a life showed such a high degree of disregard for laws and social expectations, and she knew her part of the process was the how rather than the why, but it didn't lessen her desire to understand the motivation behind these atrocious acts.

She was mindlessly picking at a hole on the arm of the chair while mulling over the current case and what had motivated it, digging more of the foam out with her nail with a rapidly cooling mug of tea in the other hand, when Jim walked into the office. Instead of his usual greeting, he waited a moment longer in the doorway and observed Bina's slow destruction of the chair and the distant look on her face. Not wanting to startle her by simply walking in, he cleared his throat to alert her to his presence. Her tea formed an almost perfect arc in the air as she jumped at the sound, and it was all she could do to keep hold of the mug. "Oh my God, what- crap!" she sputtered out as Jim launched himself in the opposite direction of the tea. "Bollocks - I'm sorry – I just thought it would be, but it wasn't and- shit, sorry – let me get some paper towels." As Jim went over to the roll of paper on the bench on the other side of the room, he kicked himself mentally You're so smooth, Jimbo - what a way you have with her. There's no way she's going to want to come out with you this week if you scare the shit out of her when you walk into the room.

He was observant enough to know there was something troubling her, and it didn't take much to work out what. After mopping up the mess he'd inadvertently caused he gestured to the seat next to her, now she had calmed down and regained her position. She smiled at him and nodded that it was OK to sit.

"Look, I'm really sorry. I didn't mean to scare you – I really thought the old 'clear the throat at the doorway' routine would be OK." He felt like a real fool. Her smile was so genuine and disarming he felt that old playground feeling rise up inside him – the butterflies and their usual ability to prevent any form of coherent speech coming out of him. "It's fine, really – I was just miles away and you made me jump, but I'm glad you're here and glad it was you." Jim couldn't help but blush. It was something he had been aware of for years – and try as he might to stop it, he couldn't and it was the bane of his life. She noticed - of course she had as his head was now bright red. Why does this keep happening? "So, I was just thinking," started Jim, already feeling yet another round of deep scarlet flushing taking over his face. "Would you, I mean are you, umm – you know, Friday night and-" Oh my God, what is wrong with me? Bina looked him in the eye and he stopped trying to speak. "I'd love to, Jim. Shall we say 7pm at The Tuppenny?" Rescued again he thought, but at least he had a date – HE HAD A DATE!!! "In the meantime, we need to look at this Reg business – I can't get past the whole cut up while still alive, minus thumbs business. That is seriously brutal, and for what? Have we got any more info on the reason that got him boxed?" Jim was still dealing with the whole date situation and wasn't concentrating, again. "Jim!" Bina was firm but considerate. She had already realised he was likely to be somewhat distracted, so gently brought him back into the room.

"Have you got anywhere on the motive behind this?" "Still nothing, I can't find any real reason for this, no obvious connection to what Reg had been up to, nothing from previous arrests, no clues from the last few car thefts. We went through them all, interviewed everyone and found nothing. There must be something we've missed, but- I don't know. I still can't get over the boxes, you know."

Jim was pacing now and had already managed four laps of the lab, tapping his hands on the sides of his thighs as he walked. "That and no evidence on weapons that would have done that having been sold, imported or received within fifty miles of here either, so there must be something else going on here that we haven't seen."

Jim stopped, closed his eyes and rubbed his temples – he was exhausted. Too many moving parts and still nothing substantial to hold on to.

Bina picked up the photos of the wounds again and went over the notes made that got them to the axe conclusion. "WAIT!" Jim almost shouted. "We've got this ongoing investigation around the markets and potential illegals - or more accurately, slavery being carried out under organised crime. Current working theory is these guys are Albanian running this. Could you show me the notes again – would you think this could be something?"

Bina looked over at Jim. She had seen that look a hundred times – he was connecting multiple strands together and this was starting to look tangible. "OK, let's have a look at some Albanian weapons then," she suggested.

TWENTY-TWO

Adrian was worried. How was he going to find a plausible method to get himself off the hook, present a 'Martin' to the police. Given that what had been explained was no trivial matter. Whoever ended up taking the heat for this was going to be arrested and probably detained during any further investigation.

They would be fingerprinted and their ID would be checked to verify who they were, so that would make subterfuge very difficult indeed. He berated himself for not having predicted any of this - he thought he had been so careful. Lisa looked over at him across the living room. He had been odd for a few days now, a little distracted when he would usually be cheerful, and he'd been a bit short with the kids, something he never was. Clearly there was something wrong, but she knew better than to ask since he would just brush it off as work and wouldn't elaborate. She looked up from her phone again. He was pacing and in and out of the kitchen without getting anything or doing anything. "If you're in need of a job," she said, softly so as not to antagonise him, "next time you pop into the kitchen, could you come back with a glass of water?" He stopped at the archway between the living room and dining area and looked in her direction, a slightly puzzled look on his face. "What?" he mumbled. "Yeah, of course - sorry." He shook his head a little as though bringing himself back into reality and pottered into the kitchen. After ten minutes he came back in, without the water, and sat down in the armchair near the sofa, nibbling at his top lip.

"What's going on, Adrian?" Lisa finally offered, in a tone as she could muster given her frustration at him. He looked across at her. His eyes were red and he looked tired, but more than that, there was something about his demeanour that reminded her of how he was just before their first child was born. He was terrified then, he had eventually admitted to her some months later – he hadn't really given much thought to what life was going to be like as a parent, what his responsibility was for this new life – and now the same look was on his face. He looked genuinely scared.

"It's nothing, just a work problem I'm trying to figure out," he said – always keeping the right side of the truth was the easiest route. Lisa was too good at working out when he lied, so he made sure what he said was true, but without necessarily giving too much away. "One of the team seems to have done something stupid, and I have been asked to bring them into the station to explain it, but I need to be able to talk it through with them first so

I can support them if needed. It's quite a big problem, they seem to have accessed some data they shouldn't have and it's, well, it's not good."

He offered this and it seemed to help him by sharing it. Lisa looked at him for a while without speaking, trying to gauge the admission and determine if this was all there was. But Adrian either didn't notice the subtle scrutiny or wasn't prepared to offer any further explanation, so she went back to Facebook and left it. "Can I at least have that water now?" she ventured.

Bina hadn't dressed up for ages and told herself she couldn't remember the last time she had gone out on a date. She could but had spent a while trying to forget that evening. What a night that was. Meticulous planning, hair done at Frankie's, makeup done by Anya – she always did an amazing job. Nails sorted – as much as they could be, given her profession. She had bought new clothes and shoes and chosen a really nice place to eat - a new tapas bar that everyone had been raving about. Her friend was partly to blame, though. It was a blind date of sorts, and Saavni had taken pity on her due to her relentless work schedule and that she felt Bina looked miserable and needed someone in her life who could "you know, look after you." Bina had laughed out loud at that suggestion. She pondered later whether she just simply couldn't see what her friends could and actually, they were right and she needed someone. But it wasn't him. Alarms bells had rung loud and clear when he turned up in some ridiculous car, that it later transpired had been rented for the occasion. A low, sporty number with a loud engine and stereo to match. Not her thing at all. Besides the car noise, the music was a bit shit too. Then there was the overall ensemble – a suit, with a t-shirt and trainers – was this the Punjabi Don Johnson or something? She had to check her phone to make sure she hadn't been transported back to the eighties. He moaned at the food, the music, the drinks selection, made rude comments about everyone in the building, went on and on about that stupid car – how fast it was, and some rubbish about litres. Not a single comment about her at all. What. A. Dick!

The doorbell chimed and she snapped back to the here and now. Another quick check in the mirror: hair – great, makeup – amazing, dress – just the right side of dangerous! She opened the door and there was Jim, looking pretty tidy - for him - in a blue cotton blend blazer, white shirt, chinos and desert boots. Just the perfect attire for the evening ahead.

"Wow," was all he could muster to start with as he drank in the sight in front of him. To be fair, he'd only really seen her in a lab coat for most of the time they had met at work, so anything different was always going to be, well, different, he thought. "You look incredible – your hair is, you know. And your dress is beautiful and so erm, elegant and you look amazing-"

"You're so erudite, Jim," she beamed. Oh yes, she thought to herself, this is how it should be. Jim opened the door of the car for her, always the gentleman. A normal car too, she noticed. Nothing flash, just a car – it was a Skoda – a nice one, but it was Jim all over. Practical, smart and considered. The music was quiet and just in the background too. He drove gently as well, no comments about any other driver, no garish hand signals and no speeding or revving the engine. The conversation flowed a little better too after he had managed to come to terms that the radiant beauty (his words) beside him was the same Bina he worked with. He was smiling too, she noticed – something she didn't often see during the working day, and it really suited him. They arrived at Cucina Toscana – his choice - and he opened the car door for her and offered a hand. They walked to the restaurant arm-in-arm, and when they got through the door they were greeted by a waiter who took them to the bar to start with, where two glasses of chilled wine were already waiting for them.

"Jim – this is all rather well-planned," she said, smiling broadly at him. He looked embarrassed as though he shouldn't have done it, but she squeezed his hand. "It's really lovely, thank you." He relaxed and hoped the other plans were going to be as well-received.

Their table was out of the way of the main area, affording them a degree of privacy and quiet so they could talk without having to raise their voices to be heard. A selection of olives and cheese with bread had been ready there when the waiter had seated them, and Jim stood while Bina sat down, then sat too and tentatively reached across the table for her hand.

"I'm so glad you're here Bina. I hope Italian is OK?" She smiled with genuine happiness in her eyes. "It's perfect, Jim, it really is – I'm glad I asked you." She giggled a little, diffusing the obvious embarrassment he felt at having to be coaxed into the date due to his inability to ask outright.

The night progressed as though it were a dream for Jim. The food was amazing, the ambience was more than he had hoped for, but it was all overshadowed by the company. Bina was captivating in her conversation, she was a vision of beauty and sophistication and Jim was aware that he was more relaxed than he had been for years. None of the conversation was about work, they must have talked about everything else during the course of the evening.

Without them noticing the restaurant had emptied around them and they were the only ones left, but at no point did any of the staff try to encourage them to leave. Eventually Bina looked around and realised it was just them and leaned over the table and whispered, "It's just us here, and the staff – maybe we ought to go?" Jim looked around and went slightly pink. Never one to want to be a burden, he caught the eye of the waiter who came over to them, a broad smile on his face. "Yes, Sir – have you anything else you need?" he asked with such a relaxed air giving them the impression that they had all the time in the world and it was no bother to the staff at all. "Oh, we had no idea you were waiting for us, or that everyone else had gone, I'm really sorry to hold you up," offered Jim, but this was waved away by the waiter. "Not at all Sir, we're glad you are here and comfortable with us. You can stay as long as you want," he said to them both, with such a genuine smile that was as much in his eyes as it was in his face. "Thank you, you've all been very patient – it's time we let you get home." said Jim, standing up and going over to Bina to offer his hand again. They thanked the staff, paid their compliments to the chef and settled the bill, shaking hands with everyone before leaving. Jim and Bina went arm-in-arm to the car. "I've never felt more welcomed in a restaurant before, it's like we were family there" Bina said as they walked. "They were so kind, and the food – oh man, it was amazing! Where did you find this place?"

"To be honest, it was a bit of a punt," said Jim. "I've never been there before but read a bunch of reviews of a few places and that one seemed to be ahead on atmosphere and food, so went for it." "Well, I'm really glad you did – I've had a wonderful time, thank you. It was perfect. It's all been perfect." Jim smiled and felt something deep within him that he hadn't felt before; Contentment.

He opened the car door, made sure Bina got safely inside and closed it, before walking around to the driver's side and climbing in. With the door closed, he turned to her. "Thank you", he said. "This has been the best night of my life". As soon as he said it, he felt like a kid and was sure she would laugh at him for making such an immature comment. "Me too," she said, "It has been wonderful, Jim. You really are lovely, a real gentleman, not that I thought you'd be anything other than that," she quickly added, "but you're just so kind and genuine. The whole evening has been just perfect." She blushed a little, aware of having repeated herself.

They drove home, discussing the merits of Italian food, their experiences of different cuisines and the plethora of options ahead of them for future dinner dates. When they arrived at Bina's house, Jim pulled up onto the drive and turned off the engine. He opened the door, got out and went around to open the passenger door – offering his hand again to Bina. At the door, they stopped – bathed in the light from an almost full moon, nerves rushing back to Jim and turning him back into a teenager again.

"It's been amazing tonight, and I don't want to rush anything, if, you know, you're not, well – if you're…" Bina took his hands in hers, leaned forward and stood on her tiptoes, and pecked his cheek. "You really are amazing, Jim – and there's no rush, we've all the time in the world," she said, and wrapped her arms around him. They stood on her doorstep for what felt like hours in this embrace, Jim breathing her in, his chest filling with happiness. He kissed her cheek, and they moved slightly apart.

"Goodnight, and thank you again," he said looking deep into her dark eyes. "Goodnight, Jim – see you in the, wait… it already is the morning. See you later," she said as she fumbled with her keys. She looked at him and a genuine smile lit up her face as she unlocked the door.

He stood there for a few seconds after she had gone in, not waiting for an invitation but just enjoying the moment. He walked over to the car and got in, putting his seat belt on while the engine started. The drive back to his house was a blur - he arrived safely but couldn't have given an account of how he had got there, the biggest smile over his face all the way home. Yes, it had been a perfect night.

TWENTY-THREE

Seamus sipped the coffee he had been nursing for nearly an hour, not paying any real attention to the temperature or lack of taste. He had been poring over the case documents all morning, trying to make sense of what lay before him.

Drugs were a given with this group. They had the scene sewn up and had done for years, but there had been no getting close to them, not in any tangible way and nothing much to talk about - that was before the op that had nearly killed him. But looking over this, they had clearly moved on at pace – rebuilt most of what had been pulled down back then, added significant scale to that part of their business and moved out into guns, and now people. People, though, that really changed things for the police - more departments needed, more operations to try to infiltrate – but this was his guy, and it was for Seamus to finish the job he had started. Kelmendi was going down, and this all happening at the market was his route in. But this time, he was going to make absolutely certain nothing could go wrong. Nobody was getting away – he had to make sure the traps were all set. Moving drugs and guns around, while not exactly easy, was a lot more straightforward than people. The logistics alone of how to get people into containers, lorries, whatever it was that they had to be squeezed into – the thought made his stomach turn. People, actual people, being torn away from families and friends, treated worse than animals, to make money for someone, somewhere. The fear that must rip through them all, the terror when they were taken and the pain and suffering as they made their way across countries to become slaves of one sort or another. Illicit factory workers, part of the drugs or arms organisations, sex slaves – none of these options were palatable in any way as far as Seamus was concerned. And it didn't end there, the anguish of the families left not knowing the fate of children, brothers, sisters or parents. One minute there, the next – who knew where?

When he'd seen reports on the news of trafficked people the reporters would say that those who survived the journey were the lucky ones, but from the cases he had been involved in, the disgusting treatments handed out – Seamus wasn't so sure. Perhaps the ones that didn't make it were the fortunate ones - lucky was pushing it a little bit.

He stopped and looked up, needing to take his eyes and mind away from all of this for just a few minutes, at the same time finally realising the coffee was stone cold and frankly disgusting. He walked out of the living room towards the kitchen to deal with the immediate issue of needing something less vile to drink. He was aware of the deafening silence around him. He had been living alone for months now - almost a year, he realised with a stab of emotion and a mounting sadness. He had been used to a house full of noise, mostly good. The kids and their games and incredible conversations about anything and everything, the background hum of the TV or music from somewhere, conversations with the dog and just that usual buzz of a busy home. But now, there was nothing at all. He could hear the clock on the wall ticking, the occasional vehicle passing outside, but mostly nothing. His mind got back to the people being taken from their own household buzz, their inane discussions about their day, what may have happened at school, or some friendly chat over a drink, before their world suddenly exploded into grief.

He realised he was crying. Leaning on the kitchen counter, tears ran freely down his face, forming a small pool on the Formica in front of him. He didn't try to stop them. The memories of that night were flooding back to him too now: laying on the ground then waking in hospital, the failure of the operation to bring in Kelmendi after so much planning, so much work. But all that was before they knew about people-trafficking, and now – their paths had crossed again. He would say it was a coincidence – but he didn't believe in them. Why here, what was it about this town that they used it as a staging post for the people they were moving – it was quiet, out of the way of a lot of the usual attention. Maybe that was it, but why did it have to be here, where he was?

He flicked the kettle on and opened the cupboard to get the coffee jar but just ended up staring at it. This was all getting very complicated, and the recent nights hadn't yielded enough sleep to really be able to process much of it properly. The fear had begun creeping in. Would he mess up - would he let this team down, like he had the last one? He reached up for the coffee but his hand was shaking and he couldn't stop it. Seamus placed both his hands on the kitchen counter and took a few deep breaths. He hated this feeling of losing control and was fighting the feelings of guilt that he was letting people down by not managing this situation, that once back in the office they would know, they would see the cracks emerging, and flags would go up. Questions would be asked – probing into why he was here, was he up to it, was he the right person to lead this investigation, was he the right person to be in charge? Should he even be here at all?

His thoughts quickly descended into what ifs – what if he really messed up and didn't make it this time? What if they all got away, what if some of the people being moved got caught up and didn't make it, what if Jim…Seamus was sweating profusely and began to feel too weak to stand. He stumbled across the kitchen and slumped onto a stool, barely keeping his balance. His head was spinning, sweat running down his back and his heart racing - the whole room seemed to be closing in on him. He fumbled for his phone that was in the front right pocket of his jeans but couldn't seem to free it. By now he was struggling to breathe and could hear his blood pulsing in his ears, desperately trying to remember the exercises from his sessions just after he was released from hospital. Just fucking breathe, he kept telling himself, getting more anxious by the second. He managed to wrestle his phone out of its denim cage but it hit the floor with a crack and Seamus knew it was likely to be out of action now.

Less than a second later he joined his phone on the tiled floor – panting and shaking, trying as hard as he could to get through the fog of this panic attack and cling onto something, anything positive that would help. He had crouched into a ball on the floor and was shivering uncontrollably and almost chanting to himself to just stop, just get up, but nothing was happening. He was just a passenger now on this sickening roller-coaster of perceived and real fear - fear that wrapped him up and made him completely unable to escape.

TWENTY-FOUR

The Peugeot was as inconspicuous as planned, but he had needed to change the plates before getting onto the ferry as there was likely to be some interest after the tennis club. Better to have an unimpeded drive to England as he really didn't need any unnecessary attention. Getting to the town was easy enough, but he needed to use a little more local knowledge from a map to get to where he needed to be. It had been a long time since he'd been here and things were bound to have changed. Many new houses had gone up, road layouts were different - the town was almost unrecognisable to him. After driving around for an hour Bariu pulled up at a row of shops to get some food and something to drink. He spotted a small group of young men at the end of the row who could well be local, heads shaved and a collection of garish and uninteresting tattoos between them, so he went into the shop and emerged with a sandwich, a local paper and some cigarettes.

Walking over to the men, eating the sandwich, they all stopped talking as he approached – looking slightly wary of the man from the dirty car. "Hi, I hope you can help me with something. I'm looking for an old friend but not sure where they are these days, I've not been here for a long while." The men looked amongst themselves and one took a step forward.

"An old friend? You sure you're not after anything else, mate?" His eyes locked onto Bariu's, searching for the reaction he usually got – fear, perhaps the intimidation he was looking for, but got nothing. Bariu smiled and stayed where he was, slowly taking the cellophane wrap off the cigarettes and putting it in his pocket. "Yes, just an old friend, no need for anything more than that, thank you. They were last at Hazelwood Avenue, but it's been so long since I was here that I can't remember how to get there."

"Do I look like Dora the Explorer to you, pal?" The man was getting looks and sounds of admiration from his friends, spurring him on even more. "Who you choose to dress up as in your own time is entirely up to you, my friend, but I apologise if I am imposing on your-" he looked at the other men- "special time." The man in front of him bristled and stood to what Bariu assumed was his full height, still not quite at eye level. Bariu smiled and offered him a cigarette, the currency of information and balance worldwide. The man in front of him hesitated, then nodded and took one from the pack. "Cheers, yeah," he said "It's OK if you don't know where it is, I'll keep looking, but I just thought you were from near here and might know." "Hazelwood Avenue - it's three streets down there on your left," the man pointed with a hand covered in italic letters and some kind of web pattern. "Thank you." said Bariu and handed the man the rest of the cigarettes and went back to the car. He checked the mirror before driving off, watching the inevitable bravado play out now he was safely away from them - hand gestures from two of the men, but just a look, all too familiar to Barui, from the man with the cigarettes.

He turned onto Hazelwood Avenue and drove as slowly as the other traffic would allow, looking for number 28. That was what his investigation had come up with as their family home. After driving the length of the road checking the numbers on one side, he turned and came back the other way. Spotting where 28 was, he then checked signs and cameras. London was full of them - where was parking allowed, how long for, could he stay unseen for long enough to monitor comings and goings of the household, give him time to create the plan and then, well – that needed some thought too. Having inspected the road he was satisfied there were no cameras, no residents-only permits required, and it didn't seem the kind of road that had too many conscientious neighbours likely to be reporting a vehicle. Bariu found a nearby restaurant and settled down for lunch and a bit of time with the local paper to see if there was anything of interest happening – may be useful, should anyone approach him, to at least sound familiar with local events.

He finished lunch and folded his napkin thoughtfully before placing it onto his now empty plate. It was time for a walk - time to get a more intimate view of Hazelwood Avenue and find the best place to start gathering the information needed for the days ahead. This part of the process had to be done properly. No short cuts could be taken here, as if there were any gaps or problems the rest had a tendency to fall apart pretty quickly. Having taken more time to get his bearings on the location of the house and the best place for a vehicle to be parked, preferably one that wouldn't draw much - if any - attention, Bariu went back to the local paper and the for-sale ads near the back. Something cheap, not eye-catching or memorable in any way, but able to conceal what was inside and have enough space to stretch out in for long periods of time. After a few minutes of scanning the ads, he found what he was looking for, Citroën van, current MOT, needs TLC, £500 cash. Bariu dug his phone out of his pocket and called the number. It was a short taxi ride to the address, and within 30 minutes he was driving away in the vehicle that would be his temporary home for as long as this would take. He was careful to keep away from major roads as there was clearly no insurance and, with tax for vehicles no longer being something that was sold as part of the deal, there were too many little issues that could attract attention.

He parked up within sight of number 28 Hazelwood Avenue and opened an internet browser on his phone. Within a few minutes he had registered the van as SORN as per the instructions on the website – one less thing to worry about. Then he got out and went to the rear left tyre which was almost on the kerb and let out some of the air to give the impression the van had been here for a while. Bariu locked the doors and walked back to the small row of shops for supplies, getting more familiar with the layout of Hazelwood Avenue and potential escape routes as he walked.

It was a beautiful afternoon, the sun sitting lazily in the sky casting light shadows around the trees that lined most of the roads. Bariu took a little time to enjoy the moderately clean air around him, the background noise of suburban life and the steady and frequent sounds of planes overhead. All these sounds were important to him; they advised him of threats from people making noise that was out of this form of ordinary. The approach of vehicles was often unnoticed as they blended into the background, but if you were to listen for a while, that background became a tapestry onto which additional, different and occasional sounds were woven. Once you understood how the sounds interacted and how the whole symphony was played, it was much easier to pick out those sounds that didn't quite match.

He sat for a while on a bench near the local playing fields and read a little more of the local news stories – car crashes, drunk hit-and-runs, alcohol-fuelled attacks on local shops. It was all similar articles, and it seemed odd to Bariu that for somewhere that on one hand seemed to be struggling to retain, or regain its identity from the sprawling mass around it, yet on the other seemed unable or perhaps, unwilling to deal with the persistent problems of those who didn't share the same view and existed in their bubble of entitlement to do whatever they wanted - and to hell with the neighbourhood. There was an advantage to this, though - it made what he was doing as good as invisible.

Bariu walked back to the Peugeot and opened the boot. Leaning in, he removed the large black bag and hauled it onto his shoulder. Closing the boot he opened the driver's door, took out some cleaning cloths and wiped down the steering wheel, gear shift, handbrake and doors. Force of habit every time he left a vehicle behind, but useful all the same. Locking the car and zipping the keys into his jacket pocket, he walked back to Hazelwood Avenue, to the van and his surveillance position for as long as it took.

Once at the van, he opened the rear and climbed in, closing the door behind him – the early dusk giving enough cover and taking full advantage of most of the street now being in the throes of making dinner and/or catching up on the soaps. He opened the bag and removed a drill, then bored a small hole in the rear door. Taking out a USB camera, he attached it to the door so the lens was almost flush with the hole, then taped the cable along the inside side panel of the van so that it was out of the way. He connected the other end to his phone and opened the camera app. Switching to the external camera, he checked to make sure it was facing the house and that he had a clear view of the front door. He needed to ensure he was aware the moment there was any sign of them entering or leaving the house. Looking through the rest of the contents of the bag, he checked that each firearm had sufficient ammunition – topping up those that were low, placed his jacket under his head and lay back, phone in hand, waiting. It took less time than he had expected for her to appear at the doorway given the time of day, but he zoomed in and made sure he captured a decent image of her. She walked to the end of the path at the front of the house, arms laden with empty cartons, plastic milk bottles and paper - all of which was placed, rather than dropped, into the recycling bin next the road. Bariu watched her go back to the house, checking the plants along the path as she went. There was no further sign of her, or anyone else, going in or out of 28 Hazelwood Avenue that night.

Bariu made some notes on the occupant he had seen, looked up the details from 12 months back and updated some of the observations from then. The morning would hopefully yield better results to understand who was there – maybe all the other occupants were already in the house, and therefore it was expected that there wouldn't be any sign of them. He looked over the previous intelligence he had put together last year - it was just over a year now, he realised as he read through it all. There should be four people in the house, two would still be under sixteen, so it was crucial to keep them away from any actions that needed to be taken. It was late and nothing was going to happen now until the morning, so Bariu decided it was time to get some rest. The van had been fitted with a roof vent, so no chance of it steaming up with him inside overnight.

He opened his bag and checked the contents again. The suppressors had been attached to the handguns already, which was one less thing to worry about when the time came. He carefully replaced everything in a way that meant each item would be easy to access when required, folded his jacket and placed it behind his head again, ready to lay down for the night. As he lay there in the van as it cooled, his thoughts - or perhaps it was dreams - took him back to the last time his path had crossed a member of this family and how things had ended up. A lot had happened in the intervening year, he had learned a lot more about their mutual acquaintance – things that had cemented his decision for action, things that had put in motion so many actions that had led him to be here, tonight. It was time to close that chapter and put to rest the questions that had been repeatedly asked by him – why and how had things come to this, and would he be able to put an end to it all? There were many more questions in his head now as he tried to sleep, but he needed to maintain focus on the task at hand and he knew he needed to be rested and alert. Tomorrow may need him to bring all his skills to the fore.

TWENTY-FIVE

Adrian had been through the whole spectrum of feelings over the past twenty-four hours, playing scenarios in his head about the impending situation. Could he find a patsy to be Martin? "I mean, they would have to be fingerprinted and a whole police record set up for them, so either someone totally unknown now and forever with a clean nose - but then they would ask me so many questions - or someone that I could pay to do that and they would bugger off afterwards." Adrian discussed with the empty space around him in the car. Alternatives went through this process and were dismissed based on merits of one criteria or another.

What could he do? Quit, but that would raise a lot of suspicion, and what would he do for money? The outlay of the van, tools, clothes and such had not been too easy to hide, but no job would be very obvious, very quickly.

There was a sharp 'honk' from behind him, and he

realised the lights had changed to green and he hadn't moved. "Shit!" he shouted, hitting the steering wheel with clenched fists. Why did he have to be so stupid and be seen with that useless bastard? He toyed with the idea of not turning up today, but that would just ring alarm bells so he needed to get some sort of story together about Martin and buy some time. Maybe he was ill, on holiday perhaps, but each idea seemed just a little too convenient and Adrian told himself that the police would see through every one of them. He hadn't eaten properly since the last meeting with the police and he was sure Lisa knew something was wrong, but there was another thing – what on earth could he tell her? She would lose her mind, even though Adrian had rationalised it all with himself and quite easily too. The more he thought about how he would approach it with Lisa should the need arise, the more it seemed to unravel in his mind.

The pressure was really piling up, affecting his sleep which in turn was impacting him during the day for everything. 'HONK!!' Another stark reminder that he was unable to concentrate. He'd been stopped too long at yet another junction while his mind raced, and tried to consider what possible routes out of this situation were available to him. It had been getting more difficult to keep this away from Lisa too. She wasn't stupid and she had clearly been noticing changes in his usually happy demeanour, however well he thought he was hiding it. But the veneer of nonchalance was wearing even thinner, as was he, and his inability to concentrate was creeping into many other aspects of his daily life.

Adrian pulled away from the lights and nearly crashed

into the car coming from his left. The traffic light had changed again without him even noticing, and he was in danger of causing an accident – collision – he mentally corrected himself. He drove away, pulled over as soon as it was safe and just sat there, staring out of the windscreen at the passing traffic, and the stares of the other motorists and pedestrians that had witnessed his near miss. He was panting, sweating and shaking. He tried to regain some composure but was certain someone was going to call the police and he would be questioned about this incident that almost was, his poor concentration – driving without due care and attention, to use the correct parlance.

His breathing was shallow and he could feel his heart in his chest. A rush of heat went up his neck and he thought he was going to pass out.

Adrian pulled up at the car park and selected the usual space and, getting out of his car, looked around, checking whether anyone was looking at him – curious since he was aware he had never been bothered about this before. But now, certainly after the last few minutes, he was expecting at least an officer to come over and address him, and overall his paranoia was such that he felt all eyes were on him. This was not a good place to have that kind of feeling.

Walking into the building he was careful to continue his usual daily routine. Straight to the kitchen, make a coffee, look at the notice board – just don't draw attention to yourself, smile and nod, smile and nod – same as you do every day. As soon as he was in the office he usually occupied, he closed the door and relaxed a bit. He was still shaking a little and needed to cool down so that the sweat patches that had gathered under his arms and down his back could dry out. He took a few deep breaths and blew each one out through slightly pursed lips. Logging on to the main system, he opened up the profile he had created for Martin and tried to think again about who could possibly help and pretend to be this employee that had been snooping about… and then it came to him.

Martin was an 'external contractor', not just to the police, but to the software support company too Adrian's company. That way, Martin had the option to leave with little notice and go anywhere. Adrian's mind was racing now with possibilities. He could have accrued holiday and decided to leave, used the holiday as notice and just gone. Yes. Yes! That would work. Of course there would be some ill feeling towards Adrian for bringing the guy in, and allowing him to just leave – but given the circumstances, how could Adrian have foreseen this person's errant behaviour, how could he have known that he would get spooked and run? Well, of course he couldn't have. Adrian then decided that Martin had given false details on his application, and while Adrian had checked in a rudimentary way, he didn't have the resources at his disposal to perform a really deep check - so what was he to do?

He sat back in his chair, genuinely pleased with himself and going over and over the idea until he was happy with all aspects, and comfortable that he would be able to explain it to anyone with clarity and consistency. So he didn't need anyone to take the heat, as Martin had clearly realised the net was closing around him and made his decision to leave. Adrian had tried to contact him, but the number he had (and had just updated on the record) turned out to be fake, or certainly not able to connect – not surprisingly, as Adrian had just made it up by using random numbers from a few he had in his contacts. The address when looked up didn't exist either – ten numbers out from the last house on the street. Clever Martin to have done that, but what was his plan, why was he looking at these people?

Adrian smiled, for the first time in a few days, and got himself prepared for if and when the next invitation would come for a chat.

TWENTY-SIX

DCI Bowler stood at the window to her office, taking in the view of the car park and municipal buildings beyond. She had just come out of a briefing on the current situation with the OCG and the updates on the potential people trafficking, the market intelligence and statements relating to the 'foreign lads' on some of the stalls and her mind came back to Reg Wilson – was he caught up in this? She had read through the report from Bina's team on what their findings were: ante-mortem injuries and conjecture on what could have caused them – the prevailing theory of an executioner's axe was causing her concern. Perhaps this was the connection, as it seemed so incongruous to have just some petty car thief hacked apart and by something as barbaric as the evidence suggested.

Dawn couldn't help but draw conclusions that people from certain locations, engaged in trafficking people, weapons and drugs wouldn't think twice to bring something like an axe to anyone getting in their way – but she still couldn't quite join the dots. She moved away from the less-than-beautiful vista and walked to the wall where she had some dry-wipe boards installed. The framework of the case was drawn out, various names, locations and details were there, the odd photo stuck on with different coloured magnets – each colour signifying a level of importance. Standing and taking it all in again, she called Seamus and then Jim on their mobiles.

Both were there within a couple of minutes, Seamus with three coffees – she knew she could rely on him for refreshments – and they all sipped and contemplated what was in front of them for a few minutes before Bowler cleared her throat. "Right, here's where I am," she started, moving towards the boards. "Reg is in this mess somewhere, but I don't know where. Did he stumble into something, a handover, a meeting – was he just in the wrong place and the wrong time, or maybe…" She tailed off, mentally filling in the gaps. "Maybe stole a car from one of this lot?" she motioned towards the pictures, pulling her bottom lip in thoughtfully.

Jim nodded slowly, as the same thought went through his mind. "So, Reg borrows a car from one of these lot, they find it – maybe it's got a tracker or something, they challenge him, he tries to talk his way out, they're not having any of it and –." Bowler's phone rang, cutting off Jim's train of thought. "Bowler," she practically barked, clearly not appreciating the interruption. "Why is this so important that you need to call me about it?" She was clearly in a challenging mood, thought Jim and Seamus, cemented by the quick look that passed between them. "Right, well, tell them to deal with it and then give me an update - not the other way around."

She ended the call and turned her attention to the wall again. "Sorry, Jim – you were saying?" She looked straight at him, and he collected himself and carried on. "Yeah, so they find him and they have a discussion about the car and then…" He tailed off this time, his brow furrowed. "Go on," encouraged Bowler. "I just don't know why or how the boxes came to be there – I mean it's possible they responded to the car getting nicked, given that is our current theory of how Reg was involved. If he was, then what – collected the boxes, were they just there for another reason, maybe another poor soul was expected to end up in them?" Jim had gone an odd colour, clearly recalling the scenes of the past few days.

"Right, so maybe they already had the boxes. Could be for a similar purpose, could have had drugs, guns, who knows what in them. But they were available, so let's just assume they were there for something, and whoever discovered Reg with the car took the opportunity to use them," offered Seamus, joining the conversation and saving Jim during his moment of recollection. "But it still leaves us with this: why leave him where he was?" pondered Seamus out loud.

Jim, very much back in the room, thoughtfully nibbled the edge of the coffee cup while looking at the board. "What if they were disturbed?" he suggested. They both looked at him, waiting for a little more, and he took the unspoken cue. "Well, look, I have no idea why they would hack him to bits. Maybe it's just a thing, maybe it was spur-of-the-moment as he'd borrowed one of their cars without asking. So they get hold of him, chop him to bits and find the boxes – and perhaps think best not to leave his parts all over the place, let's pop him into these boxes and take him back to the boss to show that the little issue has been dealt with?"

"Plausible," said Bowler with a thoughtful nod. "And it's all we have, but I like it, it makes sense. Why not take him away? They'd dicked about putting him into boxes and chopping his thumbs off, then someone came along, they figured it was time to leave, and poor Reg got left behind and here we all are." "We have a full op briefing in ten minutes," said Bowler as they were all contemplating the discussion. "DCS Bridge is coming to join. He has an op name for us and wants to add a new dimension to the planning – getting some international support, InterPol or such, to really get into how far-reaching this lot are, known associates around the UK and their European routes for all their-" she hesitated, being aware that there were people included, "-products." Seamus nodded but looked pensive. "We had a ton of info on, well, on who we think this is now – when we ran the ops in London and infiltrated a lot of the routes and some of the key players – it all came to a head during Operation Jupiter which sadly didn't yield the results we had hoped it would." He felt a bead of sweat run down his back and his heart rate increased a little. Jim had been looking his way, had clearly noticed that something was going on and quickly interjected – his turn to save any embarrassment.

"We have spent some time collating all information, Sir – and have created an expanded view from both the

Jupiter team and ours. Any of the original work has been reviewed against what we have found here, and this has gone forward as the basis for this op. It was all relevant stuff and the updates have been interesting - they sort of iced the cake, as it were." "Leave it for the briefing," instructed Bowler, keen to move along and not have to repeat the same information. "Right, make sure you've both been to the toilet. This may be a long session and I don't need any hands in the air asking for a pee break." The two men exchanged a look, - partly amused, partly suggesting a trip to HR may be needed. They left Bowler's office and headed to the kitchen.

"Have you had much to do with DCS Bridge?" Jim asked Seamus as they inspected the remains of coffee in the drip machine, weighing up the time to make a fresh pot and be a bit late but in possession of decent coffee, or make the briefing on time armed with a mug of instant. "No, only really spoken to him once, one of the fast-track brigade, likes the sound of his own voice, black belt in delegation – you know the type," said Seamus reaching for the coffee jar. "And, Jim – thanks for stepping in back there." As difficult as it had been for Seamus to allow anyone close enough to him to understand any of what went on in his head, he had realised that it was important to be able to do so, and had been really fortunate that Jim had been, well- Jim, really. Considerate and discreet and someone Seamus knew he could trust. Given Jim had spotted he was in trouble and just dealt with it, he relaxed a little more about letting him in further. "You did it for me, and I've always got your back, Sir," Jim said with absolute sincerity. Seamus smiled. "What's with the sudden formality - are you after a promotion or something?" The two men smiled at each other and made their way towards the briefing room, instant coffee steaming away as they walked.

The briefing room was almost full when they walked in, and they struggled to find a space – there certainly weren't any seats left. DCS Bridge had assumed his position at the front of the room and seemed to be engrossed by a small remote control in his hand. Having turned it over a few times and still frowning at it, he placed it on the table in front of him and took a step back, standing to his full height and surveying the room, he cleared his throat. "Ladies and gentlemen, thank you for attending today." Seamus couldn't help but smile at the irony of thanking everyone for attending a mandatory briefing. "There has been a significant sequence of development over the past few days, many of which have converged to form the view that we are dealing with a pervasive and serious threat."

He let his words sink in and nodded to the DC sat to his left, and the screen behind him blinked into life showing a wall of data. "As you can see, there are a number of moving parts to this. Our intelligence gathered suggests that the top of this OCG pyramid is Kelmendi Ahmeti, Albanian origin but current domiciliary status is transient – last known location was here in the UK. We think this is due to his business interests here increasing, and this has required him to be present to oversee. Original intelligence on Kelmendi was related to class-A drug distribution, cocaine, heroin, crack etc. and approximately six years ago he branched out into dealing weapons. I'd like to say it's small-time stuff, but let's be realistic - anything to do with weapons immediately elevates the dealer into a different league."

Seamus could feel an all-too-familiar knot beginning to grow in his stomach and his heart rate started to increase. He took a slight step back to lean against the wall in order to provide a little stability, took a deep breath and looked back to the screen ."Our latest update has come from the operation around the market here, where informants have advised us on individuals coming in and out, working on the stalls. Little to no English being spoken between them and in some cases, one or two individuals offering up information suggesting that they are being used to work for free and under duress, so - modern day slaves, to use a more recognisable label."

"CCTV in the town has picked up these." The screen changed to show images of a number of people and vehicles, clearly in the local area, sending muffled comments around the room and concerned glances. "Yes," announced DCS Bridge, "right on our doorstep". He scanned the room and spotted Seamus, who immediately moved away from the wall.

"DI Corrigan here has first-hand experience of some of these folks from his previous force role and am sure will be happy to explain the importance of coordination when it comes to us executing what we will agree over the coming days. Seamus, if you will?" Bridge gestured for Seamus to come to the front of the room. Seamus felt his throat tighten, beads of sweat suddenly appearing on his forehead, and really wished he could stay where he was, using the wall to stop him hitting the floor.

Jim looked at his boss and friend and, unnoticed by anyone else in the room, he nodded. Seamus understood the confidence Jim had in him and made his way towards DCS Bridge. "Kelmendi has a very far reach and has a large and distributed network of people who are very loyal to him. Our initial investigation led us to a significant location used by his operation and run by a trusted deputy. However, for various reasons, while we were able to shut that part of the operation down, both Kelmendi and his deputy were able to escape and regroup. We believe that this disruption cost in the region of £10-12 million so was a reasonable dent in the overall revenue stream for the wider OCG. This did, however, put a number of our team out of action. Some are still unable to carry out field roles due to their connection to the OCG and potential to be recognised and-"

Seamus didn't finish the sentence and, judging by the collective expressions in the room, really had no need to. The impact upon him was clear to see, and many of his colleagues who had harboured thoughts on why and how he 'ended up' here, now had some clarity on the history of his route and just how difficult this revelation must be for him. Jim looked across the room with genuine concern clear on his face. He knew more than most and had been involved in the broadening of this new operation from the start of interviews at the market before they had the faintest idea of what it meant.

"Thanks Seamus," started Bridge. "If I may, Sir," offered Seamus, "we need to be clear, all of us, that this man and his crew are dangerous. The network is huge and far-reaching and should they home in on you-" his breath hitched, “it is likely they will know all about you in no time, where you live, who with, where you work, how you get there, wider family members, friends. They may decide to take you out of their equation by any means necessary. We have to strike on all fronts at the same time, or they have the potential to splinter and regroup. They are extremely well-financed, so nothing is off limits if it’s needed.”

This was received by the room with thoughtful and concerned nods and murmurs. Seamus was glad he had got up and said it, all of it, as he couldn’t allow anyone here to be targeted, to have to go through what he had or deal with the nightmares he endured every night.“I think now we are all aware of the importance of cross-force collaboration here, and the need to remain vigilant at all times. As you may now be aware also, we – the broader police force - have tried to dismantle this OCG, but perhaps at the time hadn’t counted on the full scale of the operation.” DCS Bridge said this while looking mostly at Seamus, not in an accusatory way, but in solidarity with a colleague who had been more engaged with this level of criminality than he had himself.

Bowler was watching the conversation unfold and was keeping her expression neutral. She had been concerned about accepting Seamus’ transfer with this in his past, but he had proven to be a significant addition to the team, leading by example. She was worried that this operation could do him some serious damage. Her phone rang and she dug it out of her pocket and answered.

“Jim, may I have a word?” she said after ending the call. “Seems you are needed here to manage the rest of the investigation into this Burch character, kidnap and false imprisonment there are a few parents that need to be met with and you're the only senior detective we have because of this." Jim's shoulders slumped a little but he knew this was important even though he wanted to be part of the OCG operation. He looked across at Seamus and pulled a face that communicated the situation well enough between the two men. Seamus gave a slight nod and mouthed "keep me up to date."

TWENTY-SEVEN

DC Darren Shipley had had a long day and it was definitely time for a decent night out, particularly after the day's briefing. It's not every day the DCS comes in and brings the whole place together, and that DI Corrigan really seems to have been through it, he thought as he drove home.

Arriving back at his flat he walked along the path to the front door, swinging his keys around with his index finger through the ring. He stopped just before getting to the front door, aware that there were footsteps behind him. His blood ran cold and he froze, paralysed by an almost irrational fear that had gripped him. He slowly turned, a feeling of dread welling up inside him, holding his keys so they splayed out from his fingers, his breathing fast but shallow.

"Afternoon, Darren." Darren let out the breath he hadn't even realised he'd held and his shoulders dropped in relief as he saw Doris Butters, his neighbour, coming along the path behind him. "Hello Mrs Butters," he said, a smile that was much too broad for a neighbour he saw every day spread across his face as the tension fell away. "Are you OK, dear - you look like you've seen a ghost!" Doris said as she got a little closer, searching his face, a look of concern on hers.

"Yes, yes, thanks I'm OK," he said, nodding. "Just a difficult day at work, a little edgy." She smiled at him. "That's good then, you had me worried for a moment." Not as worried as I had myself, thought Darren. He was still shaken as he fumbled with his keys in the lock and when he managed to open the door, he was more relieved to no longer be outside. Darren smiled at his own nervousness as he closed his front door and placed his keys on the kitchen table. Time for a quick shower and get a bunch of friends together for a pizza and some beer and maybe an hour or two at Chester's – their local club.

There was a good number of replies on the 'lads WhatsApp group and he got ready to leave. It was a ten-minute walk into town from the flat and he had arranged to meet some of the group en-route. A handful of them arrived at the restaurant at the same time and took their places at a table, ordering a round of drinks for them and their friends who were yet to appear. The pizza came and was followed by cheesecake or ice cream, and more beer. By the time they got to the bar, the level of intoxication was such that the events of the day had all but dissipated from Darren's thoughts. The group stayed together during their time in the bar, goading each other on bizarre combinations of drinks and shots to consume based on games made up on the spot. As the evening drew on and discussions centred on their next location, a few members of the group decided to separate and leave the rest to make their way to Chester's to see who would be the last one standing.

This was fairly typical of a Thursday, even though most of them had work in the morning - they were still young enough and making the most of it. The door staff were their usual welcoming selves to a slightly inebriated group, one of whom was known to them as a police officer. Once in the club they gravitated to the bar and continued their consumption, by now in smaller, yet more expensive, vessels but none of the assembled crowd seemed bothered. Darren, buoyed by the alcohol, had been casting his eye across the bar area a few times, landing on the same young woman, with dark hair and a body to die for. He decided it was about time he introduced himself.

He walked, more staggered, across towards her and met her eye as he got closer. She offered a faint smile at his beaming face. "Hi, I'm Darren – you're gorgeous," he said, swaying slightly and only a little aware of just how much he was slurring his words. "I've not seen you here before. I come here most weekends, with my mates," and he gestured somewhere behind him with his right hand, catching the side of his head with the bottle he still held.

This brought a genuine smile to her face, something she hadn't felt able to do for the three weeks she had been here. She wondered if this 'Darren' had even the vaguest notion that she was there in a professional capacity – probably not. It wasn't her chosen career, that was certain and something she was trying to convey through her eyes but knew she couldn't tell him, at least not here..

Back home had been difficult, as the family always seemed to be struggling for money and making sacrifices just to keep a roof over their heads. Their clothes were regularly threadbare but the same applied to so many other families in the village, which is probably why she and others had been targeted. They were poor and vulnerable and easy to sway with tales of better things, money that they could make and send home to make life better for everyone in the family. It was an offer that they couldn't turn down, and little did they know at the time that it was non-negotiable. This wasn't an offer, or a choice.

Days of travelling in lorries packed with others, the smell of fear and excrement permeating the already intolerable air, made the journeys seem far longer than they were. No light, and no way to know what time of day it was, added to the disorientation they all suffered from when they finally arrived at each destination along the route. Ushered from one vehicle to another like cattle, they tried to stay together having built up a camaraderie through their shared ordeal. At one waypoint, two of the women were taken out of the group and manhandled into a waiting car. One was dragged by her hair as she tried to escape and thrown against the side of the vehicle, punched and then pushed into the back seat. The rest took this cue to be as compliant as possible, to keep themselves from a similar fate. When they eventually arrived in the town, only four of the original group remained. Others had been equally unceremoniously redirected to their unknown future, leaving Nikola and her new friends to wonder what theirs would be. She didn't need to wait long to find out. The promises of work turned out to be prostitution, something they talked about along the way here, steeling themselves for what felt like an inevitability. Being able to send money home was a lie too – everything that they were paid went to him, they got to keep nothing. Not a single penny for the sale of their bodies, their dignity and their safety. This was a level of horror none of them had anticipated. Taking stock of her new reality had taken less time than she had thought, and she had adapted with levels of stoicism she didn't even know she could cultivate. But it was all she had. She needed to keep out of trouble and find a way out, however long it took, however many times she had to perform – that was the only way she could justify it to herself, that it was a performance and that she was an actress in a movie. A really horrible, lonely and soul-destroying movie.

Darren seemed far too nice to realise what she now was and she tried to discourage his advances, but she knew she was being watched and she had a quota to meet. She let him buy her a drink and they retired to a quieter part of the club so they could hear each other. The negotiations couldn't really be done at a high volume. "I think you're really pretty," he said, a line she had heard so many times and one of the first sentences in English she had not needed to have translated soon after arrival. She offered a gracious smile and tried to steer him towards what she could offer him – but he was so drunk it really wasn't obvious to him, he just thought she fancied him. All part of the performance, she told herself.

After a few minutes in their quieter location, she spotted him out of the corner of her eye – that look on his face was clear. Get on with it, or else was the gist and she knew what would happen to her if she didn't get a client tonight. She had no choice but to be forthright about the basis of this liaison and asked him outright. "What would you like? I can do anything for the right price," she said in a thick accent. Darren looked at her, not initially understanding what was happening, and after a few seconds of cognition he moved his head back a little, then to one side, assessing her and what she had just said in his drunken state. "Blow job is £20, front sex is £80, back sex is £100, but kissing is extra," she said in as level a tone as she could manage.

Darren blinked a few times, still staring. "So, you're a-" She bit her bottom lip, not wanting him to finish the sentence and use that word, so she simply nodded. As she did so, a solitary tear rolled down her cheek. "Bollocks. I can't, I mean I'm not allowed, it's-" Darren's mind was a blur of booze, desire and surprise all at once, and he was less coherent than before. "It's because I'm in the police, I can't. I've had a meeting at work today about some guy and his business in the area, what was his name- Kelly, Kelmen – I can't remember, but he's a pretty nasty bloke by all accounts and probably does things that would make you quite angry." She was listening and understood most of what he was saying, enough to know who he was referring to. Even if he couldn't remember that name, she would for as long as she would live. "So, we are going after him soon, his whole operation, everything – I'm going to be part of the team that brings him down, might even cuff him myself," he went on, unaware he was rambling and divulging very classified police information, even less aware of who he was divulging it to.

She made one last attempt to get him in a buying frame of mind, but he was adamant that this was not a transaction he was going to be party to. She turned, he was still there but was now shaking his head, meaning she had to cut this guy loose and find another option.

Nikola politely cut Darren off mid-flow about where they were going first, and encouraged him to drink up and leave, as she knew that sometimes, failed customers would receive a reminder that wasting the time of one of the girls carried quite a penalty.

Darren finished what was left in the bottle, waddled towards the bar, placed the empty bottle down and set off in the direction of the door.

Marek strode over to her and grabbed her hair at the back of her head. "What the fuck, bitch – don't you want to earn today? You know what will happen to you now?" he spat at her, not hiding the sheer contempt he felt.

"Wait, he was policeman, he didn't want." Marek slapped her. "What did you say to him? You stupid bitch!"

"No, he told me they were coming for Kelmendi – they have many coming," she stammered, fearing yet another slap, or worse. Marek looked at her with cold, grey eyes. As soon as she had mentioned Kelmendi he seemed to back off a little, but he still eyed her with doubt. "I swear, that is what he said. They are many, coming soon and coming to here first."

Marek contemplated the message, delivered by a whore. After a short time he nodded and let her go. "Good girl - that will keep you safe for tonight."

TWENTY-EIGHT

Acting DC Andrew Gibbons was sitting at his new desk in the MCU, reviewing the details he had collected so far on the van seen on the CCTV and by the witness. He took his new role very seriously and wanted to show to his superiors that their faith in him was justified and he was a conscientious and diligent detective. It had been him that discovered the address had been empty and found the letters relating to the vehicle in question, all in the name of the deceased former owner of the house. Then he had found the name of the person who had been accessing the record of the victim that had been seen being bundled into the van, then traced the suspect's boss, and sat in on the interview.

Adrian Burch had given them nothing at all. Gibbons had thought this odd at the time but being new, didn't have the confidence on the day to mention it, but the more he thought about it, the stranger it seemed. Sure, he had looked and sounded concerned, he had stated that this Martin Collins would get fired immediately, but it felt unnatural. Gibbons dismissed it and put it down to lack of experience, but he couldn't quite shake it off completely. Digging through some more data, it was clear the owner of the house had no relatives, certainly none that had been close enough to visit regularly or notice he had departed. Gibbons thought for a moment about how lonely a life that must have been and was comforted by the knowledge that he had a close family and a wide circle of friends. He started to look more at Martin Collins. There was no mention of him within the Companies House records for the company Adrian ran, and he had asked building maintenance to share logs of access cards to the building for as far back as they kept them - six weeks it turned out unless they needed to go to a longer period via accessing an archive. It was a reasonably-sized spreadsheet, but however he filtered it, there was no entry for Martin Collins.

Moving from access cards to car park entry, still no sign of the elusive Mr Collins. Fair enough, Gibbons thought to himself. There must be a remote working policy in place so he may never have needed to set foot in the building, no - he would have needed to do the usual induction that everyone does that works here. Regardless of whether or not you ever entered the building again, you had to do this course, and it was always delivered here. Gibbons went to the desk sergeant. "Good afternoon, Sarge," he started, hoping he wasn't going to get a ribbing for no longer 'being one of us, oh, look at you, all high and mighty," and the usual bollocks, but none came.

"Yes, PC Gibbons, how can I help you?" Gibbons explained the situation as succinctly as he could to the officer on shift, who listened intently before speaking. "Let's see if we can find something that shows this mysterious person has been here." Sergeant Mason checked the records for some time, guest passes given out, temp door cards, parking passes - but nothing came back for Martin Collins. Gibbons thanked the desk sergeant, made his way back upstairs and went to find Jim Pallister to share this development, but needed to get his data together along with the next steps to present a rounded approach. This guy doesn't exist. He found Jim at his usual desk, coffee in one hand and a biscuit in the other, looking at his computer screen with a slight expression of confusion on his face. "Sir," Gibbons nearly shouted, such was his excitement about his investigation that day, and Jim looked across the room to see who it was being addressed. Realising it was him, he turned to face the incoming acting DC who was visibly bristling with a need to impart something to him. "What is it, Gibbons?" Jim asked politely, overlooking the fact he had been interrupted while trying to build a reconnaissance approach for one of the many locations on his list. "It's about Martin Collins, Sir. I don't think he exists!" Jim had to think for a second or two as the name initially didn't mean anything to him and then it clicked. "Yes, IT man checking records of disappearing thieves. What do you mean, he doesn't exist?"

Gibbons went over what he had found, or not found to be more accurate, and while doing so was trying to read Jim's expression - somewhere between amusement and interest but he seemed to be taking it all in. Once he had delivered his monologue he waited. Jim seemed to be chewing over the feast of facts he had just been served and trying to hide how impressed he was by this young officer with a keen eye for details. "That's excellent work Gibbons, really good. So, where does this take us?" Without hesitation he continued with his rehearsed speech. "Well, Sir, given this name has been presented to us as the perpetrator of accessing files and we have to link him with the disappearance of at least one of these people," Gibbons explained, "we can only really go back to Adrian Burch to see if he can tell us why this Martin Collins has never been here, ever. Since he has never been onsite he can't have completed any of the data protection training that is mandatory here and is only done here, in this building. There have never been any exceptions to this." Jim continued to look, allowing the silence to encourage Gibbons to continue with his thought process. "I've looked into the IT company that Adrian Burch runs and there's no mention of a Martin there, on their website, LinkedIn, Facebook or Companies House, which in itself isn't anything more than circumstantial, but there are two other names associated to the company on our system as well as Martin and Adrian. I've checked these out too and the same result for both. No evidence of them ever being here in this building. So that leaves us with just one person, who has been here and was probably the person to set these accounts up too. Adrian Burch."

Jim thought about the interview with Burch - how quickly he threw this Martin under the bus and how convenient it all seemed. Now, with the background work Gibbons had done, it became very obvious why.

"Brilliant, Andrew, well done. What do you want to do?" Jim asked the junior officer. He beamed, clearly pleased with the response and the opportunity to take it further. "I think we need to bring him in, as soon as possible and present him with this, the other names as well, and see how he reacts. I'd wager he may try to blame the others if we only deal the hand of Martin not having been here. He may try the 'oh, did he not do the training?' bit, but we should layer the evidence in the interview and build up to us not finding a scrap of data to prove these people have any connection to the company he runs, or indeed being actual people."

Jim nodded but then frowned. "How can we state that they may not be real?" Gibbons smiled again, Jim was really starting to like him. "I've checked the electoral roll too and can't find people with those names within fifty miles of here, which to me is too wide a catchment for this kind of job. You know, if you worked on that kind of system there are other forces that may well be more local to you, so why travel?"

"OK, let's ask him to join us. Let's say 5pm, keep him here past dinnertime so we might stir up some shit for him at home and make him late. Give him another thing to worry about and give us another element to the interview." As Gibbons walked away Jim smiled to himself. That was one sharp kid. This interview was going to be very interesting.

Adrian had expected a call and had been ready. He had rehearsed the whole thing over and over to make sure he knew how to explain his failed attempts to get hold of Martin, that the details he had given were false and how sorry and disappointed he was in how this issue had arisen. What he could do to make amends and apologise again for allowing himself to be fooled. When it happened, it was bound to be a challenging meeting, but he would get out unscathed and be seen as a victim in this too. It was just that it was almost five, and he had expected it to have happened by now. Maybe they're taking the Martin route and leaving me alone, he pondered as he began packing his paperwork up and shutting down his laptop, ready to leave.

Jim and Gibbons decided that it would be better for the strategy for Gibbons to find Adrian and invite him for a discussion in an interview room, so as to maintain the facade that it was just going to be a chat. Gibbons walked down to the office where Adrian was usually based, knocked and opened the door. "Mr Burch, would you have some time for a chat?" he said. Adrian looked up from the laptop case he had just slid the device into and attempted a smile, while inside his stomach was starting to churn. It's OK, you're prepared for this, he told himself. "Yes, of course", he ventured hoping that the young officer would just go over the story he had created and that would be that - he didn't look like he had been in the job long. Adrian glanced at his watch, it was just gone five pm and he really ought to be heading out. Mind you, a chat with a junior officer would only take a few minutes anyway.

They walked in silence along the corridor until Gibbons stopped outside one of the interview rooms and opened the door. Sitting in the room was one of the more senior officers Adrian remembered from before and his stomach-churning increased. Perhaps this wasn't going to be quite such a walk in the park. Jim looked up. "Thanks for coming, Mr Burch, please take a seat. This shouldn't take too long." Adrian sat on the other side of the table to Jim and Gibbons took the seat to Jim's right. "Mr Burch, I'm DI Jim Pallister, this is DC Andrew Gibbons, this is currently an informal discussion. We just wanted to go over the issue of the file access relating to…" - he looked in the folder in front of him for effect - "Martin Collins." Adrian nodded. "Yes, of course. As I said previously, anything I can do to help." "That's good to hear, thank you," said Jim.

"Tell me about Martin Collins, if you will - how long has he worked for you, what kind of employee is he generally, how long have you known him, usual background stuff," he continued, watching Adrian for any reaction or tell that may be giving away his position. Adrian almost relaxed. They'd fallen for the whole story, all he had to do now was roll out the stuff he'd come up with and he would just about be home in time for fish and chips.

"I haven't known him long, and we haven't had anything outside of work between us. He was a good developer and tech support guy, according to his CV and the remote interview I carried out with him. Answered all the questions I had set him, explained scenarios well, and he seemed like a good prospect to assist in the role I had open." It was going as per his mental script, and it looked like they were both buying it too. "I did the usual checks on him, address, previous employer, social media stuff and he checked out, so I made the offer to him. He got up to speed quickly, always did good work, and I had no need to doubt anything he had said to me, until all this happened."

Jim watched Gibbons out of the corner of his eye and saw he had noticed the same thing - a slight movement from Adrian when explaining background then moving the subject quickly on to the issue that had brought them all to the room. Perhaps he was just sensitive to the importance of what had been noticed and wanted to demonstrate his support, or more likely he was weaving a story in front of them and didn't want to dwell on certain aspects. Adrian continued. "As soon as I heard what had happened, I spoke to Martin and immediately dismissed him. I then advised I needed to ensure his device had no data on it, so requested a screen share so I could see he had removed it all, and the remote access software and configuration so he had no route back, which was done. "I then explained that I needed to meet and explain the situation and its severity, in person. I went to the address that he had given and the people there had never heard of him, so he must have given false information. I tried to call him but the number no longer worked."

He followed this with his rehearsed script and allowed both officers to absorb all the actions he had taken: how bad he felt that the details no longer checked out and he could no longer contact Martin Collins. Jim nodded at Gibbons. Time to play the first card. Gibbons took the subtle cue and picked up the file which was now mostly the data he had gathered. "Thank you, Mr Burch. May I ask, in terms of our mandatory data training, I see you had attended the session here. Was Mr Collins at the same session, or did he attend a later one?" Adrian tilted his head as though thinking back to the course. "No, he didn't attend the same one as me. He attended a later session not long after he was brought in, possibly in September last year - yes, that rings a bell."

Gibbons made some notes, capturing what had just been offered by Adrian, then put his pen down and looked directly at Adrian. "As you know, these courses must be held here, onsite. We have the record of your attendance, when you signed in and accessed with your pass, and the escorting officer to have got you to that part of the building. What we don't have are any corresponding records of Mr Collins taking the same route - no access or visitor card, no escorting officer's signature, no sign-in for the course, nothing." Gibbons remained leaning on the desk, his eyes locked with Adrian's.

Adrian looked thoughtful and shook his head. "I would have thought you would have that. Perhaps it was an oversight on the day but given the revelations I had discovered about his address and phone, it is more likely he told me he had attended but never did. Most of what he has told me has less credence the more I look into it, so it's difficult for me to trust or believe many things he advised me of." Gibbons waited to see if Adrian was going to offer any more, but the man opposite didn't seem to have anything else to say, so it was time to go to stage two. "I see. As I said, we looked into the attendance data for the training and found no evidence to support Mr Collins having been onsite here, but also there is nothing to support his ever having been here. No card requested, no visitor pass provided, no entry to the parking, nothing." Adrian raised a hand to stop Gibbons. "His role was performed remotely, so it makes sense that he hadn't been here, apart from the course he told me he had attended, but like I said-" Adrian knew he didn't need to continue that sentence, so left it there. Gibbons smiled thinly. "Yes, that would make sense, except-" he opened the folder again and removed some pages. Placing them on the table, he tapped his pen on them a few times. Adrian tried to see what was on them but the print was too small to read from his position.

"We also looked around online for Mr Collins, and were quite surprised to note that he doesn't seem to have a digital footprint - you understand what I mean by that, I assume?" Gibbons allowed Adrian to nod and fill in the gaps a little. "Yes, social media etc., I know what that is," Adrian stated. "Exactly," said Gibbons in a matter-of-fact tone. "No Facebook profile, nothing on LinkedIn, no other social media that looks anything like an IT guy from around here. I take it he was reasonably local?" Jim smiled to himself. That was a nice move, sliding that little gem in like that- he has a future as a detective. "Well, all the information he provided to me suggested he didn't live very close to here - probably twenty or so miles away, which is why working remotely made more sense. But as I've already said, his details didn't check out, and there is a possibility he deleted any social media accounts - he clearly doesn't want to be found."

"That is certainly a possibility," added Jim, "and one we had considered, to be fair. But social media leaves a trail too, old pages from searches, that and the electoral roll, we couldn't find anyone by that name for over 50 miles from here. Even if the address you had for him turned out to be false, it is feasible that it would have been an address reasonably close to the real one - if there is a real one, of course. Our problem, Mr Burch, is that we can't find anyone by the name of Martin Collins around here, with any association to you or your company, or this site, anywhere. So we need to understand how that is and what it may mean."

For the first time, Adrian seemed visibly nervous and now it became clear that his story was beginning to unravel. "Before we continue, I need to advise that the rest of this interview will be carried out under caution," said Jim in a calm and level tone. Adrian moved his head back a little and shook very slightly. "You do not have to say anything. But it may harm your defence if you do not mention when questioned something which you later rely on in court. Anything you do say may be given in evidence. If you would like to have a solicitor present, we can either appoint one for you or you can request us to contact your own. Should you wish to wait for a solicitor, we can suspend this interview until they arrive."

Adrian simply stared at Jim for a few seconds as the room seemed to close in around him. "Sorry, what is this for - why am I being cautioned?" he managed to ask. "We need to determine the facts around the breach of confidential data, as it directly relates to individuals that have been identified as missing, and the information to date does not correlate with your descriptions so far. If you do wish to have a solicitor here, we will pause this interview and reconvene on their arrival." "Look, I have shared with you what I know, and that the person has lied to me and given me false information and I can't speak for them or their reasons for having done this. I don't think I need a solicitor, so we can carry on, but I really don't know what else I can tell you."

"OK, if you are happy to continue, I will advise that this interview is being recorded both for audio and visual purposes," Gibbons added, happy to continue to apply pressure, and more than a little pleased that no brief would turn up to advise Adrian to 'no comment' for the rest of the evening. "Interview commenced, 17:22, those present - DC Andrew Gibbons," (he hoped it was OK to miss off the 'acting' part) "and DI James Pallister, MCU," Jim added. Gibbons looked over to Adrian and raised his eyebrows. "Adrian Burch," said Adrian, a little robotically. "Thank you. I'd like to check about the details of some of the other people you have listed as employees or contractors on the system under your management and are shown on our system as reporting to you. Given what our investigation has shown on Mr Collins, we are concerned that similar issues may be discovered for the other names. Let me ask you to provide some details on the following people and we can see where this takes us." Gibbons went back to the folder and removed four pages and placed them on the table in front of Adrian. Each one had the name of a person who had an administrator-level account on the computer system, and a list of other details. Starting with Martin Collins on the left, Adrian scanned each one, nodding slowly as he did so. "As you can see, Mr Burch, we have carried out the same level of investigation on all the people you have advised the service that are working with you on the system, and cannot find evidence that any of these people have been to this site, have any connection to you or your company, they don't appear to have any social media presence. Quite specifically, we would have thought that they would at least be connected to you on LinkedIn given it's a professional networking site - most people link themselves to the company they work for. So, if you could help us understand how this may be the case, that would be very informative."

He sat back and observed how Adrian was now clearly concerned. One could say he seemed cornered. Quick-witted as he may be, having all this presented to him in one go seemed to have unbalanced him. Faced with the information in front of him, Adrian was struggling to concentrate, so much so that he hadn't noticed his phone ringing in his inside jacket pocket. "Can I please have some water?" he asked a little feebly, trying to buy any time he could to come up with something, anything that could sound even halfway real about these names - every one of them had been created to disguise his accesses of confidential data, allowing him to create his list in the first place.

"Of course," said Gibbons who walked to the other side of the room, just behind Adrian where there was a chilled water dispenser - and was back at the table in a matter of seconds, handing Adrian a plastic cup. Adrian accepted it with shaking hands, not quite able to make eye contact. "Thanks," he said in a barely-audible whisper. "I- ummm- don't know why they haven't got any social media accounts or why they aren't connected to the company, but they do provide ad-hoc support. They're freelancers so they don't work directly for me." Even as he said it he knew it was a weak story, but it was all he could come up with. "Now, Mr Burch - currently we are only really looking at falsifying documents and accessing confidential records, which is serious enough, but we are concerned that some of the people whose records were accessed, as we mentioned when we last met, are missing. There are more records that have been accessed, and thankfully, to date, none of those people have been reported missing. So, it may be coincidental, and presently we don't have sufficient evidence linking the record access directly to the disappearance of these people, and therefore to your- let's call them aliases. Because of this, we are going to conclude this interview and you will be released under investigation."

"We will be in contact to arrange a further interview in due course, so we will ask you to stay locally, you are under no obligation to do so - however, it is recommended should we need to bring you in at short notice. Do you understand everything that has been said to you this evening, Mr Burch?" Gibbons was in his element. This was his investigation and his suspect, and he was managing the whole interview like a seasoned pro. "Yes, I think so," Adrian mumbled, now very pale and displaying none of the confidence he'd had when first taking his seat. "Thank you, interview terminated at 19:23," Gibbons announced, then leant over the table to turn off the device that had captured the conversation for the last two hours.

He remained standing, opened the door and gestured for Adrian to exit the interview room and follow him to the reception. They reached the front door and Gibbons turned to Adrian. "Please don't go far - it is likely we will need to speak to you again very soon. Thank you for your time this evening," and he held the front door open. Adrian stepped out into the evening air with legs of jelly. The churning in his stomach had turned into a solid knot. As he walked to his car his thoughts turned to what was going to come up next. How could he get the people out of the pit without them coming after him straight away, what would he do about work, what the hell was he going to tell Lisa, as there was no way he'd be able to go back in the morning and carry on as normal. His mind went to damage limitation and how to get himself out of this appalling mess.

"Track his car and his phone, I want to know exactly where he goes." Jim said as he walked up behind Gibbons. "I'll deal with the warrant now."

TWENTY-NINE

Adrian drove away from the police station, his mind whirring and trying to find answers to his dilemma and what he had to do. There was no way he was going straight home. Lisa would just keep asking questions about where he had been. What was he going to tell her? Certainly not the truth, that he was implicated in the disappearance of four men and in possession of a list of many others. He couldn't tell her about the interview, about the fictitious staff members, none of it. He needed to sort out the mess, and he needed time to think and come up with something she would buy.

All this time he felt he had been so careful, having planned so meticulously how to keep one step ahead, remembering all he had seen on so many forensic TV documentaries about keeping off the networks, away from view of ANPR cameras, away from CCTV and crucially, no witnesses. At least so far all they had was data access, and he kept telling himself that they wouldn't find anything that could directly link him to the men in the pit, and anything they may have would be too circumstantial to get through the CPS. The only way to be absolutely certain was to deal with them, the van, everything, anything that connected the list of names, via 'Martin' and back to him.

Instead of going home, he headed for the house. He needed to get to the van and to the pit and find a way to get them out before the police could connect him to any of it. They don't know about the van being mine, or the house - they just know about the data access, was all that kept going around in his head. In his state he wasn't able to process basic thoughts - his rationality had deserted him and he was unwittingly getting careless. His phone was on and in his jacket pocket as he pulled up to the house.

It was getting late and was already dark. Adrian went into the garage and found the ladders he had used when checking the pit on his inspection of the farm, making sure it was acceptable for what he needed. When he had done his reconnaissance, he wanted to make sure there was no way anyone could escape once they were in there, and the ladders were just long enough to get him in and out, at a bit of a stretch. He managed to get the ladders onto the van roof rack and tethered them as best he could for the short journey to the farm. He started the van and drove off the driveway, the ladders bouncing a little on the roof and making quite a noise, but Adrian wasn't really paying attention to this. His mind was elsewhere. All he needed to do was give them all a way out - they couldn't identify him - he had made sure of that throughout. Once they had made it out, he would be miles away and given who they were and why he'd chosen them, he was certain they wouldn't go anywhere near the police. As soon as it was done, he could get another job somewhere, far from here doing something different, maybe change his name and this would be a dim and distant memory.

Once he arrived he drove as close to the edge of the pit as he could get so he didn't need to carry the ladders too far, leaving the engine running. He undid the tethers, removed them from the roof and threw them into the pit. As soon as the last one landed, he ran back to the van and jumped in and drove off at speed, not waiting to hear anything being said by his soon-to-be-escaped captives.

The sound of the ladders hitting the ground woke all four men from their fitful slumber on the ground. For the past few days the only things that had landed near them had been bottles of water, packets of cakes and crisps, nothing of any nutritional value but enough to sustain them. They had never seen who dropped any of these things in, nor did they see tonight, but the latest delivery didn't sound like food or water. The men got up and walked over to where the sound had come from. While the night sky was clear, the moon light wasn't illuminating the floor of the pit so they edged forwards with caution. On discovering what had been thrown down to them, they were initially sceptical - even though immediately after waking they had heard the sound of a vehicle driving away at speed, none were certain this wasn't some sort of test or trap. James went over to the ladders checking what state they were in, then assembling them to their full length along the ground, making sure the rungs seemed secure. "What the fuck is this?" said Sean as James stood back from the gift from above. "Mate, I dunno, they seem OK, but just seems dodgy, you know." They all seemed in agreement. "Why bung these in now, what's the deal?" asked Gary looking at the ladders and other men. Rob paced along the length of them with the same look the others had, clearly thinking along similar lines. "What if he's gone, maybe he changed his mind. Whatever the reason, I don't care about you three, but I'm getting out of here and taking my chances," said Rob, a steely look in his eye. "If all four of us go up, and he's still there, then we'll just chuck the cunt in here and see how he likes it". Rob was never one to mince his words, but the others agreed. "Even if he has got a weapon, like a baseball bat, he can only get one of us at a time, so the others can disarm him and then sort him out." This odd assortment of men, who had quite literally been thrown together, lifted the ladders to the side of their muddy jail and began to climb up.

The first up helped the others clear the gap between where the ladders ended and the edge of the ground, levelled out, showing a camaraderie that had developed between them during their time together, each making sure the other was safely out before pulling the ladders up. "If he's here and we chuck him in, he's not having these back," Sean sniffed in the direction of the ladders now laying on the ground in front of them.

Even though they were tired and hungry, their ascent had injected each with adrenaline, and they quickly looked around in the growing moonlight to see if their captor was still around. After a few minutes it was obvious he had gone. "Right - where the fuck are we?" asked Gary as they stood in what appeared to be a farmyard. Clearly the pit that they had been in was part of this, so they looked for buildings, maybe a house, but decided that if there was a house, there was a chance he could be in it. They chose to head for the road and then on to town. Walking through the yard, they found the long drive to the road and as they reached it, saw the sign - a little battered and worn, but still legible - Sykes Farm. "Remember that, it might come in useful," suggested James. "Useful for what - coming back for a fucking holiday?" Rob clearly had no intention of having any more to do with this place and made his feelings very clear. "I don't need to remember the name of this shit hole, why would I want to?" "Because we have to speak to the police. That fucking nut job needs finding and sorting out."

The others looked in the direction of this last statement, and Gary stood before them, an imploring look on his face. "I'm not messing about. That bloke could do it again, and kidnapping, I mean come on, that is some serious shit. Look, I know we're not your typical grasses, but this is next-level shit, and - anyone?" There followed a reasonable debate. What had the police ever done for them, they were all fascists, the usual crap from the other three, but eventually they came to an agreement. "You're right," said Sean. "He can't be allowed to get away with this. Maybe we do need to talk to them, and besides, we might even be being looked for as missing persons, or whatever they call it. Probably worth it, at least this time, yeah?" Standing on the edge of the road they looked around. No phones meant no sat nav, so it was going to be luck if they went the right direction until James made a suggestion that seemed to be sensible. "Look, out here there's no street lights, right, so if we look in the sky and see like a glow, you know - we ought to go in that direction as it is probably street lights. I've seen something about it on TV once - light pollution. What do you reckon?"

The night sky was clear out here and they could see stars everywhere - something that was unknown before their incarceration, having been in the large town for their whole lives, the light pollution preventing such beauty from being visible.

Over the past few days they had talked, discussed their lives and backgrounds after the initial bravado wore off and they came to realise they needed each other. So many attempts had been made to get out, but none had provided the result they needed, but rather than just give up they kept trying, their bonds improving each time. Being more aware of what was around them had a profound effect on them all, their appreciation of teamwork and the importance of being able to rely on others brought a different perspective to each of them. Now it was time for them to find who had captured them, but rather than taking it upon themselves to mete out justice, they knew this was something the police had to do. Looking across the horizon, the orange glow of street lighting was a halo of hope and something to aim for, so they set off, following the road as a group with a clear and single focus.

Adrian brought the van back and nearly crashed into the garage, such was his haste to get away from the farm and ditch the van. He got out, wiping down the steering wheel, door handles, any surface he thought would hold his fingerprints, even though he had worn gloves and been very careful about what he touched to minimise contact points. He stood next to the van contemplating what to do next. He was still a few steps ahead of the police, so anything that he could do to keep his name out of this needed to be done. Thinking of options, he went into the garage to see what combustible material might be in there. Fire gets rid of everything - he'd seen that enough times. There was an assortment of paint cans, rags and white spirit. The previous owner must have been quite handy, Adrian thought as he scanned the shelves around him. Gathering armfuls of tins and rags he placed some in the van, on the seats as they were likely to burn well and went in search of a source of ignition. He spent some time repeating this process by filling parts of the house with similar material. There'd be no sign of him ever having been here by morning.

Setting the fire in the house first, Adrian then turned his attention to the van, making sure both were fully alight before getting into his car. As he drove away he could see the flames engulfing the house in the rear-view mirror. A feeling of relief and satisfaction came over him, taking the place of the worry and dread that had been plaguing him all night. In his mind, all tracks were covered, and there was nothing left that would link any of this to him: no post, no vehicle, no prints and most importantly, no prisoners. All loose ends tied up. During his drive back, he had to work out what to say to Lisa. He had been out for hours, and she would need some sort of explanation for this - something plausible to deflect attention from the wider issue of what was most likely to happen next, how to describe the events of the evening in terms of what he could say, not what actually happened. He didn't really notice the smell of burning that had managed to attach itself to his clothes, the mud on his shoes from the farm or the paint residue on his hands and sleeves. His phone started to ring again in his pocket and he stopped abruptly in the quiet road. A feeling of absolute dread took over every sinew in his body. "My phone, my fucking phone," he exclaimed, his head dropping with the weight of what this meant. None of what he had done had any value now, there was no way he could talk his way out of this, and there was no way he could go home.

He looked around the car for something to remove the SIM card tray from the phone. Opening the glove box he delved around and found some documents held together with a paperclip. He removed it and pushed it into the small hole on the bottom of the phone, the small tray coming out exposing the card. Taking the card out, he opened the window and threw it onto the road. Sliding the tray back in, he closed the window and drove away, although he had no idea where he would go.

THIRTY

It had been a very long day for Jim, with many facets of the OCG case coming up for discussion and a lot of concern about his boss and friend. By the time he got home it was late, too late to eat as he really didn't need another night of heartburn. Given the events of the day, he had a feeling he would have trouble sleeping anyway. The whole issue with this Adrian guy was troubling him. The list of records Gibbons had found that had been accessed was pretty long and if this guy had made up the staff, all of them, then it seemed like a bigger issue. Only two of the names on the list had been notified to them as missing, but given their backgrounds, it wasn't that surprising that no one had come forward. They probably spent long periods away from home, family and friends. Jim needed to understand the full picture. He had seen the list of names, been involved in updates on the two who were reported missing, but where did they fit together? What was he not seeing? It was too late and he was too tired to think. What if Adrian had abducted them, what if there were more than the two they knew of - and where were they? He also had the distinct impression that Adrian Burch was going to be hard to find after today. The end of the interview saw the man leave the station looking very distracted, and that was a look that was usually followed by disappearing. That said, the warrant had been issued pretty quickly so tomorrow he would see the phone data of where he had gone after leaving, and most likely, where he'd be next. But there was nothing he could do about it tonight, so Jim went into the kitchen and poured himself a small glass of Beckford's caramel rum, added a few ice cubes to it and on returning to the living room, eased himself down onto the sofa.

The aroma of the rum was delightful and a small sip through the ice was just what he needed. Holding the glass against his chest, Jim lay his head back on the sofa and closed his eyes. His thoughts drifted to Bina and their date. The evening had surpassed his wildest expectations for so many reasons, but the biggest one was he actually felt she genuinely liked him for him, warts and all. She knew what he did for work, she knew the odd hours and the horrific things he got to see most days and better than most, knew what they could do to someone and how long it could take to process them. But she liked him, and that was something he wasn't used to. "She actually likes you, Jimbo," he said to the empty room and allowed himself a smile. Jim took a long drink from the glass warming in his hands and felt the smooth liquor run down his throat, diluted only slightly by the melting ice. Outside there was hardly a sound and given the hour he was pleased it was quiet. This was a nice location on the outside of town and the mortgage had been a bit of a stretch to start with, but his lack of a social life and working all hours meant he didn't really spend any money, so it was bearable until his promotion had come through. Even now, he wasn't living the high life but at least he had a few quid left over at the end of the month. Until recently, he hadn't had anyone he wanted to spend time with and treat every now and again.

He woke up several hours later, still on the sofa and with a dull ache in his lower back. He stretched, arched his spine to try and straighten himself out a little and gingerly stood up, rubbing his bleary eyes as he walked over towards the hallway and up the stairs. Once there, he thought it would be a good idea to use the toilet - it was 5am and he wasn't about to have a shower, much as though he felt he should. Instead he had a pee and blew his nose, noticing that he was finally on the last roll of toilet paper from the multipack he could have sworn he bought last year, a privilege of living on one's own and rarely being at home.

This brought his thoughts back to Bina and a whole host of 'what if' scenarios in his now fully-awake mind. Would they make a good couple, would things progress to staying at each other's houses, what would her family think - and a hundred other ridiculous and childish questions that really didn't need to be flooding his brain at this time of the morning. Jim dropped the paper into the toilet and flushed it away, picking up his toothbrush and giving his teeth a once-over. He climbed into bed and stretched out, happy that the ache in his back had almost gone, then plumped up the pillows and closed his eyes.

The rest of his sleep passed with strange dreams about the OCG case and Adrian had taken the role as the leader of the whole organisation. This funny little IT guy was in charge of people, drugs and arms trafficking and all of it was being done from the station, right under their noses. He made them all look stupid as he used his IT skills to push them all off his scent and covered his tracks by deleting records from the PNC. When Jim finally woke he was relieved that none of it had been real. His back was still a little stiff, the duvet was nowhere to be seen and he really didn't feel refreshed in the slightest. He sat upright, ran his hands down his face and pushed out a long breath from between his fingers. It was time for that shower now. Feeling a little more human, Jim checked his phone as he always did in the morning. There were no missed calls or messages, so he made his way into the kitchen and switched on the TV.

The missing persons cases had made the news, finally. Jim was pleased that there was a decent amount of public interest, largely due to the background of those involved and their usual contempt for the police. At least there seemed to be a bit of a swell of public opinion that the police were doing a reasonable job of trying to find them. His phone rang and he looked at the number, which was coming from the station. "DI Pallister," he announced. "Sir?" It was Gibbons, at 7:45 in the morning and already in the building. "We've got the data from Adrian Burch's phone and you're going to want to see it," he blurted out without any introduction to explain the call. "OK, I'll be there in twenty minutes," Jim told the eager young constable and ended the call. That lad was good and there was bound to be something very interesting that he had uncovered, bearing in mind it was him that had put most of this case together already. Jim was certain this wasn't trivial.

Getting into his car he felt his excitement levels increasing. He had a feeling that this was going to be a good day for him and Gibbons, although he suspected the same couldn't be said for Adrian Burch.

As Jim pulled into the car park four men walked into reception. They were all muddy, smelly and exhausted, but for the first time in their lives they were happy to be in a police station.

THIRTY-ONE

Lisa was beside herself after not being able to sleep all night. Just where the hell is he? She must have said it a hundred times and was still no closer to an answer. It just wasn't like him to not come home and not say anything about it in advance. She packed the kids off to school and rang her mum. "Just take a deep breath, darling, and tell me what's happened," Lisa's mother said calmly when she picked up the call, her daughter a sniffling wreck on the other end of the line.

"Recently he's been coming back late, but nothing like this. I must have called him a dozen or more times last night, and each one went to voicemail and I have no idea where he is, or what he's doing, or who with, or if he's safe or- oh, Mum," and she descended into sobs. Her mother listened and tried to offer comfort where she could but without knowing anything about the current situation, there really wasn't much she could do. Adrian has always been a gentleman, she thought and reminded herself of holidays they had shared as a wider family, the summer BBQs and his always thoughtful and considered gifts for birthdays and Christmas. Alice tried to glean what she could between sniffs and tears. "Just lately though, Mum, he's been coming back late and saying it was work drinks or something. You know it starts like that - someone new and exciting while the old bag is at home, ironing shirts and helping the kids with their homework. I feel such a fool because he's seemed different for a while and I should have noticed and done something, challenged him about it or- I don't know." She trailed off.

"Listen, darling. Something could have happened to him on the way home. You know Adrian, he's just not the kind of man to look elsewhere - he absolutely adores you and the kids. Have you called the police? Maybe they might know something, perhaps he is still at work due to some major problem, these IT systems can be very complicated and its very important stuff he does. Perhaps you could give them a call, put your mind at rest?"

Begrudgingly Lisa agreed, ended the call with her mum and looked up the number for the police station Adrian often worked at. The tightness in her neck and shoulders that had started the night before was increasing in intensity, and she could feel a headache coming on. Using the thumb and forefinger of her right hand, she massaged her temples while waiting for the call to connect.

"Mayfield Road police station, this is Christy. How can I direct your call?" came a very chirpy voice that immediately riled Lisa. She didn't need happy little voices, she needed serious people who could understand the gravitas of the situation. Shaking some of the tiredness out of her head and trying to regain a level of rational thought, she replied.

"Hello, my name is Lisa Burch. My husband Adrian works there in your IT department and- well, you may think I'm overreacting, but he didn't come home last night and that never happens, he is usually really punctual, especially when it's fish and chips night and he hasn't seen the kids all day and he-"

Lisa realised she was gabbling. "Sorry, I-"

"Mrs Burch, there really is no need to apologise. Let me take some details and I will assign this to an officer to look into. Now, when did you last see your husband?" Lisa did her best to provide as much information as she could about yesterday morning, his recent later nights and that this was completely out of character, trying desperately not to cry. Once the PSCO had taken all the details on offer she thanked Lisa, hung up the phone and made her way to the main part of the building to the MCU. "Hello, I've just taken a call from a lady who said her husband didn't come home last night. Very unusual by all accounts, according to her." Acting DC Gibbons allowed the rest of the summary to complete before offering his hand to take the notes being discussed. Reading them quickly he looked up at the PSCO. "Lisa Burch? Did she say what her husband's name is? Oh wait, it's here. Thank you - I'll take this one."

Jim looked at his young colleague from across the desks they had been sharing since arrival. The phone data was indeed very interesting, just as Gibbons had suggested earlier, and tables and maps were splayed out in front of them. He raised an eyebrow as the conversation came to an end and Gibbons turned back to him. "Well, good job we didn't have a bet on him not going home, or one of us would be buying cakes!" Jim said with a smile. They shifted their attention back to the papers on the desk. "Right, let's try and find where our Mr Burch has gone," said Jim, his brow furrowed. The phone data mapped Adrian's route the night before right up to the point he had thrown the SIM card out of the car window onto the side of the road. There was no doubt he was now directly linked to the house that had been used for the address of the documents for the van, and it wasn't a stretch to connect him to the van either. During the night a call had come in from a member of the public, concerned that a house on the road was alight. When police and fire services arrived on scene there was little left of the van, and the house was well ablaze. As the events had been fed back to the station, the team had advised the duty sergeant who in turn had updated ADC Gibbons on his arrival. "He torched the house and the van last night then left in the direction of Calne, but then we lose signal, like his phone was turned off. But why turn it off then and not here, or wherever?" Gibbons was thinking aloud, trying to piece together what lay in front of them and not getting it.

"I reckon he just forgot his phone was on, what with everything else going on. Does his housekeeping jobs, sets light to the evidence and starts to drive home then," Jim leaned over to the pile of spreadsheet printouts, "gets a call from Mrs B and remembers his phone has been on the whole time, panics and turns it off. But we're still no closer to working out his route after that little revelation."

"I've got some info on family members, but they're all miles away. Not saying he wouldn't drive out to them but it's a good five hours to his folks from here," Gibbons said, and Jim looked over and opened his mouth to say something. "And I've been in contact with the local force to get to the parents and let us know," finished Gibbons. Jim closed his mouth and smiled. "I've also started going through his social media to see how many Facebook contacts he has, and from that list how many have an open profile, so we can message them and see if they'd seen him in the last twelve hours or so." Christ this guy is thorough, Jim thought as Gibbons continued to list everything he had done in the last two hours. "Mind you, given what we have learned about his 'colleagues', some of these friends might be fake, so it's going to take some time, but I'm ploughing through them and I'll update you during the morning."

"Right, coffees are on me - what do you want?" Jim asked the young DC, who seemed to perk up even more. God, I remember being that keen, thought Jim. "Oh, thank you, Sir. Could I have a caramel macchiato please?" Jim just looked at him for a second, blinked a couple of times, nodded and walked in the direction of the exit.

"The youth of today," he muttered to himself as he left the building.

THIRTY-TWO

Following a long night's drive, Adrian stood on the coastal path looking out to sea. Even after destroying the van and house, letting the men out and trying to cover his tracks, he was acutely aware his whereabouts were now common knowledge with the police due to his phone data being pulled. No amount of running would make this go away, but at least they wouldn't know where he was now. He had driven his car to within thirty miles of where he now stood, then walked and took public transport the rest of the way. All the police would find would be a car in a car park, with a note on the driver's seat. When he'd pulled up at the car park in the early hours he needed to try and structure his thoughts and get to a decision about the next few hours at the very least. There was nothing but darkness in his mind.

He had opened his laptop bag and removed a pad and pen, and just sat there trying to start writing something.

He couldn't work out what or who it needed to be for. Eventually words had started to come out, just a few to start with, but then they poured onto the page - a maelstrom of regret, anger and fear. It was essentially a full confession and apology to Lisa and the kids. His despair at how he had felt when cornered by the police was combined with how devastating the whole episode would be for them, not just now but for who knew how long. As he stood on the wall, metres above the swirling waves, all he could think about was Lisa and his kids and how he had let them down. Tears mixed with the foam being blown into his face and he sobbed uncontrollably, his hands on his knees and saliva and mucus streaming from nose and mouth. His chest hurt from crying, but also from the knowledge of what he had done.

He couldn't go back home and he couldn't go to anyone else. Who in their right mind would allow him into their home after all this eventually came out? The severity of his actions, and the clear consequences they would bring, weighed heavily on his mind and prevented any rational thought. All he could focus on were the jagged rocks below and the sea that would take him away from all this mess, forever.

Gibbons had already been onto the RPU and requested ANPR data for Adrian's car before he had finished for the previous day, so was already a few steps into the process of tracking him down. He had updated the Roads Policing Unit and advised them that the owner was a suspect in a kidnapping case, and that he needed to be notified as soon as the car was sighted, irrespective of the time. It was this information he now approached Jim with. "Sir, we have received the ANPR reports that had tracked Adrian Burch's car to a Sainsbury's car park in south-west Exeter, and local units found it there. There was a handwritten letter on the driver's seat - reads a bit like a suicide note, to be honest." Jim took all this in, nodding slowly as he processed each piece of news being imparted, and waiting to see if there was anything else. When nothing was forthcoming he ventured a question. "Why Exeter? Seems a long way to go, so what's the draw - family?"

"Not that we could find Sir, no - no prior address there, didn't go to uni there so no direct connection to the place-" Gibbons stopped and frowned. "Just a sec," he said, moving back to his desk and opening Adrian's Facebook profile. Jim walked across and looked over the young detective's shoulder, mentally noting that Facebook had been the undoing of many a well executed plan before. A few clicks of his mouse later, Gibbons sat back a little and pointed at his computer. Images of Adrian and his family on holiday filled the screen and, as Gibbons scrolled, many from a year or so back were clearly in the same place. The caption read 'Staddon Point Battery.'

"Worth a call to local units there, Sir?" asked Gibbons, bringing up Google Maps on the computer and finding Staddon Point. "Looks like Plymouth would be closest," he said, and looked in the direction of his senior officer. Jim nodded. "I'll call them now - you try and find how he may have got from Exeter to there." Jim had his phone in his hand before getting back to his desk, and put an internal call request in for the right number at

Devon and Cornwall Police. He was connected to Hampton Street in less than a minute and appraised them on the situation as best he could, requesting that officers be despatched towards Staddon Point immediately but to proceed with caution on arrival, the potential suicide note very much in mind.

The Sergeant who had taken the call confirmed that officers were on their way, that he would be the liaison from now on and all updates would be via him. Jim cupped his hand over the phone and gave the news to Gibbons, who was mid-call with the local bus company who ran the route. "They have onboard CCTV images of a man that matches Adrian's description taking a bus from Exeter to Moretonhamstead, then they lose him until he boards another bus five and half miles away at Bovey Tracey and on to Newton Abbot, and then gets another to Plymouth. Paid cash for each leg." Gibbons was still talking when Jim took his hand away and updated the local sergeant. "Looks like he will be there, or thereabouts, he's taken a few buses from Exeter in the direction of Plymouth so I think we can safely assume that Staddon is his destination." Jim sighed, looking at the Google Map and trying to work out the distance. His head dropped. It was over one hundred and sixty miles, and that was in a straight line at least three hours from where he was standing. He knew he needed to get the local team to do this, and he would need to meet them there. He ended the call after asking that as soon as there was an update on Adrian's location and they had him in a car, they were to call.

Adrian sat down on the steps that went to the lighthouse

and pulled his knees towards his chest, the cold wind penetrating his clothes and the spray from the sea below soaking him, but he didn't notice. His thoughts were on his wedding day - Lisa resplendent in ivory, her hair curled and falling over her slender shoulders, the way she looked at him with happiness in her beautiful eyes. He could see her smile and how she held his hands to stop him from shaking. Always there for him, his best friend for so many years. His kids appeared next, their happy faces and scruffy hair and pure innocence, boundless energy and enthusiasm for everything they saw and did. He lifted his head and looked out to sea, and as he did so his heart broke again, the sobs becoming guttural.

Two police cars approached from the direction of Fort Staddon. One stopped at Watch House Battery, its occupants taking the coastal path, the other continued along past Bovisland Beach and crept up towards Staddon Battery, the officers inside scanning the road and adjacent buildings and paths. The officer in the front passenger seat spotted Adrian on the steps and gestured to their colleague to stop just ahead. The car pulled up a few metres away and both officers got out, as the crew from the other vehicle emerged from the other side of the building, having navigated the path and curving route to the road. A brief discussion confirmed their strategy, and the negotiation specialist took the lead and approached the man sitting on the lighthouse steps.

She stood on the step just behind him. She could see he was crying and used this distraction to be able to gently get past him and take a position on the step two below him. Waiting for a gap in his breathing she tried to get his attention. “Adrian,” she said in a soft voice. “I’m Rachel. I’d like to help you if you’ll let me?” She placed a hand on his arm.

He had a feeling there was somebody there - perhaps it was Lisa coming to say goodbye, and he hoped the kids weren’t there to see this. He didn’t want his wife to see him jump either but she had been there for everything else, so it seemed right she was here now. Through the fog, he felt the light contact on his arm and could hear a voice, saying his name. It didn’t sound like Lisa - it was soft but different. He opened his eyes and saw the person sitting in front of him, auburn hair and green eyes. This wasn’t Lisa. She looked kind, sympathetic even, and he heard her say his name again. “Adrian, please come with me so we can get a cup of tea and maybe talk a little more?” Her eyes seemed to plead with him. “Erm- right,” he managed, as though regaining consciousness and not really understanding what was happening. The stranger helped him to his feet and they walked up the steps back to the road.

A blue car was parked and the back door was open, and Adrian realised he was being directed towards it by the woman, her hand still on his arm. When they got to the car, other people came into view. Two in uniforms, one in a suit. The latter moved towards Adrian and took something out from an inside pocket. “Adrian Burch, my name is Detective Sergeant Colin Walsh and I’d like it if you would come with us, please.” Adrian nodded his assent and climbed into the car. Walsh walked to the other side, but before getting in he called DI Pallister. “Sir, we have your Mr Burch. We’ll take him to Hampton

Street and hold him until you arrive."

Jim put his phone in his pocket. "Grab your coat, we're off to Devon," he said to Gibbons. The two men smiled. "You have done an outstanding job, Andrew, and you deserve to make the arrest when we get there, this whole investigation is from your work. What a way to make an entrance to MCU, crack a multiple kidnap and imprisonment case, uncover illegal data gathering, fraud, identity theft, arson- I mean, greedy comes to mind!" Jim said, beaming at their latest addition to the team. Gibbons grinned and tried to sound as nonchalant as he could - "It's all in a day's work, guv!" - but it was clear he was as pleased as Jim to have been able to follow up on his initial hunch.

THIRTY-THREE

Seamus apprised Det. Supt. Bowler on the events of the last twenty-four hours and she listened, with a growing scowl that this had happened right under their noses. However, she was consoled to an extent by Acting DC Gibbons and that he had practically managed the case from the start, so accepting his permanent move into MCU was an easy decision.

"What time's the first raid scheduled for next week?" she asked her DCI, moving the conversation on to the OCG operation that was still having the finer points added. "Thursday at 5am, ma'am, and all sections have been fully briefed on location, strategy, exit routes that may be selected as well as two other locations that may be beneficial to hit simultaneously," Seamus reeled off, as though he had said it for the fiftieth time that day. "Right - so hit them hard and early. Good. Seamus, sit down a minute." Bowler looked pensive, so Seamus did as asked and took one of the seats in front of her desk. She leaned on her elbows and tented her hands, placing both index fingers on her lips for a moment. "The last time you tried to take this guy out, you said he knew you were coming. Any idea how that would have been?" She looked over her hands at him, trying to read his face. "He must have had someone in the station on the payroll, that's the only explanation we ended up at. We lost some good officers at the end of it, they just couldn't come back, so our guess was it was one of those, but none of the investigations went anywhere. The place wasn't empty though, but we just assumed it was sacrificial stock - enough for us to think we had something, but not enough to really damage him."

He suddenly looked tired, perhaps more than that. She let the silence ask the next question for her. "We have got the sites under surveillance and will do until we arrive. There has been no suspicious activity, no additional traffic in or out compared to usual. If he had been tipped off there would have to be a fleet of vehicles needed to empty those three buildings and we'd see it straight away." He looked at his boss as he said this, and she seemed on edge still. "It's still a few days away and anything can happen yet," she said, "and we can't afford any fuck-ups."

Seamus leaned back in the chair. You don't have to tell me that, he thought as he had been there before. "We are monitoring all sites, 24/7, and have everyone on stand-by in case anything changes. I won't let him get away this time." Bowler shot him a look. "And what if he isn't there on the day? Are you sure that Kelmendi will be in attendance at the location?" "Our intelligence shows he has a visit planned, hence the date for the raids, so we are confident he'll be there."

But Seamus was having his doubts, although he wasn't prepared to share them with Bowler - at least, not yet.

THIRTY-FOUR

Bariu had been awoken by what turned out to be a football hitting the side of the van, at pretty much the spot his head had been at the time. Since this startling event he had been splitting his time between checking on the house from inside the vehicle and making short walks up and down the road, partly to stretch his legs and partly to try to get a different view of the house.

As expected there had not been any sign of people coming in or leaving overnight, so he waited to see what a Saturday morning would bring, and after getting coffee at a nearby shop he didn't need to wait for long.

A car pulled up at the end of the path to the house and a man got out, carrying a bag from a supermarket chain. There he was, right in front of Bariu. He didn't look any different really to the last time they had met which was a blessing, since it made it a certainty he was the target. He watched as the man walked to the door and rang the doorbell. That struck him as odd. Why ring the doorbell to your own house? The door opened and the woman Bariu had seen the day before stood there on the threshold. The meeting seemed awkward, as though this was not a regular event. There was a strained hug and the man entered, the door closing behind him. Bariu opened the black bag and removed a small, black box. Pressing an almost hidden button he opened an app on his phone and synced the two devices. Putting his phone down, he slipped out of the van and walked in the opposite direction from the house, on the other side of the road, crossed and made his way to the recently parked car. Using one of the oldest methods around, he stooped to tie his shoe and at the same time covertly attached the black box to the underside of the car's right rear wheel arch. Standing back up he walked to the end of the road in search of breakfast.

He sat in the cafe on the corner, the same place he had got his coffee from earlier, and was settling down with the paper, expecting a short trip to tail his target later, mulling over what he had just witnessed. The meeting was clearly strained between the two people, as though it was a rare event and there was tension there. Breakfast finished, Bariu left the cafe having thanked the staff for their hospitality and complimented them on the food. Walking along the road past the house, the car was still there and a few more had arrived. One pulled up and children got out and excitedly ran up the path, each bearing a gift. Must be a party he thought and made the decision to wait a little longer to move in.

With more time on his hands he did something he hadn't

been able to do for a long while. He walked to the National Trust park and immersed himself in the beauty of the local area, marvelling that even in this part of the city there was green space in abundance, trees and parkland, a wetland walk, so much to enjoy. His years of doing the work he had to do had stopped him from being able to appreciate what was around him, to stop and just be in the moment. He took a seat on a bench after walking through the rose gardens and just listened to the world. People laughing and talking, making plans for this weekend and what tonight would entail, children playing and running around with nothing to worry about. The sky was clearer here - even with the proximity to the city beyond the park, he could see birds and clouds and of course aeroplanes to and from nearby Heathrow airport. He was happy to lose an hour or two here, and he closed his eyes.

The app on his phone sent a notification that the device was on the move, emitting a 'ping' sound that jolted him and Bariu opened his eyes and watched the dot on the map moving along the road. He remained on the bench and put his faith in the tracking device to do its job. It would most likely be a quick tube ride and a walk and then they would meet and he could do what was needed.

Barui spotted a garden centre and wandered around it for a while, marvelling at the normality of his morning. This is what normal people do on a Saturday, spend time with family and look at plants. He bought a coffee and began walking back to the van.

He had expected another notification to advise that the tracker had stopped, but nothing had happened. He opened the app and realised that it was still moving, no longer in London but heading west on the motorway. Perhaps he is on a job or having some course to attend Bariu considered, as he watched the dot continue its progress. Maybe a different location to the one he had planned would provide a better situation he considered as he walked. Wherever it was to be, it looked like he needed to make a longer journey than he had anticipated so he increased his pace a little given he now needed to get items from the van, then get to the car he had parked up a few streets further away. By the time he had reached the car, the dot was nearly 100 miles away and hadn't moved for about 20 minutes. Bariu headed out of the city, taking note of the fuel level and calculating the distance he would be able to travel, and which filling station he would be best to stop at along the way without needing a major detour.

Arriving at the outskirts of the town he pulled over and checked the app again. The dot was still in the same place which meant it was still active, and either the car and its occupant were within a reasonable vicinity, or it had come off and was just on the road and he'd lost his quarry. A few minutes later his question was answered as he rounded a bend in the road and saw the car parked up in a residential car park. He drove off along the road until he found somewhere he could leave his car, and retraced his route on foot. Why was it here? This was a long way from home for him and even further from work - surely this wasn't part of an investigation. But then he remembered the stilted meeting he had seen and things began to fall into place. Walking around the building adjacent to the car park he noticed that it was front-to-back flats, all accessed by a communal door and what appeared to be a staircase and lift on one side. All he needed to do now was determine which one he needed to get into.

Seamus flicked the kettle on again. This rugby match was dragging a little so it was OK to step away from it to get another drink, nothing much had happened over the last twenty minutes, so nothing much was likely for the next five. Settling back down on the sofa with a fresh mug of coffee, he turned his attention back to the match and tried to ignore the feeling of loneliness that had been creeping its way into him since the morning, not to mention being made to feel very much a stranger to his daughter on her birthday. He was brought into the moment by the sound of a car alarm going off. He walked over to the window and noticed it was his. Going into the kitchen, he grabbed his keys and walked back to the living room and pointed them at the car. A press of the button - and silence. He tossed the keys onto the sofa and resumed his previous position.

Bariu had been watching the windows after rocking the car to make the alarm sound, so spotted the figure appear on the second floor. Making his way to the side of the building, he brought out some lock picks and gained entry. His standard uniform baseball cap pulled down enough to prevent his features being seen on cameras, Bariu climbed the stairs to the second floor and as suspected from the outside view found there to be only one flat taking the whole space. He pondered for a moment about just ringing the doorbell, or letting himself in. Whichever option would probably result in a similar outcome, most likely there would be some sort of scuffle, but it wouldn't last long and he would be able to get down to business.

He opted for the former and with his finger bent, pressed the mid-joint onto the button.

"Who the bloody hell is this?" Seamus demanded to the empty room. He pushed himself up from the sofa and went to the door, not checking the security viewer in his annoyance at the interruption. As soon as he had opened it the door was flung into his face and a man pushed his way into the flat, kicking the door shut behind him, and forcing Seamus up against the nearest wall.

"Please don't try to do anything that may get you hurt," Bariu said in a low voice. "This doesn't need to become difficult." Seamus was still struggling with what had just happened, his arm up behind his back and starting to hurt, and he really wasn't in a position to argue. "OK," he just about managed. "Take the car keys, whatever else you want, and just leave, alright?"

Bariu almost laughed. "That is not why I am here, Mr Corrigan. I already have a car, thank you. I also have a gun, so when I let go of you, please don't try to attack me." Seamus was even more alarmed but agreed given the circumstances and nodded his assent.

"Excellent," said Bariu, letting Seamus go from the arm lock, and stepping back to allow the two men to see each other. Seamus turned slowly, not knowing what to expect, but when he saw Bariu standing there in his flat he froze. Dread enveloped him and images from his past flooded into his mind. His heart pounded in his chest and he couldn't breathe.

"Relax, please. I'm not here to hurt you. I need your help."

THIRTY-FIVE

"Sit, please, so we can talk," Bariu said, gesturing to the sofa. Seamus just stared at him, not really sure what to say. After a minute of silence he looked at his surprise house guest and walked to the kitchen. "Let's have a drink then," he said, opening the fridge and taking out two bottles of beer.

He re-entered the living room, handed one to Bariu and they both sat down. The air felt electrically charged. "It is clear that you remember me, Mr Corrigan, and I can assume you recall the situation we ended up in, but I need to fill you in on some details." Seamus tilted his head to one side and frowned. "Please, let's just- you know I'm a police officer, and should arrest you, right?" Bariu smiled. "For what? Setting off your car alarm?" Seamus nodded. "Fair point, but what's this about?" Bariu looked like he was arranging his thoughts as he took a drink from the bottle. "Listen, we have a common goal, you and I. When we last met we were trying to do the same thing, and those people need to be stopped. But I can't do that on my own, much as I have my methods, I don't have access to information that would be- beneficial." Seamus just looked at Bariu. "What are you asking for exactly? In my home, a known criminal, asking for help- I'm sorry, but that's insane. I can't collaborate with you. Why would you think this could work?"

"Mr. Corrigan," Bariu started. "We both need to get Kelmendi away from society, you want to see him in jail and I want to see him- well, jail is a reasonable idea, but we both know he won't get there or stay there." Seamus shook his head. "You're probably right, but like I just said, I can't get involved with you. Why is that such a difficult concept for you?"

Bariu had expected resistance as this was a long shot, but he also knew his skills in negotiation would have to come to the fore. "I think it's a little early to say no," and this was delivered with a genuine smile which caught Seamus off guard. This was a man who had spent his life dispatching people all over the world, and he was in his flat talking about working together. "Listen, I really don't know who you think you are coming here, or if you think I'm going to be intimidated by you having found me and all this crap about wanting my help. Frankly, it's all a bit far-fetched, to be honest. The last time we met, you nearly killed me." Seamus was on his feet now, looking down at the man referred to by everyone as The Shepherd. "It is funny how you remember things, don't you think? My recollection of the same moment is very different. Had it not been for me, you would be dead.

Even though you managed to put my own knife into my leg, it wasn't for you. It was for him."

Seamus shook his head slightly and looked at Bariu through narrowed eyes. "You see, I knew you were all going to be there that night, so I figured I could blend into the chaos and take him out, and I was so close." Bariu stared into the middle distance, recalling that scene, and frowned. "But you-" he looked at Seamus with disappointment in his eyes, and blew out a long breath. "You stopped me from doing what we both wanted, so now here I am to see if we can have another bite at the apple." Bariu sat back and took a long draught from his beer and regarded Seamus, reading his expression as one of piqued interest. He was clearly going over the events of that night, but it was very likely he had no idea after the arrival of Kelmendi.

"Let me make you an offer, Mr Corrigan. We work together and you get to take down Kelmendi and his organisation. Keeping your country safe, getting all that shit off the streets and saving those poor people and I, well I get to finish what I started. You do what you need to do but with some inside knowledge and some of what you know, I could know. It must be a win-win, right?"

"You really aren't listening to me, are you? I will have to say it slowly so you can understand. I am a police officer, I cannot, no - I will not collaborate with you. If I did, everything I have held close in my career would mean nothing at all. You are asking me to forget my sworn oath to preserve justice. You must be-" but Bariu cut Seamus off. "You won't get him without me." He let it hang in the air for a moment, fixing Seamus with a steely stare.

"You can't, he will always win. He will escape, or he will evade a trail or - most likely - will derail one. Jurors have had a history of disappearing before. He is everywhere, Mr Corrigan, and you need me to get to the parts of his organisation that you and your team can't. So yes, I very much understand and have been listening, but I feel it's you that hasn't." Seamus sighed. It was clear the man in his flat had a point and was right. This Kelmendi was not someone he could allow to get away this time, and he was already having doubts about the operation. But there was no way he was going to say a thing about it to this Bariu guy - not a chance.

"You can call me Seamus. This whole Mr Corrigan thing makes me think you're my GP." Bariu smiled. "Then you must call me Luan. Shall we get some food, Seamus? We have much to discuss."

"OK, what do you fancy? Even though it's not London there's plenty of choice for takeaways." They agreed on Thai, twenty minutes later the door buzzer went and the two men sat at the small table and ate and talked and drank.

At 1am Seamus excused himself to go to the toilet. He considered sending Jim a message, but what would he be able to tell him? Oh hi, Jim, there's an international assassin in my house and we're drinking vodka together was probably not going to achieve the result he needed. It would keep until the morning. It was 4am by the time the conversation came to a reasonable point that Seamus offered Bariu the spare room and they called it a night, although he couldn't sleep. The idea made sense to him, the outcome was what he had been trying to achieve for a long time, but the execution of it - well, that was something that he still couldn't settle. Seamus lay awake staring at the ceiling and going over scenarios in his head about how he could make it work, but without actually agreeing to anything or knowingly feeding information on intelligence gathered. The cost of that coming to light would be devastating to a lot of people he knew well and trusted. He couldn't help thinking what would Jim do? And he thought he had his answer.

"You can stay here as long as you need to, I have to go to work but please try not to draw any attention to yourself," Seamus said as the men met in the kitchen just three hours later. Bariu laughed out loud, then checked himself. "Sorry, you are very generous, thank you. The idea of me drawing attention is very funny." He chuckled as he said it.

"I will have coffee, maybe toast, clean up and be on my way. But I want you to think about what we have talked about. I will be nearby, you can call me on this," and he held out a phone. "Jesus, a burner!" Seamus said, eyebrows raised. "What is your number?" he asked Seamus and typed it into the phone as it was called out to him, then made a call so that his was on the phone Seamus now held.

Seamus bit his top lip as he considered what to say next, and levelled a gaze at his temporary guest then took a deep breath and let out a long sigh. "I need to think about it," he finally said, much to his own surprise. He nodded at Bariu, and left.

THIRTY-SIX

When DC Gibbons and DI Pallister arrived in Devon, Adrian was in a holding cell with an officer on watch with the door open, as he had been assessed as a potential suicide risk. On the drive down, the two detectives had discussed the evidence so far and what had come from those men who had escaped from the farm, Gibbons being coached in the art of only really being able to accept facts as they had been presented, not allowing assumptions or supposition to cloud his judgement. "It's really important that you only refer to what you can back up with data, documents or images," said Jim. He had learned that the hard way early in his career, when his exuberance had nearly blown a case as he admitted to introducing information during his testimony that hadn't been fully proven. He wasn't going to allow this young officer to fall into that trap. Statements had been taken from the four men who had presented themselves at the station at the end of last week. They had all been allowed home but asked to be available as needed should further information be required. Gibbons and Jim were slightly surprised at how amenable they had all been given their history with the police, as well as how willing they were to return as needed. The statements were almost identical - no real recollection of a vehicle, no description of their assailant, nothing about the location until the ladders had arrived and they had managed to escape. All except Gary. The last man to have been abducted had been able to see the van and gave some description of the person who had attacked him, but it wasn't enough to make a clear identification. Jim hoped there was enough evidence linking Adrian to these men already. There certainly was enough connecting him to the van and the house, phone data showing he was at the farm, and CCTV footage from when he had bundled Gary into the van. It felt solid enough to take to the CPS, but he was never certain of their decision until they called.

It was time to interview Adrian on the abduction and kidnap of four men, identity theft, fraud, arson. It was a long list and this was going to take a while. Jim walked over to the CO of Hampton Street. "Do you have any objections to us conducting the preliminary interview here, then we can get him charged and be out of your hair?" The station commander raised his hands in mock defeat. "You may as well, DI Pallister," he said with a warm smile. "Mi station es su station," and walked to his office, pointing to the interview suite as he left. Jim was shown to a room and opened the door. Switching on the lights, he motioned towards Gibbons and the duty sergeant went to the cells to fetch Adrian.

Once all three were in the room, Jim closed the door and took a seat. "Mr Burch, would you like to call anyone before we start? You are aware of your rights to legal representation, so is there someone we can contact?" Adrian's eyes were red, and it was clear he had been crying for some time as he raised his head to look at Jim. "Could I call my wife, please?" he almost whispered. He slumped towards the table and was clearly tearful again. Gibbons took a mobile phone out of his pocket and placed it on the table. "Do you know the number, Mr Burch? You can call her now, if you do." Adrian picked up the phone and dialled Lisa. "Adrian, where are you, what the hell is going on? Me and the kids are going mental here." Her voice was loud, high-pitched and desperate, and it showed on Adrian's face that she was clearly distressed. "I'm- I'm in Devon, and I'm with the police," he managed through tears. "It's OK, I'm not hurt or anything but I- Lisa, I'm so sorry. I need you to call our solicitor. I'm at the police station-" Jim leaned over the table. "Mrs Burch, we will be taking Adrian back to Swindon soon, so it would be better to ask your solicitor to meet us there.". "OK, right. I'll call him now and erm, yes, I'll let him know to go to Swindon and-" Lisa took a deep, shuddering breath, "-what have you done Adrian?"

The journey to Swindon was long, and Adrian considered sleeping but couldn't manage to settle his mind enough. Lisa's voice was ringing in his ears and all he could hear was the pleading tone and fear. He had really messed everything up, but maybe John could sort it all out, he'd be home by the morning and then they would be able to craft a plan.

As the small group arrived at the police station, they signed Adrian in and moved to the interview room that had been allocated to them. John Muir was already there and was waiting to be called from reception. He had received a call from Lisa and realised the gravity of the situation. He'd been their family solicitor for over ten years and had only needed to support them in buying their house and a few minor jobs. This was a very different job and the solicitor had thought it was somewhat out of his area of expertise but didn't have the heart to say so.

Gibbons went to reception to meet the new arrival, and as they walked to the interview room the solicitor was trying to get up to speed on the events of the past few hours so he had a fighting chance of knowing what he was about to walk into. On arrival the feeling in the room was sombre. Adrian was pleased to see John and looked with pleading eyes, hoping that he would find a way out of this.

"If you don't mind, gentlemen, I'm going to need some time with my client before we get started, if that's acceptable?" John said in a matter-of-fact tone. Jim nodded and gestured for Gibbons to leave the room. "Can I get either of you a drink while you talk?" he offered, and John spoke for both men. "Please, black coffee, one sugar for each of us - thank you." When they were alone, John turned to face Adrian. "So, what's happening here? What has gone on since we last spoke, and how are Lisa and the kids bearing up?" Adrian couldn't meet his eye and muttered his response to the table instead "I just wanted to help - do some good, you know - and take some pressure off the police with all these repeat offenders-" and the whole story poured out in a garbled and completely uncoordinated flow of words. By the time the officers returned with the coffee, John Muir was apprised of the history but concerned for his client. "Are we OK to start?" Jim asked as he placed the drinks down on the table, and received a nod from the solicitor. "Good - I appreciate it's late, so let's get on with it." Jim pressed the button on the recording unit. "Interview with Adrian Burch, present in the room are DI Jim Pallister, acting DC Gibbons-" Jim nodded to John. "-John Muir, representing Mr Burch," and in a meek voice, "Adrian Burch."

"This interview is being audio and video recorded, the time is now 20:26 and I'd like to just start with a reminder of the rights and that you do not need to say anything as you may have been advised by your solicitor."

"Can we start with the data access? During the course of our investigation, it became clear that there had been access made to confidential police records under an assumed name, that we believe had been created specifically for this purpose." Jim had decided to go with the less impactful components of the overall allegations to try and break down the barriers he was expecting to be put up, given the seriousness of the kidnapping and imprisonment charges. John leant over to Adrian and whispered into his ear, and Adrian nodded. "No comment," Adrian managed feebly, and he leaned back in his chair and placed his hands on the table. Jim nodded. This looked like it was going to be a long interview if he had to squeeze all the answers out. Longer still if it was going to start as a 'no comment' and potentially carry on that way. "Our records have shown a number of accounts that had been set up on the system, and we understand that these had been created for the purpose of farming information on individuals. We have been unable to validate any of the details that have been provided for identification. Can you elaborate on this?" Jim was trying to keep things fairly light and needed to get to the nub of why these people had been targeted without Adrian closing down.

"You don't need to respond to that," said Muir, placing his hand on Adrian's arm. "I- well, it was-" Adrian began, but Muir shook his head. "No comment," came the response and Jim nodded, flicking through the notes in front of him. "OK, let's look at the records that had been accessed. Many of the names on these had been notified to us as victims of abduction, four of whom have come forward to give evidence." What colour remained in Adrian's face drained at this comment. It was clear he hadn't been made aware of recent events. He had assumed that the people he had put into the pit, and subsequently let out, had just gone back to their usual lives, and they were so anti-police it hadn't crossed his mind that they would report anything. His shoulders dropped and his hands fell into his lap. "Listen, I-" Adrian started, but was immediately stopped by Muir. "Please keep our conversation in mind, Adrian - these are some serious allegations and we need to maintain our position." But Adrian looked away from his solicitor and moved closer to the table. He moved the coffee cup out of the way and rested his elbows in front of him. "Sorry, John, but I need to explain this," Adrian said. Jim and

Gibbons exchanged a glance. "I just wanted to help you, that's all. These people are such a burden to you all and I couldn't deal with seeing them using up your time day after day, getting let out and committing the same offences. I thought I could do something that would make a difference." Gibbons looked across at Adrian as the background of this whole thing began to unfold in front of him. His experience so far had only really been on the periphery of the broader picture that was being presented across the table. It was all he could do to stop his jaw dropping. "When the idea came to me I needed to create a method to keep my name out of the limelight, so I had to set up some other logins and use them to look up people on the system that had been - you know - busy." Adrian seemed incredulous and the officers tried hard to keep their expressions to themselves.

John Muir placed his hand on Adrian's arm again and silently pleaded with him to be quiet, but Adrian just shook his head. "I have to," he said simply. "I needed to do something to get these people away and the idea had been brewing for a while, so when I found a location on an old farm the rest of the plan started to formulate and, well, I needed to take action. I had to find a way to get things moving. The first step had to be who to target and how to keep my name out of everything." "I think we need five minutes," announced John Muir. Jim nodded in agreement, even though things were going well from his perspective. He and Gibbons got up. Jim announced for the recording, "interview suspended at 21:09," and the two officers left the room. John turned to his client once they were alone.

"Adrian, what the hell are you doing? Do you know what this is all about? If they charge you for kidnap and false imprisonment then you are going to prison. You have got to be careful with what you are saying, or this is not going to go well for you. We can agree on the van insurance and registration issues, that's not a big deal, the data access is a bit more of a challenge but navigable. The identity theft is something we can deal with since there wasn't technically a direct victim, as the person whose details you used was deceased. You can't just hand out the rest. If they haven't joined the dots yet, you can still get home tonight." "What do you mean, still get home tonight? You said you would get me out tonight and home to Lisa and the kids," Adrian blurted out. "Listen to me. Kidnapping people and chucking them into a hole in the ground is a major thing. You won't be eligible for bail - you'll be remanded until a trial date comes up." Adrian just stared at his solicitor. "Comes up? What do you mean, comes up?"

There was a knock on the door and Jim peered through the glass. "Can we resume?" he asked, and John looked across at Adrian. "Ready, and keeping with what we talked about?" Adrian nodded, but Jim could see he wasn't bought into whatever plan had been discussed and was hopeful that the rest would come out.

"Interview resumed at 21:20. Adrian, let's see if we can pick up where we left off. You were talking about how you needed to keep your name out of it - keep your name out of what, specifically?" John leaned into Adrian. "Please keep to what we discussed." "No comment," was the only response Adrian gave. "You mentioned that you needed to use the aliases to determine who to target. Target for what, Mr Burch?" Muir practically hit Adrian's arm. "I needed to be able to compile a list while keeping my name out of the system, so I could stay onsite to gather data under at least one other name while I decided what the next steps were going to be." Muir sat back from the table and took a deep breath, letting it out in a long, slow sigh. "The next steps, Mr Burch - what did these involve?" It was the turn of Gibbons to ask questions this time. "Could you explain how you went from a list of people to, well, to what next?" Adrian leaned on his elbows and put his head in his hands. "Getting people, these repeat offenders, out of the way was what I needed to do. All that happens is the same people just keep coming back out and knocking cars and buggering up people's lives. You guys just waste so much time on them, so they needed - you needed - some help."

"How did you decide on who was included in the list?" Gibbons asked, genuinely interested in what Adrian was likely to say. "Anyone with more than twenty offences made it since they were clearly a drain on the force, so it made sense to focus there and then get them sort of targeted to take some action. That's where the whole thing with the van and the house occurred to me. I found the house and realised it had been empty for a while, and worked out the old owner had passed away. It seemed the perfect opportunity to, you know, get things done." "So, once the list was created, how did you go from names to-" Jim was interrupted. "Collection?" offered Adrian. "I looked at who was nearest and spent some time working out their movement patterns to be able to get them at a time when they would be alone." "Mr

Burch, I need to understand a little more here. You have created a list of repeat offenders, you have accessed data from the Police National Computer, under one or more aliases, assumed the identity of a deceased person, and used their address to register and insure a vehicle that was used for- how did you put it-" Jim referred to his notes, "-collection.

So you have admitted to illegal data access, insurance fraud, identity theft and stalking so far. I do need to remind you of the seriousness of all of this." Jim was trying to give Adrian a chance to back up a little. "Yes, that's correct. I had to find how to help you guys," said Adrian in an almost defiant tone, like he had mentally switched back to absolving his actions. "These people just consume so much of your time, so I had to deal with them, and when I found the old farm it all came together. The disused slurry pit was the perfect place. I knew they wouldn't be able to get themselves out once I'd got them in, and then they couldn't cause you any more problems. So, you can see I was doing this for you guys." Jim had a decision to make but Adrian was in full flow, the whole saga spewing out of him. The more he spoke, the more virtuous he sounded. "Once I had the first one in, the others were easier - well, up to the last one, Gary, was it? He took a bit more effort and he was-" and he trailed off, his demeanour changing back to how he had been when they brought him in, with the realisation of his last victim being the key to his undoing.

"OK, let's bring this to a close for tonight and get you somewhere to sleep," said Jim. Adrian suddenly looked shocked and turned to his solicitor. "John, I thought you said I could go home?" he said with panic in his voice.

"Mr Burch, we need to speak to the CPS to understand the position here on the allegations, but from what you have just shared, it is likely they will recommend that you stay with us."

Jim stood and announced to the machine "Interview terminated, 22:37," and he went to the office to make the call.

Five minutes later he returned to the interview room and asked for everyone to follow him to the front desk. They all walked through the station with Adrian lagging slightly, until they got to where the custody sergeant was waiting for them.

Jim read out the charging decision he had received from the CPS minutes before. "This is Adrian Burch, to be charged with the following offences: illegal access to police data, insurance and vehicle fraud, identity theft, kidnap and false imprisonment. CPS have advised that due to the severity of the last two offences, bail will not be granted and you are to remain on remand until a date can be set for your hearing." Adrian's knees buckled and he slid to the floor. "But Lisa will be worried about me, and what about the kids, John, you- but-" He was panting the words out as Jim helped him up and led him down to the cells.

Jim could hear Adrian's sobs as they walked back along the corridor towards the front desk.

THIRTY-SEVEN

Seamus was pacing while Bariu sat on the sofa with his coffee. "Listen. I should just arrest you now and take you in, but I just-" He let out a long sigh. "Just you being here is a problem and could cost me my job, whatever benefits we feel could be had." "There, you see - you're already thinking about it!" Bariu almost shouted. "Whatever benefits we feel- we- you see, you are getting there. It makes sense we take Kelmendi out of the picture, and nobody else needs to know how. I can help make you very successful and all I want is to get the whole empire taken down. We both get what we want and that animal can't hurt anyone else." Seamus just stared at his uninvited house guest. Taking a deep breath, he let it out slowly as he walked to the kitchen, picked up the coffee pot and refilled his mug. Can this work? What am I even saying?

"What is it you think you need from me?" Seamus finally

asked what had been playing on his mind for the last few hours but was afraid to ask. But before any answer came, his phone rang. Jim's name showed up on the screen and a brief feeling of guilt washed over him, given his company. He shook it off and took the call. "Boss, we've charged the guy we collected from Devon. Kidnap and false imprisonment times four, identity theft, fraud, illegal access to confidential data and a couple of other minor bits. He's on remand and his solicitor is trying to negotiate bail, but that's not happening. His wife is on her way down. I'll fill you in on the details later."

Seamus took all this in while eyeing Bariu, who was still on the sofa and had switched on the TV, possibly to ensure none of the conversation could be heard. "Thanks for the update, Jim - excellent work on getting him." "It was almost all down to Gibbons, to be fair - had it all worked out and nailed him. Clever lad, that one. You coming in today? We've got to brief Bowler and we have a session on the upcoming op."

"Yeah," sighed Seamus. "I'll be there later - just finishing a few things off here." He looked across the flat at Bariu, wondering how best to get him out of the way while he got himself updated on the operation that was planned to start by the end of the week. He was worried enough given the history with Kelmendi and- his thoughts went back to when they had last met, and a bead of sweat rolled down his back. It was time to make a decision. He knew there was no way he was going to share any of the op details and even less chance anyone back at the station was going to know who he had accommodated. But Seamus knew that Bariu was right - between them, they would be more effective and get the results they both wanted, no- needed. He closed his eyes and exhaled. I can't, I just can't do this. What if he kills someone - how would I manage that, knowing that I would be complicit? Bugger this.

"Look, I have to go and you can't stay here. I need to think about this a lot more, and I can't do that with you here," Seamus announced as he walked back to the living room. Bariu looked up and smiled. "Of course, I will start getting myself somewhere to stay so I am local when you need me." Seamus shook his head. "Please just make sure you're not here later. I have too much to do and I can't concentrate with additional layers." Bariu stood and walked to the kitchen, rinsed his mug out and placed it in the sink. Seamus watched this and inwardly smiled, he had had house guests that would have happily left everything in the living room. "Right, I will leave now and we will talk," - Bariu pointed at the phone he had given Seamus - "on this," he said. Seamus almost laughed and looked at the ceiling. Once in his car, Seamus hid the phone in his jacket and started his journey to the station. The team needed him focused so that the planning would be done right. There was a lot riding on the raids and he had to make sure there was no room for error.

Marek made the call. "Boss, I have to tell you about plans I have been made aware of, the police will be-" but he was cut off as Dushku bellowed at him down the phone. "What are you talking about, where did you hear this and what facts do you have?" Marek was taken aback but carried on as he wanted to make sure he got all the info he had squeezed out of Nikola the previous day, leaving her beaten and broken despite his promise she would be OK. "There was a policeman in the club and he told one of the girls there was to be a raid and she came to tell me, she couldn't get any business from him so her news paid for the evening-" again Dushku erupted at him. "It's not for you to decide if a girl has covered her costs to us with this bullshit information. It sounds to me like a prick showing off to a pretty girl - it's just talk, you fool. There is nothing here for me to take from you, so leave me alone and get some fucking sense.

Do you have any idea how much it would cost to move our operations around, how much disruption it would be? No, you don't, so think these things through before talking such shit." With that, he ended the call. Marek just looked at his phone and thought about what he had just heard. He went back into the basement room of the club and walked over to where Nikola lay and continued where he had left off, putting a hard kick to her abdomen. "You stupid bitch, you have made me look shit, you will pay for this." By the time he left her she had barely any fight left but at least she hadn't mentioned that the police officer nearly got Kelmendi's name - it was her only way out if the whole business collapsed. She had to keep herself alive and get away, back home somehow. Dushku slid his phone into his pocket, pulled his cigarettes out from the other side of his jacket and lit one. Blowing smoke out he considered what he had just heard and immediately dismissed it, making his way down to the unit he had come to check on, to make sure all the product was up to scratch and the money was correct, this was the important issue today, not spurious tales from a whore that couldn't sell her shitty body to some jumped-up prick pretending to be a policeman. There was a lot to get done this week to get the new product ready for sale and there wasn't time for imbeciles. Dushku made a mental note to make an example of both of them when he had time. As he walked into the unit the men at the door seemed to straighten up as though standing to attention, he liked that. Going into the secure part of the building he looked over the tables of people manufacturing the new pills. These were going to cement their position in the market, pushing into their clubs first then get the streets opened up. Over the last year they had lost some of the share of these routes to competitors and it was starting to cause issues for Dushku.

He had made a promise to Kelmendi he would build up the business on this product and test it locally before getting into wider distribution, so it had to work as his reputation was at stake. "Are we on target?" he asked the man known only as Dem, his approach to people matching that of the bull he resembled. He made certain that everyone did their job and nothing went wrong, nobody would dare do anything else. Dem simply nodded, a man of very few words. Dushku smiled thinly and continued his inspection. Their unique mark on the bags, all centered and clear, this was good. Attention to detail was important to him and he made sure it was adopted by everyone involved in production. He took his time to look over each area, noticing how everyone he came into contact with seemed to stiffen up on his arrival, demonstrating his reverence in the organisation. He was pleased with what he had seen so far and this gave him confidence in the upcoming push. It was time to check the rest of the units, there was a lot of preparation to do and he needed to use his time wisely to make certain everything was on plan. Back in his car he called the next team to make sure they were ready, much as he enjoyed surprise visits, today he needed everyone to be on point.

The previous conversation had been forgotten and he was feeling confident about next week. There had been a lot of preparation and now everything was in place. Dushku took a moment to relax for the first time in months, they were about to retake the UK, club by club, town by town. A smile crept across his face as the sun slowly sank into the horizon.

THIRTY-EIGHT

Detective Superintendent Dawn Bowler stood at the front of the room, DCI Seamus Corrigan to her right and DCS Bridge on her left. The team were slowly assembling and taking the available seats, some choosing to stand irrespective of furniture. She was more nervous than she had been in years and was carrying some concern over Seamus. This would be a significant step for him and while she didn't want to undermine him or allow him to feel as though he didn't have her full confidence, he had history here and there was no way anything could impede this operation. "Right, settle down, everyone," she boomed, taking herself slightly by surprise with the volume. "Tonight is a significant moment for all of us, our opportunity to put a stop to this OCG and bring control to our streets, not to mention safety. The drugs business here is going to be hit hard, but we cannot underestimate the rest of their business. We have armed support for each location as we have intelligence that in addition to the drugs being manufactured, weapons are being stocked on some sites. Take no risks tonight, don't get complacent and expect problems. This way we will all be vigilant and more importantly, get home in one piece."

She scanned the room, each of the officers looking back at her, nodding and clearly keen to get on. This had been a long time coming and the level of excitement and apprehension in the room was palpable. Bowler turned to Seamus and saw a fleeting look of concern in his eyes, rapidly replaced by his steely focus she was pleased to see. He was very much ready for this. "Thank you Ma'am, let's get the teams together and mobilised." Seamus issued instructions to each team that were allocated a unit and each ensured the lead was appraised of their role and responsibilities. The armed units introduced themselves so everyone knew each other. This made a key difference in these operations, just knowing the names of those around you gave that bit of confidence needed in difficult situations. Once the teams had bonded a little more over the notes per unit and some pizza it was time to get the vehicles ready. The armed units were ready with the vans, weapons stowed and each team member was provided with vests and helmets as well as bodycams. Nervous chatter was replaced by serious murmurs of who was going to be first out on arrival and replaying the rehearsed tactics making sure everyone was clear. Seamus took a moment to appreciate the dedication of so many people to carry out this operation. More people he couldn't let down and the stakes were higher than before, more sites, bigger targets since the whole business had expanded significantly and- he stopped himself mid-thought. This was not the time to have doubts.

The teams set off from the station, each leaving in a different direction to arrive at their assigned site to make sure the raids happened simultaneously as planned. Their instructions were clear, arrive at their location and wait for the command to approach. It was time. As the first team arrived they could see lights on in the building. First person out was the drone operator to do a sweep of the site, to make sure they had enough information on potential threats. Nothing showed up on the thermal imaging camera although that didn't mean there was anyone outside. Next out were the armed officers doing their assessment of the site, access to the building, exit routes for those inside. The two teams shared what they had seen and formulated the onsite plan, positioning officers at the road and path routes that had been noted. The rest agreed on the doors to enter and protect from escaping people and then waited for the signal. This pattern was being repeated at the other four locations so that each team had all they could gather and were ready. Seamus had joined the team at the most recent unit where the intelligence had shown mass production of drugs at an industrial scale. He wanted to be there when they got in.

The order came over the radio, it was time to go. The entry team smashed the doors open and the vestibule was filled with the shouts of "Armed police, stay where you are and keep your hands where we can see them!" Officers piled in and with the obvious chaos those inside initially froze, it was 3am and the night shift didn't seem to have the wherewithal to run. Most were arrested and cuffed within minutes but some braver ones tried to escape but the teams had anticipated this and all ended up apprehended. Just ten minutes on site saw all occupants in handcuffs, not a single problem and the update came over the radio. One other site had a similar status, this was clearly the optimum time to have made these raids, but the team on site three hadn't updated after twenty minutes. In the building, the initial entry had gone to plan. Most of the staff had been taken by surprise and had been held but this site had more than one business being operated within and three of the people in the building took the initiative to defend. Running into a separate room they opened a wooden crate containing assault rifles, each taking one and running back to the main area, now filled with police. Aiming the weapons at the armed officers, they pulled the triggers only to hear a series of clicks. A brief moment of panic took over as the police turned to see three rifles aimed at them. Without hesitation they took aim, the laser sight dotting the chests of their would-be attackers. Each man dropped their gun and dropped to their knees, this was clearly not the time to be brave and surrender was a much preferred option to getting shot. Safely in cuffs, they were led out with the rest and the update made.

Meanwhile, across the county at the largest location on the raid plan, two black Range Rovers were making their way along the lanes towards the building. Seamus and the team had managed to follow their approach to the letter, every person they had found onsite were being loaded into the waiting vans and the armed team were doing a final sweep. Unfortunately, nobody had noticed that there was a room within a room, which is where the call had been made from to Kelmendi. The head of the OCG was in the back of the lead car, while those around him were arming themselves he was still and quiet. This could not be happening and he was considering if it was just one site or more. His thought process was accelerated as each number he called wasn't answered.

The other sites were either down already or in the process of being raided so he had to save this one. There was far too much product here to allow it to go without a fight. As they arrived it was clear the police already had the upper hand in terms of most of the people being taken outside. The only ones not in custody were those in the clean room where the call had come from. The driver of Kelmendi's car positioned it out of line of sight of the police vans and one of the men stayed with their boss, the other three got out and moved to be able to provide cover, weapons out and trained on the officers stationed at the door to the building. They made sure their earpieces were in and working so they were able to receive instructions. The second vehicle parked up, but not blocking the road out allowing the police to be able to leave and all four men got out and took up stances behind the doors of the Range Rover, giving them some level of cover should a gun fight ensue.

Kelmendi surveyed the situation, weighing up the actions that may be needed to protect his site given the police presence. "Get us in so we can assess once the vans have left. There may be officers that remain, but just deal with them if they cause you problems." The first of two vans drove out, the second close behind with multiple detainees on board. The team were pleased that the raid had gone without issue and that everyone onsite had been gathered. Only three officers remained onsite, the DCI and two armed sergeants to make sure the clearance team knew where to go when they arrived to empty the building of its contents. The first of Kelmendi's men made their way to the front door and entered the building, gun up to his eye throughout his approach. Listening out for any sounds of people he soon heard voices to his left and made his way as silently as possible in that direction.

Seamus was discussing the successful operation and was pleasantly surprised at how well it had gone when out of the corner of his eye he spotted movement. The armed officer, Sergeant Bloom, noticed the change in Seamus' demeanour and turned just as the shot was fired. The bullet tore through the vest and almost came out the other side, dropping the target to the ground instantly. Both Seamus and Bloom froze as their would-be attacker lay in a growing pool of blood.

Half a mile away hidden in bushes with a heat scope attached to his long-range rifle, Bariu smiled. One down but the sound of the window having blown in on impact would have alerted the others, so he didn't have time to congratulate himself on the shot. He turned his attention to the Range Rover and removed the driver and rear passenger that had been hiding behind their doors, in rapid succession. Due to the location of the vehicle, Kelmendi hadn't seen these two hits being made and was still under the impression that his team were taking the unit back since he had seen the police leave. In the building, Seamus and the armed officer had met up with their colleague and were trying to piece together what had just happened when another shot rang out, echoing in the large space. Sergeant Bloom span, blood spattering the other two officers from a hole in his left arm. Instinctively Seamus pulled him to the floor and he and the other sergeant dragged the injured man to the cover of some cabinets as the gunman advanced towards them. Seamus could see him and the one immediately behind and gestured to the sergeant to his right. The armed officer raised his MP5 and fired off a salvo of bullets, the first ones hitting their target of the gunman in front, the second salvo taking out the man behind. The three men moved towards the back of the room keeping cover as much as they could while taking care to keep out of sight.

Dushku's phone rang again and this time he woke up and answered without looking at the screen. Kelmendi's voice was loud and impatient "Get yourself to unit five now, we are under attack. Police seem to be in the building still, there have been shots, you need to get here to protect your part of the business, you promised me it was safe" and the call ended. He threw on some clothes and made it outside to his car and was on the road within five minutes of waking. At this time of the morning traffic was not a problem and he made good time, covering the eleven miles in just over seven minutes, sliding into the yard at speed and nearly colliding with one of the Range Rovers. The first thing he noticed were the bodies on the ground, the other two men now crouched in the trees motioning to him to the building. Dushku took a pistol from his car, checked the clip and chamber to ensure it was loaded and went in the direction being advised. Two steps away from the door there was the unmistakable sound of glass breaking and Dushku spun around to see the windscreen of the second Range

Rover had exploded. Rather than go towards the car to investigate, he pressed on into the building, this was too important to be distracted and he was sure that the men Kelmendi would have brought here knew how to manage themselves. In the Range Rover, the driver was slumped over the steering wheel while the front seat passenger had clambered into the back to protect his boss. Kelmendi, now flanked on both sides was frantically trying to understand what was going on, he couldn't see anyone outside that was firing anything so who and where were these bullets coming from?

Bariu moved to his next chosen spot and lined up the sights on the heat source in the second car. He checked his ammunition and counted seven bullets left in this clip and took aim. With two shots in rapid succession both men on the back seat who were either side of the original occupant had been shot and Bariu watched their position move as they slumped down. Kelmendi was on his own. Two more and the men standing on either side of the gate, who had positioned themselves as sentries at the gate. From this vantage point, the two in the trees were clear. He took the first out, quickly resighting to the second and got up to get closer to the building. One left. He had seen Dushku turn up and make his way through the door and was unable to see from this position where the police officers were. He continued to move closer to get to his other prepared location should he need to manage anyone coming out from the front. Once settled in position he scanned the area, the Range Rover containing Kelmendi was stricken, both front and rear windscreens were gone and its sole occupant was clearly distressed and not willing to venture out.

Dushku made tentative steps into the building, gun raised and ready to take on whatever or whoever may turn up. He had a feeling there were some of his people in the clean room so he made his way in that direction to get to the bottom of what was going on. The hairs on the back of his neck suddenly stood up and he stopped moving. Breathing as quietly as he could he looked around, the room was a mess, clearly there had been a lot of activity during the initial raid the evidence of that was all over the floor. Bags of pills were scattered everywhere, boxes of packaging had been overturned and tables upended and there was no sign of people. He stepped around the mess and then caught sight of two bodies and as he turned, laying there surrounded in their own blood. He recognised their clothing as Kelmendi's men and let out a sigh, it was unusual for them to have been taken out, more so where the police were involved as they most often went to immobilise rather than kill, so his mind started racing that there was more to this than first appeared.

His next steps were far more trepidatious than before given the scene he had just witnessed. The quiet was interrupted by his phone ringing and he swore that he hadn't turned it off or at the very least, put it on silent mode. For the second time that morning he brought it to his ear without looking at the screen and was met with the same voice as had called him earlier. "Get outside and get me out of here, there are men coming who will clean this up." Dushku shook his head and turned to leave. He retraced his steps and made it outside, thinking about those on the way and what they might be walking into while being cautious not to become the next victim of their mystery attackers himself. He skirted the edge of the building keeping his back to the wall and gun raised ahead of him and made his way towards the Range Rover parked a hundred metres away. He could see someone, he assumed it was Kelmendi, waving at him to hurry up. Still being careful he got to the car and pulled the former driver out and climbed into the seat in his place. "This is a mess, you told me you had no issues and now this and the other UK units have been pulled apart by the police. This car is fucked, you and I need to get out of here so we have to take your car, get me to it and get us out." Kelmendi shouted. Dushku got out and slid over to the rear of the car and opened the door, all the time looking around himself to see if there were signs of anyone that could cause him and his boss harm. Inside the building, Seamus was making Bloom as comfortable as he could as he knew they had to move. Blood was still coming from the wound but it had been padded as much as possible so it was as good as it was going to get. The three men moved along the wall keeping away from the windows, as they had no idea what had happened to the first gunman and couldn't be sure if he had been collateral damage or an intended target and weren't keen to find out.

Just as they moved away from the side of the room, voices could be heard on the other side of the wall. Seamus looked at the other two and raised his eyebrows, none of the men wanting to speak in case there was anyone else there waiting for them. Sergeant Brown motioned to Seamus and Bloom to keep moving and he put his ear to the wall and frowned. He nodded and put up two fingers then paused, pushing his ear harder and then changed to three fingers. Seamus assumed this meant he heard three different people and held down the emergency call button on his radio, knowing they would need help to get out and having no idea what might be waiting for them outside. He was doing all he could to hold it together, the memories of the last operation where Kelmendi had been involved were flooding his mind and creeping up on him, threatening to derail his focus and potentially put him into a very dangerous place, again. Dushku opened the rear door of his car and ran back to the Range Rover to get Kelmendi and made sure he stood between his boss and the tree lined edge of the property. Bariu watched this unfold in front of him, keeping his adrenaline under control just like he had been trained to do all those years before, both of these men in the same place at the same time was a gift. Although he was acutely aware he only had one bullet left and he didn't have time to change clips over in case these two got into the car while he was doing it. So it did reduce his options and he had to make a decision on what made most sense. Seamus crouched away from Brown, keeping Bloom to his side and shuffled along the route that had been agreed for their exit. Brown had taken a short amount of time to check if Seamus had undergone firearms training, and satisfied with the response he agreed with Bloom that Seamus should take control of his MP5 and Bloom would retain his Glock pistol so both men would be suitably armed as they made their way outside.

Brown meanwhile made his way along the wall he had heard the voices on the other side of, looking for a door or some way to get in, gun raised as he moved. He had turned his radio down as the last thing he needed was noise from that, but was conscious that he would need to keep in contact with the others. He dug into his pocket with his free hand and pulled out the earpiece and pushed it into his ear, plugging the other end into the radio. He could hear the arrangements being made to deploy more armed officers to his location and he was happy to hear the cavalry were on their way. Not that it gave him the option to relax, certainly not while there were at least three people inside and God knows how many outside. Seamus and Bloom got within twenty metres of the door and stopped behind some of the tables to provide some cover while they worked out the next part of their exit plan. Outside there was a distant sound of sirens as more armed officers made their way to the site, it was a welcoming noise to the officers on the ground. However the men in the clean room were unlikely to be as pleased to see them and this had the potential to ignite a situation that could rapidly get out of hand and be the cause of some less than favourable decisions.

Brown found the door but waited, not knowing what was likely to be on the other side and knew he needed to come up with some sort of mechanism to either get him in or them out in a contained way that would not result in discharging any weapons. He looked around him and found a table leg that had become detached during the earlier evacuation and measured it to determine if it would reach the door handle with him safely out of the way. His concern wasn't just based on whether or not those inside this room were armed, but also he was on his own and may not be able to apprehend multiple people single handed.

It occurred to him that he was carrying smoke grenades, used to disorientate people and create distractions, so he hatched a plan to arm one and open the door and throw it in. Gingerly he approached the door with his recently acquired tool and expected there to be someone directly behind it ready to ambush or rush him, but nothing happened. He took the pin out of the smoke grenade and tossed it into the room and closed the door. The effect was immediate, he heard coughing and spluttering and within seconds the door opened and three men walked out, each with one hand in the air the other covering their nose and mouth shielding their lungs and throat from the smoke.

Brown shouted to Seamus for cuffs, and pulled his own out from their pouch and he quickly used his to attach two of the men to each other, and as Seamus ran up with his and Bloom's cuffs, between them they secured all three men. "Is it just you in there?" Seamus barked as they led the men towards the main door of the building. The men appeared to agree in unison, terrified at their situation, clearly unarmed and not there to protect the site but given their attire seemed to be more aligned to chemical work as they were in overalls from head to toe.

Bariu watched the shadows moving towards the door with one eye still on Kelmendi and Dushku. He too was aware that the sirens were getting closer and he was running out of time to take action and get to a place of safety. He saw his chance as Dushku and Kelmendi walked around the car, one man slightly in front of the other as Dushku was protecting his boss keeping himself between the man and the tree line where he was sure there was someone lurking. With only one bullet left he made it count. It entered Dushku's chest just next to his shoulder joint and exited his body millimetres from his spine but as it left Dushku it hit Kelmendi square in the chest splintering on impact with his heart. Both men dropped to the ground, Dushku cried out in pain and began gurgling as blood made its way into his airway, coughing as his right lung collapsed. It was a matter of seconds before he realised there was no sound coming from the man now underneath him. Kelmendi looked up with dead eyes. His reign of terror had come to an end.

THIRTY-NINE

Bariu was pleased he had made the shot and detached the magnetic bag from the side of his weapon that had held all the spent cartridges so nothing was left behind. He collected all his equipment and moved away from the trees back towards his vehicle. Careful to keep hidden as the rest of the police began to arrive, he crept from tree to tree with his focus on being silent as he made his exit.

Seamus, Bloom and Brown walked out of the building with their prisoners in front of them as the ARVs turned up and more armed officers poured onto the scene, and all three felt a little more comfortable being outside. They scanned the environment in front of them and saw a number of bodies but couldn't correlate them to having heard that much gunfire, but each seemed to accept it for now and put it down to the stress of the operation.

Dushku stayed as still and quiet as he could, his breathing laboured and pain still searing through his upper body.

He knew the next few minutes would be the difference between getting arrested or getting away. He lay there and watched the officers move around the site, checking the bodies that they came across as they approached the building but hadn't got to the vehicle he was next to. There was enough noise around him to cover most of his movement but he grabbed his jacket lapel and put it into his mouth to dampen any other sounds he might emit as he moved. Slowly he slid under the car, letting out a groan as he did so but stifling as much as he could, his entire focus on getting to the driver's side without being seen. Just a few more feet.

Finally he emerged from the underside of the Range Rover, and pulled himself to his knees, reaching up to the door handle. Opening the door, he hauled his damaged body into the driving seat and pulled the door, allowing the auto close mechanism to finish the last centimetre or so silently. He put his head back onto the headrest and let out a long breath. Nearly free. He checked the route in front of him, noticing that there were vehicles almost blocking his exit but figured there was just enough space if he was careful, although the pace he needed to drive at was unlikely to afford the care needed to navigate the gap safely. There really was no choice, it was now, fast or he was going to be caught. Dushku started the engine, put the car into gear and floored the accelerator. He managed the gap, just brushing the front left corner of one of the parked ARVs, and was away down the lane. Bariu looked over his shoulder at the sound of the high revving engine, just in time to see the tail-lights of the Range Rover disappear into the distance. He initially assumed it was a lucky foot soldier taking advantage of a car being there and making a getaway and didn't give it much thought. He was too far away to see who was driving. The senior firearms officer surveyed the scene in front of him and assessed it quickly, issuing orders to the team to secure all doors and check the remaining vehicles then giving instruction over the radio relating to the fleeing car. He walked over to the three men by the entrance and dropped to his haunches to look Seamus in the eye. "What happened here? Seems we aren't needed now." Seamus was exhausted and still somewhat disorientated following the last hour's events and struggled to get a cohesive sentence together. "We arrived at the allocated time, waited for the-" "I don't need the full debrief just now, Sir. What I need is to understand-" he gestured around him, "-this." Seamus looked around in line with the other officer's hand and saw what he meant. The time he had been inside the building much had occurred out here. Stricken vehicles and bodies peppered the immediate landscape and his head was spinning. He could hear reports from the other locations that each site had been secured with minimal issues and no casualties. The overall operation had been a success, yet his location seemed to have more than its share of difficulties. He leant his head against the wall, closed his eyes for a moment and took a deep breath.

"We were inside, I- well, we haven't seen this until now. There was a lot going on in there and we needed to secure the product and staff, out here." This time it was Seamus who waved his arm in front of him. "No idea." He knew how bad that sounded. As the senior officer on the site he should know all aspects of the operation irrespective of where he was. He was supposed to be in control of all people on the ground and all moving parts, so to come out to chaos and not be able to explain it was a potential problem. It took some time to clear the site and get everything secured. The clean room was first to be dismantled and catalogued, the rest of the boxes and equipment got loaded onto vehicles once the CSI team had cleared each section.

Detective Superintendent Bowler had arrived and was discussing with some of the team before coming over to Seamus. He looked awful and was clearly still agitated following the events over the last few hours. She studied him for a moment before approaching him, considering her opening words. "So, looks like you got him, then," she started, watching for his reaction as her words seemed to just wash over him. His focus wasn't with her and he was visibly shaken, understandably so, but she needed him to talk it out. He sighed and slowly nodded while he gradually turned his head in her direction. "Yeah, I suppose we did, I suppose we did-" he repeated with a distant look in his eyes. He suddenly snapped back into the present. "Who escaped?" she asked him. "It can't have been him, he's there in the ambulance," Seamus said and pointed to one of the black vehicles parked up on the edge of the site.

"He's in a bag, I saw his face, it wasn't him, it must just have been a lucky one to have managed to get away. But we'll most likely see them trying to get into one of the other sites, or the club or -" he trailed off. Bowler could see his mind was racing with a host of possibilities about the vehicle that left at speed. She needed him to drop it, but at the same time realised he was tenacious and clearly dealing with a number of threads, least of which was a seemingly incongruous number of people in the morgue.

The debrief on site took a number of hours and the ammunition count was creating a wider puzzle - not enough rounds spent for the bodies taken from the site. Eleven down, ten rounds used. Bariu had as usual, done his homework and ensured he used the same calibre ballistics that the police would have had in their firearms. He knew what would be checked, any of the bullets in people or lodged in vehicles were going to be scrutinised so it was important to keep attention on the only weapons expected to be there.

Once the sites were all secured Bowler brought everyone back to the briefing room. Those with fewer complications regaled each other and the rest of the teams with how easy it was and the speed in which all those on site were apprehended. Seamus was at the back of the room and staring at the floor, the discussions going on around him as he struggled to maintain focus on any of the threads. His mind was still reeling and trying to organise the thoughts and information he had received over the past few hours. He kept seeing the gunman in front of him right there, gun poised and then-He exhaled a long, slow breath and became aware some of the team were looking at him, Bowler included. He shook himself out of it and looked at his superior. She gave a subtle nod which he returned. The full session lasted over three hours, by which time each team had provided their updates on arrests, seizures and closures of each building. The reports had detailed and catalogued everything they had found, no other site had shots fired so the ballistics reports were short. CSI had updated their side, it was just Seamus' team that had to extend the rest of the meeting. He stood at the front of the room, giving details of the arrival of the other vehicles, the bodies and everything that had happened, but it was as though he was watching himself - he was completely disconnected from the proceedings.

As soon as it was over he made his excuses and almost ran to the nearest toilet and locked the door of the nearest cubicle. Fear, guilt, relief and much more flooded through him and he broke out in a sweat, shaking and holding the sides of the small space as he felt it closing in on him. His breath quickened and his heart felt like it was going to burst out of his chest. Minutes passed but felt like hours as he struggled to regain some composure. His shirt was soaked now and he needed to sort himself out. He got out of the cubicle and felt a vibration in his jacket pocket.

It took a few seconds for him to work out what it was, and he reached in and pulled out the phone he had been given. No missed call, just a text message. We have what we needed. That was it. The answer to the puzzle he had been struggling with. It was the phone Bariu had given him - there was no doubt who the message had come from and what it meant. He looked in the mirror but he didn't recognise the person looking back at him. His overactive mind had already joined the dots. The phone had been on his person the whole time. Bariu would have been able to find him with it. He had led him straight there. It was all Seamus could do not to shout. He gripped the edge of the sink, his knuckles white, and he sneered at his reflection. He shook his head and made his way to the hand dryer, doing what he could to dry his shirt before going back out. Walking back along the corridor he tried to tidy himself up before getting back to the conference room. He put his hand on the door and stopped. Taking a deep breath, he pushed and entered.

Bowler could see there was something wrong, but rather than make a fuss she just gave Seamus a smile and watched as he took a seat. He'd tell her soon enough, but it had been a busy few hours and there was history there. This time, though, Seamus had got the prize. Sure, there were repercussions and there was bound to be some decompression needed, but for now she knew he needed thanks and reassurance - and, judging by the state of him, some very strong coffee too. There was something else she could see in his eyes, something she wasn't sure she wanted to delve into just now.

By the time the ballistics report had concluded, there were no questions left to answer. Rounds expended tallied based on one having taken out more than one assailant, so no further investigation had been recommended. Seamus relaxed a little, knowing that was the biggest question from the events earlier in the day, but still he couldn't shake the feeling that it may come back. He looked over and noticed Bowler was watching him, a slight frown on her face - possibly concern, or maybe something else. She walked over, gesturing to the remaining folks assembled in the room that it was time for them to leave. She took a seat next to Seamus and placed her hands, palms up, on the desk. "What do you need?" she opened with. Seamus tilted his head to one side and looked across at his boss. Her expression was passive and open, yet her eyes gave her away. He knew she wanted him to open up, it was obvious that he was struggling to keep it all in, and Seamus was acutely aware he needed to talk about it. But he didn't know where to start, let alone where it would end.

FORTY

Lisa spent an hour getting the kids ready for school, fighting tears back each time either of them asked, "Where's Daddy?" She gathered them up and got them into the car for the short journey, but while sitting in the driver's seat she couldn't find the keys. It was more than she could manage, and she burst out crying and began slapping the steering wheel in desperation. The last forty-eight hours had been a tremendous strain on her, trying so hard to come to terms with what had happened - the news she had needed to try and deal with. It was bad enough that he had disappeared and then to learn he had been arrested, but now this was all too much. The don't worry, Daddy will be back soon line was no longer viable, not since John Muir had called to tell her Adrian was in custody and unlikely to be released any time soon.

The whole appalling reality of it still hadn't hit home yet. She had been told the basics so far, as Muir had felt it best to fill in the blanks in person, so Lisa was still confused as to how it had gone from him being picked up in Devon to being held in remand in Swindon. She had so many questions and no real answers, and she really wasn't sure she wanted to get them right now. She was starting to question everything he had said to her the whole time they had been married, every time he had been out of the house, but the only thing that was coming from this was more stress and anxiety. It was taking her down a very dangerous path but Lisa was oblivious to just how much this was affecting her. She had worked to convince herself she was dealing with it well, keeping a steady ship for the kids and putting a brave face on things. At the end of each day, though, when the door was closed and the curtains drawn, she felt it - the pressure pushing down on her making it hard to breathe, never mind sleep. She couldn't maintain this for much longer and needed to know what was happening with Adrian. She had to be able to prepare for what the future would hold and - more importantly - how she could hold the family together.

After getting back from the school drop-off she let herself into the house and went into the kitchen, flicking the kettle on as she passed it. Normally she'd have checked the water level, but her mind was everywhere and nowhere so it would have to just manage. She pulled her phone out of her pocket and with trembling fingers dialled her solicitor's number.

John Muir answered after just two rings. If Lisa had hoped that the call would have helped, she was very wrong. As soon as it ended she just stood in the kitchen and stared at her phone, the black rectangle reflecting a distorted image of her face. Finally after what could have been hours she hurled it across the room and screamed "bastard!" at the top of her voice. She slumped to the floor and drew her knees close, one hand on top of the other as though trying to console herself by gently rubbing her thumb across her wrist. How could he do that, to us, to me. I mean, why? There were so many more questions and she had no answers to any of them. The landline rang and it woke her from the daze she had been in. For how long, she couldn't tell, but Lisa was aware her legs were numb from being on the kitchen floor and she was cold.

Pushing herself onto her knees, she could feel pins and needles. They threatened to stop her getting up but she slowly stood. The phone had gone quiet by the time she managed to lean on the worktop. Whoever had called was persistent, as it rang again. She leaned over and grabbed it from the charging cradle. Lisa pressed the green button on the handset. "Yes, what?" she practically whispered, and didn't realise how curt she was being. "Mrs Birch, it's Linda from St. Mark's. I just wondered what time you would be able to get here since pickup is almost over, and-" Lisa looked at the cooker clock. It was 15:50, and she should have the kids almost back home by now. What had happened to the time? She had only dropped them off an hour ago, surely. She cut Linda off. "I'm sorry, I'm coming now, just a minute, thanks," and ended the call, dropping the phone onto the worktop and making her way to the front door.

On the way to the school, Lisa was distracted by the

conversation she'd had with John Muir. Adrian wasn't coming home this week, possibly not even this month, if at all. John hadn't held back many of the details this time, having told her it was only fair that she was in possession of as many of the facts as were necessary to be able to make arrangements and stop supposition. He'd said that in his experience it was essential to prevent the latter as much as possible, as this led to worsening of the fear that was always associated with arrests and detention. She was inclined to accept this.

Tears clouded Lisa's eyes as she tried to navigate her way across the junction near the school, making it difficult to see what was happening to her left. A small number of kids gathered outside the shop were teasing one of their group, gently shoving them and pretending to push them into the road. As Lisa rounded the bend a child lost her footing and stumbled sideways and into the road. Instinct shook Lisa out of her thoughts just in time to see the young girl step out onto the tarmac. She somehow managed to stop herself at the same time that the brakes went on and brought the car to a screeching halt. Their eyes locked for a fleeting moment of mutual understanding, and the girl's friends grabbed her and pulled her back towards them. Lisa took a deep breath and let it out through pursed lips. Putting the car into first gear, she checked her mirrors, took one last look at the girl to make sure she was safe and out of the way, and continued on to the school.

Adrian hadn't slept, even though he was exhausted. There was no peace in this place. It wasn't just the sound of the other prisoners, but also the constant noise in his head replaying the events of the past few hours - the interview, and the discussion with his solicitor advising him of the severity of the charges and the lack of options for him. John Muir had explained to him as best as he could. Knowing Adrian wasn't in the best state of mind to take this information in, he had chosen his words carefully to have maximum impact. Even though he had been told what was likely to happen, Adrian was still trying to remain as positive as possible - largely by ignoring the advice he'd been given. He hoped he would be allowed home at some point later that day, the whole thing would be dealt with quickly and he'd be able to spend the night with his family. This thought remained with him for a while as he sat on the bed in his cell. A slight smile crept across his face as he recalled the usual breakfast time conversations with his kids, getting them ready for school and hearing about which parts they preferred, and the lessons they would rather not bother with and why.

His world came back into sharp focus when the door opened and Jim and Gibbons stood in front of him. "Mr Burch, we're taking you to Erlestoke today. We need the cells clear and this is our standard process for offences such as yours." Adrian just looked at both men, lips parted as though he was going to speak, but no words came out. He simply stared. Eventually he mumbled out, "Erlestoke, the- prison?" "Yes, Mr Burch. As an offender of this magnitude we will be transferring you to Erlestoke today. Your solicitor is aware and should have advised you already on this stage, and the option for you to have visitations planned shortly after arrival, so you'll have the opportunity to get that organised."

Gibbons had rehearsed this a few times. He was conscious that he needed to sound like he had made this speech many times, as it was his first time advising anyone on their position for being remanded. He was quietly pleased with his performance but couldn't let it show on his face. Adrian stood up and walked slowly towards the officers, arms outstretched awaiting cuffs or some kind of restraint. Jim just smiled and gestured for him to walk past, following behind him. The three of them walked to the edge of the custody suite together. Gibbons spoke with the custody sergeant and was handed the paperwork he needed for transport.

"Ordinarily, Mr Burch, we would use G4S for the transport but I think you'll be OK in the car with us. We do need to put these on, though." Gibbons put down the paperwork and removed his cuffs from their pouch. This time, when Adrian put his hands out, they were attached. Paperwork collected and prisoner signed for, the three men walked to the car that Jim had brought to the door. He positioned Adrian in the back, strapped him in and then got into the front. "We should be about an hour, so make yourself comfortable," said Jim as he started the engine. Adrian spent the journey looking out of the window taking in the scenery, part of him realising that this might be his last opportunity for a long time to appreciate the landscape around him.

As this thought continued to grow, a tear rolled down his cheek but he let it fall. He turned his attention to Lisa and the kids and what he would say when - if - he saw them again. How to explain this to them all, get her support and be able to get past this and back to some sense of normality?

But his thoughts were interrupted by their arrival at HMP Erlestoke, and a feeling of dread washed over him. The place was bleak, surrounded by high wire fences - a carbuncle on the Wiltshire countryside - and this was where he was going to be for the foreseeable future. *I'm going to be sick - I need the car to stop.* Jim brought the car up to the gate and got out to sort the paperwork and get them through security. When he got back into the car he looked across to where Adrian was sitting. His face was ashen and tear-streaked, which was as expected given the situation, but nevertheless Jim couldn't help feeling a tinge of sadness about what he knew was coming next. Getting to the door was one thing, but once the prison gear was on and the cell had been assigned, the real fear kicked in. That was Jim's main concern. How was this mild-mannered IT guy going to deal with it? They got the transfer complete and watched as Adrian was escorted into the main body of the prison. Jim took himself to one side and pulled out his phone. Bina answered after just a few rings. "Hello, you - everything OK?" she said, smiling to have a call from Jim during the day, but also considering it may be work-related too so she did her best to maintain an air of professionalism. "I just wanted to say hi and I'm looking forward to seeing you later," he said in a quiet voice. She smiled and then caught a tone in his voice that brought butterflies to her stomach. "What's going on, Jim - are you alright?"

He thought for a moment before answering and smiled a little to settle himself. "Yeah, I'm OK. It's this guy - he seemed so normal, you know, and he's-" Jim stopped before swearing. "He's screwed, he won't be out for a long time and he's going to be a prize in there. They'll just have to keep him safe." Bina listened while Jim talked as she knew he needed to express this. His concern for his prisoner was real and even with the list of offenses it was clear Adrian had just overstepped some level of normality in his attempts to address what he saw as injustice. It was clear that Jim could see the wider impacts and consequences and even though he didn't have his own family, it spoke volumes about his desire for his future. She felt something inside her that she had never felt before, deep within her - a sense of hope. "I'll see you later - please take care on the way back," she said to him once he had said all he needed to and they'd said goodbye. She made a short list of things to get from the supermarket on the way home. He sounded very much like he needed some time and attention, so a nice dinner at hers would help.

Jim went over to where Gibbons was waiting, the younger officer looking decidedly uncomfortable in his current surroundings. Safely back in the car, Gibbons let out an audible sigh and Jim looked across at him. "You OK? First time here?" Gibbons looked at his SO and smiled thinly. "Yes - it's not erm, very nice, is it?" Jim almost laughed out loud. "Not very nice - this week's biggest understatement. It's a prison, not the Ritz, man!" Jim drove off and Gibbons took in the juxtaposition of the horror of the building they had just left and the beauty of the surrounding fields and villages. It had been a difficult morning for all of them, although for Adrian it was about to get significantly worse.

After processing and being moved to his wing, Adrian was shown to his cell by the guard for the remand wing. As was explained to him along the short walk, a lot of the prison was for remanded offenders awaiting trial and there were a lot of activities he would be able to participate in while here. His spirits were lifted a little now he knew he wouldn't be breaking rocks or sat in his cell for twenty-three hours a day. The tour, such that it was, had introduced him to where things were: the 'restaurant' as the guard had ironically referred to the cafeteria, the gym, library and some of the work rooms where - from what Adrian had understood - he could learn all manner of things.

During the initial processing, Adrian was advised of the visitor list that he needed to start and how to do it. This was something he paid absolute attention to and asked, in what he was aware was a very meek voice, how soon he would be able to submit it. He followed the instructions he had been given and was aware that it would be at least three days before his first visit would be able to take place. He sat in the library later that afternoon and filled out his part of the form to add Lisa to his list, along with John Muir. After some deliberation he added his mother to the list too. This was a reasonable start for his first day but was advised that it wouldn't be taken up until the next working day.

All he had to do was wait. He realised with a feeling of increasing dread that he needed to do a lot of that for now. At the end of the evening he was reminded of the location of his cell. There was no getting over that word. It wasn't a room or dormitory or anything remotely welcoming. It was a cell. He was going to be spending the night in a prison cell. Adrian thought about lounging across the sofa and then padding to the kitchen in his slippers to fetch another glass of wine. Now he was scared to even venture out of the tiny space he had to occupy.

The moment the door closed his heart broke. He was in prison. It wasn't supposed to be like this. He had been helping the police, and now- Adrian took in a deep breath and scanned the small space he was now in for what could be months. He lay down on the bed, pulled the thin pillow into his chest and sobbed.

FORTY-ONE

Everyone else had left the room, and Seamus was aware it was just him and DS Bowler. He put his head back against the wall and closed his eyes, waiting for - well, he wasn't sure what he was expecting. Dawn went over to the drinks machine in the corner of the room and, minutes later, came back with a black coffee for Seamus and a hot chocolate for her. Placing both cups on the table, she took the seat to his left. He picked up his coffee and was about to speak, but she beat him to it. "It went well, considering all the extra noise," she said, underplaying the obvious. Seamus blinked and looked up at his boss. "The noise? Kelmendi's blokes all over the place, gun shots and one of ours getting it in the arm." His voice was rising with each word, and he was aware that something might end up getting said that really needed to stay very quiet. Seamus stopped mid-sentence and took a deep breath. "Sorry, ma'am. It's just that there was a lot happening and we could have lost one of the team. After we'd started clearing the site, the boss turned up and then-" He shook his head. He took a long sip of his coffee and carefully put the plastic cup down, tracing his index finger along the ridge between two of the desks that had been put together to form the conference table. Looking out of the window, his attention returned to the conversation and the thoughts whirling around in his head about Bariu's message to him. He was aware Bowler had been talking but wasn't sure what he'd missed. She pushed her empty cup away from herself and stared at Seamus, one eyebrow raised, waiting for an answer to the question he had missed. "Well, have you?" she asked again. He looked at her, his lips parted, but she had pre-empted this and repeated her question, "Did you call Bloom today, to see how he is?"

"Yeah, yes of course I did. He's fine, all things considered. A bit sore, as you'd imagine with a hole in the arm, but a little time off will have him sorted out soon enough." Seamus was concerned about the direction this was taking and really wasn't sure he wanted it to keep going. Time for a change of tack. "What's the next step now we have Kelmendi out of the picture and his enterprise in our control? Where does the intelligence tell us things sit with the wider routes and network - is it the case that now we have the head of the snake and all that?" Bowler looked pensive as she considered her response. This was a complex situation and, while she was sure Seamus was more than capable of managing it any other day, today was a different story entirely. She really didn't want to push him over any edge he might be teetering on. "It's a fluid situation that's evolving by the hour. Right now we're aware there has been a significant blow dealt to the whole operation, leadership gone and pretty much everything they had in the UK is in our possession. It does, of course, put a serious target on our facilities where this shite is being stored so we're moving it tonight, then again into a few different locations." Seamus nodded along with the update and made some mental notes. "I suppose there's a deputy somewhere, but will they have the same connections and access to the distribution and customer base?" It was more of a rhetorical question, but certainly gave them both a lot to consider. "Right," said Bowler, "you need to go home, clean up and get some rest. It's been a long day and we need to look at what to do with the data we have and close all this down here. We will pick it up in the morning, there are folks from NCA all over it and they will be here tomorrow to go over where we all fit in."

They both stood up. Dawn looked over at Seamus and did all she could not to hug him. He had been right in the thick of it with Kelmendi, again, and got out the other side in one piece- sort of. Jim walked across the main office as Seamus came out from the kitchen area, two mugs in his hands. "How was your day, then?" Seamus asked his friend and colleague. Jim smiled but it didn't quite get to his eyes. Seamus put his hand on his shoulder. "Tell me yours, and I'll tell you mine." The two men walked down the corridor to find a quiet room. Jim gave Seamus the full breakdown of the interviews and subsequent charging of Adrian and updated him on the trip to Erlestoke.

Seamus nodded at the explanation and Jim didn't hold back. "We need to deal with the tidal wave of shite this operation will have uncovered and what that will mean to us lot. I'm sure you can imagine the next few weeks will be unpicking this, and we'll be crawling with National Crime Agency bods from tomorrow." Jim shrugged. "We ought to get some decent coffee then - you know what they can be like." Seamus managed a smile and the two of them went into the main office. "Gibbons needs to make the move to the team full-time," Jim said after a while. He had been updating his report and it was an obvious decision, so he just needed to get the DCI to approve so he could initiate the detective training for the young PC. Seamus stopped his own typing and leaned back in his chair. "Yes, absolutely, mate. He ran rings around you, didn't he?" and winked.

Bina took a while longer than usual in the supermarket. While she wasn't the greatest cook, she was always appreciative of a little help and this evening that would come in the form of a Marks and Spencer's ready-made meal for two. She took her time choosing some wine too. What was it he said he liked? Wine was not one of her strongest subjects and Jim had mentioned he liked a couple, but for the life of her she couldn't remember. Thankfully her memory was assisted by the contents of the shelf. Malbec! She popped a couple of bottles into her basket along with the food and a nice-looking but not-too-fancy cheesecake. If they didn't have it tonight then it would be perfect for lunch tomorrow. When Bina got home she tided the downstairs to make it presentable. Given her job and the meticulous nature of how she worked, her house was always spotless. Her friends always commented on it when they came over, made the odd joke about it too if a spoon was out of the drawer, even if it was being used. But she always felt it needed a little extra if anyone was coming over. Bina plumped up cushions on the sofa and put the cheesecake in the fridge while fussing over what to wear. She was suddenly nervous - no, excited about seeing him again. More than that, it was dinner at hers. What would he think of the house, the kitchen- Oh, come on, woman - get a grip! she told herself. A quick run around with the vacuum cleaner and a wave of a duster, and she felt better about the place and settled down a little. Before heading upstairs for a shower, she dimmed the living room lights. Jim was at his desk finishing a coffee and reading over the situation reports from the operation that had just concluded, the one he had almost been on too. He scratched at his chin as he skimmed line after line of detail on entry, containment, arrests etc. and just happened to glance at his watch as he turned a page. "Shit, bollocks!" he erupted and leapt to his feet. A few colleagues were still in the open-plan office area and Jim apologised before stuffing the documents into his bag and practically running out of the building. By the time he got to his car he was panting, he wasn't nearly as fit as he thought he was.

He opened the driver's door, threw the bag onto the front passenger seat and climbed in, folding his impressive frame into the car. He knew he was going to be late but didn't want to attract any unwanted attention. Contrary to popular belief, a traffic officer was more than happy to arrest another officer for speeding. Jim kept within an acceptable percentage of the speed limit and made it to Bina's just five minutes after the time he had promised to be there. He hated being late for anything, and he really didn't want Bina to feel that anything was more important than her. He hadn't had time to stop and get her anything, which made him feel even worse, so when he got to the house it must have been written all over his face. "What's that look for?" Bina said as she opened the door, her head slightly tilted. "I'm really sorry I'm late and that I haven't-" but he didn't get to finish the sentence as she leaned forward and planted a gentle kiss on his lips. He looked surprised for a second.

She thought she had massively overstepped the mark, but his face softened immediately and he pulled her into his arms, his head resting on hers. She felt him take in a long breath and let it out in a longer sigh, but clearly one of relief. "Thank you," he said, lifting her head so he could see her face, and returned the kiss. "I really am sorry for being empty-handed, I just-" and for the second time that evening she stopped his apology with a kiss. "It's fine - you're here, I have food and wine, and all the time in the world. Come in off the step, will you, and let's get a drink." They walked into the kitchen and Bina reached for the bottle she'd opened earlier. Someone she had met had said it, or maybe it had been on TV - either way the advice was to let red wine breathe, whatever that meant. Take the cork out a while before drinking it, but it's a screw top, does that count? As soon as he'd taken a sip, the last few days seemed to fall away from Jim.

There he was in Bina's kitchen and she was making them both dinner, they had wine, and it felt so natural. As she walked past him he reached out, held her hand and looked into her dark eyes. "Thank you," he said, realising it seemed to be the phrase of the evening for him, but he struggled to find anything else that could convey what he needed to. "This is-" he hesitated for half a second and said earnestly, "-perfect, absolutely perfect." Bina put down the tongs she was carrying and turned to face him. She shook her head and took his other hand in hers. "I'd wait for you all night, every night, Jim - just to know we can have time together. Minutes, hours, days, weeks - it doesn't matter, as long as it's with you." He simply beamed at her.

He couldn't muster a single word in response to that wonderful and yet simple sentence. She had managed to articulate in a handful of words everything he felt - all the complex emotions that seemed tangled within him were right there. She just wanted to be with him. He chewed his bottom lip while trying to come up with something to say in return that wouldn't sound pathetic but nothing came, except tears. He couldn't stop them. It was a combination of pure unadulterated joy at being here, with the woman he loved - yes, he loved her - and having spent time with Adrian today, witnessing a man's world turn upside down with no one there to help. And now, he had Bina there, whatever happened. "I'm so lucky," was all he managed to say, and immediately berated himself internally for such a feeble reply. But she just smiled at him, warmth in her eyes. "Yes, you are, James Pallister - but then so am I."

The meal was a success, and Bina secretly thanked Messrs Marks and Spencer for their fine dining options and handy instructions to boot. To be fair, she would have probably burned everything had she not set the timer on the oven, distracted as she was. They sat together on the sofa. By now Jim was on lemonade, but he drank it from his wine glass and pretended it was champagne, pointing his little finger out on each sip. The night was everything she had dreamed of and more. They were just so relaxed together, and when it got past midnight she started to feel saddened that it would end soon and he'd go home.

A little under thirty miles away, Adrian lay on his bunk. It was mildly more comfortable than the one in the cell he had spent the previous night on, but this was his bed for - well, he really didn't want to contemplate the length of time. He hadn't got used to the noise at the police station, the constant comings and goings of people throughout the night, a stark contrast to home where, although they were on an estate it was a quiet one and their house was on a close, so no passing traffic interrupted his sleep. Tonight, though, he was kept awake by his thoughts - fear, uncertainty about his future, worry that Lisa and the kids were by themselves and the sounds of the other prisoners. The other prisoners he repeated to himself a few times, other prisoners, I'm a prisoner, I'm in prison.

People were shouting but he couldn't decipher what about or where the sound was coming from. It might have been from outside for all he knew, as he was still somewhat disorientated and had no idea where he was in relation to this huge, rambling complex of buildings. Finally fatigue got the better of him. He drifted into a fitful and shallow sleep, images of Lisa and the kids flashing in and out of his mind. Sometimes they were coping, other times they were all together and crying, and each time he woke he was soaked in sweat. During the induction he had been told that sleeping tablets were available if needed and were quite commonly prescribed by the prison doctor for new intakes during their first week or two. He decided to request a visit in the morning and tried again to sleep.

FORTY-TWO

Dushku pulled over into a wooded layby after having travelled a reasonable distance to give him a little time. He checked again to make sure he hadn't been followed, although he had been looking in the mirror every few seconds after speeding away as the place filled with more police. His shoulder and back were hurting so much he thought he would pass out and he was aware that he'd lost a lot of blood. The car seat had absorbed a reasonable amount that had soaked into his trousers.

Climbing out of the car, he realised how weak he was. He almost fell to the ground and grabbing the door was the only thing that stopped his descent. He fished around in the door pocket for the phone he had dropped in there and scrolled through the contacts. "It's me, I need help. Can you come to me?" he croaked down the line when the other party answered. "Fine, I will be there," came the reply and the call ended. Keeping the phone on he grabbed a coat from the back seat, shuffled away from the car and found a spot in the trees that sheltered him from the road yet maintained a view of oncoming traffic. Folding the coat and placing it on the damp ground, he lowered himself gingerly onto it and leaned against a tree, wincing in pain throughout. With Kelmendi dead, the empire was his. All he needed to do was survive the night and get to safety, then he could execute the plan he had been preparing for months. It was always Kelmendi's wish to have Dushku as his successor, but neither had expected it to be like this. There was still so much he didn't fully understand, but now he had to learn on the job.

After what felt like an eternity, a large black Mercedes pulled into the layby and stopped. The engine was killed and a large man emerged from the rear dressed in a long, black leather coat. Dushku sighed in relief. This was a man he had seen many times over the years. Esat was the 'cleaner', the guy that turns up when a mess needs to be dealt with. Dushku knew that he wasn't the mess, and given the news would have reached the clan by now of Kelmendi's demise, nobody would be sending Esat out after him. The new arrival surveyed the layby and the damaged Range Rover before returning to the car and opening the boot, extracting two petrol cans. He doused the Range Rover's interior with petrol and threw the empty plastic containers in for good measure. He turned his attention to the trees and found Dushku, offering his hand to his new boss and helping him to his feet.

"We leave now," the cleaner said, ushering Dushku to the Mercedes and opening the rear door, helping him inside. Once the door was closed, Esat casually lit a match from a book he had removed from his jacket and tossed it into the Range Rover, then took a seat in the Mercedes and nodded to the driver.

The engine started and the car swept away from the layby, the flames starting to engulf the Range Rover visible in the rear window. As comfortable as the car was, Dushku was in agony from the change of position, having been leaning against a tree for the past twenty minutes. "Not far now," said Esat, clearly aware of his new passenger's plight. Dushku nodded, even this motion bringing waves of pain across his upper body. The car arrived at a large industrial building at the edge of a village. Dushku had a vague recollection of having been here before but was aware that he was losing consciousness so the timing couldn't have been better for his extraction. He was carefully taken from the car and put into a wheelchair, only peripherally taking in his new surroundings. Dark corridors were followed by bright white walls and strong lights - then nothing.

When he woke he was in a medical bed, the kind he had seen in hospitals, but he was certain this was not one of those establishments. Various pieces of equipment surrounded him and he was connected to at least one of them. There was no one else there so he hadn't anyone to ask what time it was or even what day it was. He had no concept of how long he had been there. He closed his eyes and, for the first time in what felt like days, he felt relaxed and safe. The pain wasn't there either, he realised, as the pillows seemed to swallow him. He was gently shaken awake by someone who appeared to be a nurse, not helping in his quest to understand where he was. She spoke in hushed tones to simply advise she was checking him over and updating his chart, but did ask if he needed anything now he was awake. "Yes please, water - and what time is it?" he just about managed through dry lips and an even drier throat. She smiled and looked at her watch while walking just out of his line of sight, returning with a tall plastic beaker and a straw. She helped him sit up a little, positioned the straw by his lips and made sure he managed to drink some of the water. "It's eleven-fifteen pm," she told him and smiled as she checked he was still drinking. He nodded and wanted to ask which day it was, but decided against it. He would soon know, and there was little point in the detail anyway.

He motioned to the nurse that he had finished with the water, so she placed it on the table beside him and withdrew from the room. Dushku lay there looking around him. Aside from the machines and his bed it was fairly sparse in there - plain walls and no windows. That struck him as very sensible, given the likely clientele that would be treated here. Although he did consider it had been put together just for the purpose of his convalescence but shook that thought away when he thought about the timing of his collection and arrival here. It was ideal for now and he chose to take the opportunity for some more rest. The next time Dushku woke there were people in the room with him - three men in suits and all with very serious looks on their faces.

For a moment he wondered if they were all doctors and were about to impart some very grave news, but as the fog of sleep cleared he began to recognise them: Esat,

Vedat and Mjek, the doctor. He frowned as he tried to focus better and Vedat came closer to him so they could speak without needing to raise voices. Dushku thanked his now right hand man for being so considerate, which was dismissed by a wave of the man's hand. "Shef, we are blessed that you are well and that we are able to assist you," Vedat said with reverence, and bowed at the end of the sentence. "We have much to discuss. The English business has sustained significant losses and we must consider our options. Our suppliers are nervous, as are our customers, so I have taken the liberty of putting some reassurances forward to them, that you are in place at the helm of our Clan and things will soon improve."

Dushku took a deep breath and held out his hands. Taking the cue, Vedat placed both of his hands into Dushku's. "We will prevail, brother, we will take this time to assess our location strategy and rebuild here. This is a good market, our products are all very well received. Yes, this is a setback, but I have faith that we will return stronger." All the men in the room nodded in agreement to this. Dushku allowed his hands to open and Vedat took a step back. "Yes - with your leadership, Shef, we will become more than we have lost."

Dushku beckoned Mjek to him and gestured for him to lean close. "Tell me, Mjek, when can I leave here?" The other man looked pensive for a moment then smiled. "Shef, you may leave when you wish. But I would advise maybe two or three more days. You were very ill when Esat brought you here and we need you in full strength to lead us. So, will you take my humble advice?"

Dushku expelled air through pursed lips and shrugged.

“If you say I need two days, I will agree with two days, but bring me a laptop and a phone. If I have to be in this bed I need to be able to see the extent of the work ahead of us all. But for now, please leave me, as I am aware I must rest.”

Mjek bowed his agreement, joined the others and gestured for them to leave, giving a final curt bow to the leader before retreating through the door himself. The nurse returned a few minutes after the men had left and tended to her patient. His brow mopped and water offered, Dushku was beginning to feel more like his usual self. His thoughts went to his former boss and mentor, and the events of the morning of the police raid. Something was niggling away in the back of his mind, but the pain relief and fatigue were still too much of a barrier for him to get through to determine what it was.

He decided to leave it for now - it would no doubt come to him in due course. Now was the time for planning the future and not thinking about the past. The raids had hit all their warehouses, all the UK products had been seized by police, so they must be storing it all somewhere. His first task was to find out where. There was a lot of product so there would most likely be multiple storage locations and he knew the police would keep things on the move given the nature of what they had in their custody. There would be a number of opportunities to infiltrate it in transit, rather than having to find and enter any specific sites. There were some of his men on the inside within the police forces, just not the local one here, so he decided to change that at the earliest chance he got. He would make some calls to those he was aware of and see what feelers could be put out there to find out if anyone knew where his stock was and whether there were any transport schedules available.

Dushku was going to get as much of it back as he could - there were people higher than him that they owed some of that money to, and they would soon be asking for it. These were not people you could keep waiting, nor the kind that could be appeased with cute stories about when they would get paid. They wouldn't care about what had occurred, except that they might impose more rigorous security controls on their part of the inventory and cash. Luckily cash wasn't as popular as it used to be - gone were the days where there were piles of it stacked up in warehouses.

Thankfully most of the transactions were now electronic and encrypted, but they still had a good few hundred thousand packaged up from street dealers. It was time for another rest, as it was going to be a tiring few days getting this ship back on course.

There was still one loose end to be tied off. The Shepherd must have been there and it was more than likely it had been him that fired all the shots. As far as that man was concerned, Dushku was dead. He'd let him think that for a while longer as he and his closest men constructed a plan to deal with him. He could wait another day or so.

FORTY-THREE

Seamus got out of his car having driven home with a whirlwind of thoughts going through his mind, although each thread seemed to bring him back to Bariu. It was him onsite somewhere that had shot those people, that's what his message had meant. We have what we needed. He blew out a long breath and just stared out of the front windscreen for a few moments before shutting off the engine. Unclipping his seat belt, he reached for the door handle and stopped. He picked up his phone and called Jim.

"Jim, what's the story with the computer guy? Did he have full access to the PNC and our local stuff?" he said without introduction. Jim hesitated a little. "We could see he had access to offender records, that's how he had created his list of victims and he must have had wider access to get the records for the deceased guy whose identity he stole. But outside of that, there's no evidence to suggest he'd looked at anything else. What's on your mind?" Seamus was silent for a second or two before answering, scanning the parking area as he did so. "Well, the operation took a lot of stock out of those sites and we have it all somewhere. If the guy has been able to gain access-" He stopped, gathering his thoughts a little better. "Is it feasible he could have given himself access to more than just offender lists? I mean, have we found all the accounts he had set up, and checked what they can do?" Jim couldn't quite follow the thread as the two cases didn't seem to share many similarities. It became clear to Seamus that his colleague was struggling a little. "My point is, your guy is on remand and accessible to who knows what kind of people. If the reason for his incarceration is made known to them and they squeeze him to give them details, then they could use the access he has set up and have a nose around. We have to be certain that we've closed all the routes." The penny finally dropped and Jim agreed. "Got it - I'll make some calls now and get back to you. We'd found two other accounts and played these back to him but hadn't asked if there were more and he hadn't volunteered. We'll use the same details to check and then go and see Mr Burch in his new lodgings and ask him."

"Right. Don't alert him to the specifics - it's probably bad enough for him in there without the fear of someone slipping into his cell and having a chat, you know," Seamus added but didn't seem to have much conviction in his voice, which Jim did pick up on. "Maybe. Or perhaps a subtle hint wouldn't go amiss?" Jim suggested. The two men agreed and ended the call.

Seamus opened the door, unfolded himself and stretched. It had been a very long shift and Bowler was right - he really needed some sleep. He locked the car, walked over to the communal door of his building, opened it with the fob and made his way to the stairs. He always preferred them over the lift, even just to get his step count up for the day. Once in his flat he locked the door and kicked his shoes off, making sure they were neatly lined up against the wall. He padded into the bathroom to run a bath and caught a glimpse of himself in the mirror. Shaking his head at the sight of a very tired, ageing man, he placed the plug into the hole and opened the taps, adding some bath foam to the running water.

Taking advantage of the time he had while the bath filled, he opened a cupboard, withdrew a large wine glass and then pulled the cork from a bottle on the counter. He poured its contents into the glass and placed the empty bottle into the recycling bin. Moments later he was shoulder-deep on the bath, wine in hand, and finally starting to feel the tension of the day abate. He sipped the wine even though his head was at an odd angle as he lay there, shoulders against the side of the bath. At least this time I made it out without ending up in hospital, he thought, then immediately admonished himself as he remembered that Bloom hadn't been so fortunate. He replayed the scene in his mind seeing the wound, but bigger as his imagination played its tricks due to exhaustion and adrenaline.

By the fourth or fifth version, the poor man's arm had been completely removed with bits of bone and flesh spattering Seamus' face. He woke to find himself almost fully submerged, and the wine glass somewhere under the now cold water. He sat up and shook himself awake, retrieving the glass and placing it on the small drawer unit next to the bath. Hauling his tired body out was hard work, as so much of the water had gone so he seemed several times heavier but after the second attempt he managed to exit and grabbed a towel. Rather than go to bed, he put his bathrobe on, went into the living room and sat down, picking up the TV remote and turning on the news to see what else had been happening. He was pleased to see none of his recent work had made it to the media yet and very soon slipped into a deep sleep.

This time he was woken by his phone ringing. He blinked a few times to get some focus and stared at the screen before sliding the green disc upwards. "Jim?" he managed to say, with what felt like a mouth full of cotton wool. "We had a look around the system, based on what we knew from the other accounts and found nothing. Gibbons is on his way over to Erlestoke now for a chat, and I've told him to impart enough to keep Burch on his guard but not the depth of the issue in terms of the wider OCG background. Should be enough to keep him twitchy and hopefully open up if he has set anything else up - I'll update you later. You OK, by the way?"

Seamus was still trying to bring his level of awareness up to something resembling consciousness and merely grunted to start with. "Yeah, fine, cheers. Sounds good. Are you happy with Gibbons on his own with this?" It wasn't said with any criticism, just making sure nothing would either be missed or get unnecessarily complicated. "He's fine, I trust him to not be a knob about it," said

Jim in his usual manner. This brought the first smile to Seamus's face for a while. "OK, and I'm buggered to be honest. It's been a challenging few hours and frankly I'd rather be on holiday somewhere or just, well, not doing this for a few days. I'll be in tomorrow so let's have a chat then - you can apprise me of the Burch situation and we need to look at the stock movement to get it out of our building." Jim agreed. "Yep, just take some time. Make sure you've had some rest, otherwise you'll be a waste of space tomorrow and I'm not sure we have enough coffee to keep you going." "Fair. See you tomorrow," said Seamus and ended the call. Putting his head back on the sofa, he knew he needed to go to bed but couldn't bring himself to get up, so he tucked his knees under his body and snuggled up with a few pillows. Of all the times he really needed her there, this was one of them.

He drifted off and imagined her arms wrapped around him.

By the time he made it to the office in the morning Seamus had ruined some more toast. He nearly left the flat with it still on the worktop but knew he would be thinking about it all day, so cleaned it away and tried to make it to the office without a detour but was alas, unsuccessful. Walking into the open-plan area, he spotted Jim and handed him one of the coffees he had purchased along the route. His colleague nodded his thanks and scanned Seamus up and down. "Cheers, you crash into a pastry bar this morning?" he laughed. Seamus looked down to see the evidence of his pit stop still mostly stuck to him again.

"Gibbons is at Erlestoke," Jim said as they walked to

some desks to get their day started. Seamus nodded thoughtfully, recalling the discussion the previous evening. "What's he been briefed for?" he asked, looking across at Jim, who had opened his laptop and was frowning. "What?" came the reply. "Gibbons - what have you told him? And what's up?" Seamus asked as Jim's expression seemed to clear a little. "Right, yeah - just to ask about access, account names and indicate that someone in there may approach him about how he had managed to get into the PNC. Try to give him a dialogue to use that was close enough to the truth but with some extras to keep them, assuming it happens, off his case."

"And?" Seamus pressed. "Note from Bina - she wants to see us in the lab when we're free. She has something on Reg." "Oh?" said Seamus, raising his eyebrows. "This I've got to hear. Fancy a drive?" The two of them closed their laptops, made the short journey through the corridors to the car park and got into Jim's car as it was closer. Seamus looked around himself and then at Jim. "This is nice," he said, gesturing with his hand to the interior of the car. "Thanks, I like it," Jim replied, smiling, "not the old-school Skodas of their day, right?" They travelled in relative silence to the lab, parked in one of the staff spaces and made their way to the reception. Showing their ID, more of a formality since both were greeted by name, they signed in and waited. A matter of minutes later Bina arrived to let them through. Seamus couldn't help but notice a look that passed between her and Jim, and inwardly smiled.

"Good to see you, Seamus," she said in her usual professional voice, and ushered them into her office.

"Right, then. Our friend Reg was a bit of a conundrum for us all until yesterday. We had been trying to understand what it was that had been used to segment him and managed to narrow it down to some sort of axe, but-" Bina stopped as she could see Seamus was looking impatient. "We found an old axe in the back of one of the vehicles from the site yesterday. We took some samples from the blade and there's blood on it. Preliminary tests have given a match to Reg, so while we wait for the full report, it's reasonable to assume this was the weapon used. Fingerprints come back to one of the bodies also recovered at the scene, ID for them is in the post, as it were. Non-UK, not on our system or Borders', so at the moment we're at a loss. We have a murder weapon and a suspect but no clear motive, which is where you boys come in."

She blushed for a moment as she thought that last comment was a little over-familiar, but when Seamus smiled she relaxed.

"That's excellent stuff, sort of," he said. "At least we have the axe and the axeman - sorry, axe person - and I'd wager old Reg borrowed one of their posh cars and they caught up with him. Doesn't explain the thumbs, though - but at least it's feasible," he concluded. Jim looked at them both and smiled at Bina. "Thanks, this is really excellent. At least we now have some idea on how he ended up the way he did, silly old bastard." Jim checked himself immediately. "I mean- you know what I mean. We can assign this to Gibbons when he gets back, then get in touch with Reg's mum and tie it all up."

FORTY-FOUR

Gibbons arrived at HMP Erlestoke and parked up. Signing in, he was escorted to the visitor area where Adrian Burch sat waiting for him. He looked very different to the last time they had met - thinner, maybe, or was that a trick of the light? He certainly looked tired. "Mr Burch, good morning," said Gibbons as he approached and Adrian stood up to shake hands. "Please," said the young detective, waving towards the chairs to encourage the man to retake his seat. Adrian nodded and sat down, folding his hands in his lap. Gibbons pulled out a chair, sat opposite and took his notebook out of his jacket pocket. "Thanks for seeing me on such short notice, Mr Burch. I need to just ask you a few questions on the IT system access if you don't mind." Adrian looked puzzled but nodded in acceptance. "Yes, of course. Anything I can do to help I will."

"Thanks. Listen, we need to check how many accounts

you set up and what level of access they were given. I'm not going to mess about as this is quite important - there's a reason we need to get this detail now. You see, if you have created a number of different accounts other than those we had discussed with you, and they have access to a wider data set than you had used for your-" Gibbons paused while he tried to find the right word, but just went with the simplest option, "-list, then we need to know so we can close them and any method of remote access down."

Adrian looked even more confused. "But I'm in here - what do you think I could be doing?" he asked. "It's not what you might do, Mr Burch," Gibbons said in a very serious tone, making the colour drain from Adrian's face. "You see, if others find how to use the access and the accounts that may still be active, then there is a chance they could discover information we would rather they didn't." Gibbons hoped he was keeping to the brief about being vague but, given the look on the other man's face, he may have said too much already as Adrian looked terrified. "What kind of people?" Adrian asked in almost a whisper, not really sure he wanted to hear the reply.

Gibbons sat upright and took in a breath. "Full transparency, Mr Burch - we have recently undertaken an operation where a significant amount of illicit items were removed from a number of sites belonging to an organised crime group-" In for a penny, he thought to himself. "This is all currently being held in a few police storage units and these people will use any means necessary to get it back. So, if there is a possibility that you have created some sort of- back door, shall we say, and they apply sufficient pressure to you so that you tell them where it is, then the sites could be compromised and the products taken back. This is not a situation we would be pleased with."

"I'm sorry, are you telling me that there could be people in here-" Adrian swept his hand around himself, "-that are connected to whatever you called it, and could find me? I mean how would they know about me, let alone what I had done, and - just what the hell are you saying?" He was clearly agitated and Gibbons was inwardly worried he had gone too far, but given he couldn't take any of it back he decided to press on. "The organised crime group, yes. It is feasible that there are representatives here and that they may have already been able to ascertain the reason you are here and gathered details of how you had been able to get the list of names. Now if they join any dots then they may assume that you will not yet have had the opportunity to close down any routes and would be able to share the details of how to access our systems with them."

He took a pause to allow this to sink in. "You can't, I mean you have to just- you've got to get me out of here or some protection or, you can't just leave me here at the whim of these people. What if they attack me in the showers or drop something on me at night and make an attempt to just-" Gibbons could see that the man was clearly worried, and his rambling only cemented this. "Mr Burch, it may not happen. But if anyone does approach you, we need to have been able to close anything down so you have nothing of value. They'll leave you alone if you know there is nothing that they can use. Our experience is that these kinds of discussions are done quietly and without raising any suspicions, so they don't do anything physical to you."

Before Gibbons had really been able to finish the sentence Adrian blurted out, "to me, they won't do anything physical to ME, but if they can find me in here, then they can find my family out there," and he wildly pointed towards the windows. "Can you keep them safe, at least?" The reality of the wider implications of his actions seemed to hit him like a train and knocked the wind out of him, and he heaved. Gibbons instinctively moved back in case he got an impromptu shower of prison breakfast, but nothing came out - just a cry of anguish. "What have I done?"

After a cup of water and some time to calm down, Adrian spent the next hour providing as much detail as he could on everything he had set up, all the access methods, software that had been installed, all the accounts that had been created and how to close everything down. By the time he had finished, he felt a little calmer given what Gibbons had said - that once he had nothing to offer, 'they' would leave him alone. Even so, he couldn't shake the fear that something would happen to Lisa and the kids. He needed to get hold of them, so decided he had to ask Gibbons if he could help.

Gibbons listened and made appropriate sounds, but Adrian didn't get the impression that he was actually listening. It turned out he was right - Gibbons had moved to self-protection mode as he had come to the conclusion that he'd been a little too articulate. Adrian stopped talking and waited for Gibbons to react. It took a few seconds, but the officer's eyes seemed to refocus and he tilted his head to one side. "Everything alright?" Gibbons asked, and Adrian lost his patience. "No, everything is not alright. My family's at risk out there, and I am stuck in here and I can't do anything, and I need you to help me!" It all came out in a rush, and it was very clear he was scared. Gibbons licked his top lip and nodded. "OK. I'll get a uniform patrol to your house today to ensure they keep an eye on them all, and we'll discuss with the governor here about keeping you in a safer place ."Can you at least get Lisa here today?" Adrian pleaded. "I'll see what can be done, but I can't promise. I can ask if we can speed up the process that you've already started and get in touch with Lisa to get her details on the visitor system. In the meantime, you need to keep as low a profile as you can."

After Gibbons had left Adrian was allowed into the main population recreational area. He couldn't relax and was constantly looking around at everyone and trying really hard not to make eye contact. All he could think about was Lisa and the kids and what he had exposed them to. A plan was forming in his head about tomorrow, when he hoped Lisa would be there in person and he could try to explain it all to her since he hadn't had a chance since Devon. That was, if he was going to make it to the morning.

Gibbons made the call to Jim from the car before leaving. He omitted some of the details from the discussion but relayed Adrian's reaction and request as well as a summary of the data gathered that would soon be with their own IT team to act upon. Jim placed his phone on the desk and looked over at Seamus. "He's got it all - accounts, remote access details, the lot. We'll have people starting on it as soon as he is back and that should be it, all routes closed - well, at least from this fuck-up, anyway." Seamus acknowledged the language and considered that Jim was under more stress than he had initially let on. "OK, let's get an update once the techs have done their thing. How is our Mr Burch holding up?"

Jim shrugged. "He didn't say, but I can't imagine he's in good shape. He said he'd asked for some uniform to check on the house, so I've put in a request already. We ought to check in with Erlestoke at the end of the day, make sure he's alright." Seamus looked over at Jim and frowned a little. "You OK? You seem a bit short with this guy." Jim shook his head. "Not really. I get he's a middle-class office bloke who's found himself in a shitty situation, but come on - he kidnapped people, what did he think would happen? We'd let him go home to his wife and kids, pat him on the head and say nice things to him? No, he has to realise that these are the consequences of his actions and take some responsibility for them."

"Right," said Seamus. It seems that Jim had taken this in a different way than he'd assumed he would. It didn't take long for Jim to break.

"He dragged his family into something that has potentially put them directly in harm's way. He took people off the streets and put them, no, threw them into a hole in the ground, and left them there. How long would they have been there if he hadn't felt us coming up behind him? These are people's kids, family members, you know. Just left there and now he's worried about his, he's a fu-" he stopped himself and edited his language. "He's a hypocrite. You can't do that and leave us exposed like that."

Jim just shook his head and Seamus saw another side of his colleague. He already knew Jim was pretty sensitive but hadn't fully expected this kind of reaction.

He placed his arm around Jim's shoulder and pulled him in a little. "I get it, and you're right, but still - we have to be mindful that he will be terrified."

Jim nodded and smiled thinly. "I know, I'll call them in the next couple of hours, make sure he's being looked after and check uniform are being dispatched."

FORTY-FIVE

Lisa received the visitor request via email and deleted it. She walked around the kitchen a few times, occasionally glancing back at her laptop. She perched on the bar stool at the side of the counter, retrieved the email from the deleted items folder and read it again.

"NO!" she shouted at the message. Her shoulders slumped as she thought about him there, surrounded by who knows what kind of people, and knew he needed her. But she was angry at him, at who this person was that called himself her husband. The things she had been told by John Muir came back to the forefront of her mind, and she slammed the laptop shut.

She'd managed to get the kids to school this morning without incident and had even gone to the shops and made it home with groceries, but on arrival back home she had fallen apart again. The pressure of trying to seem normal was too much. To then be greeted by an email from HMP Erlestoke was more than she could manage. When John had called her, she had asked so many questions about the charges, what they meant and what Adrian had actually done. Mostly why he couldn't come home, surely there was bail? she remembered asking, only to be told, in no uncertain terms, that his actions were in a category which meant bail wasn't an option. She'd cried more at that part than anything else. This was what kept going through her mind: 'his actions were in a category that bail wasn't an option'. A few minutes on Google hadn't settled her concerns when she read through offences that bail wasn't applicable for. John had given her a lot of details, but kidnap and false imprisonment just lay there in her stomach like a heavy meal. Lisa had called her husband many things over the last few days, but between these outbursts he was still the man she married, the father of their beautiful children, the man who encouraged her in all her pursuits and comforted her when she needed him.

She opened her laptop and the email, clicking on the link to accept the invitation. All things considered, she thought, he was alone and scared and needed her. Her phone rang. She nearly knocked her tea over as she was so lost in the process of completing the form and trying to juggle all the thoughts that this brought up. She didn't recognise the number but answered it anyway. "Hello," she practically whispered, placing the phone to her ear. "Mrs Burch? I'm Acting DC Gibbons from Swindon Police and I'm calling about your visit to HMP Erlestoke." That was fast, she thought to herself - she had only just clicked 'send' on the web page. "Erm, yes. Is there a problem? I've just replied to the email," Lisa explained, hopeful that she had filled the form in correctly and still trying to work out how the response was so immediate. "Everything is fine, Mrs Burch. I'm calling to ask if you'd like us to collect you today and take you there. It's not far from you but I appreciate it is quite an emotional thing to do, so if it makes it a little easier for you-"

Lisa's eyebrows went up and she wondered what this was about, even if it was a genuine call. "I don't know. I, erm, should be OK, thank you. Like you said, it's not too far to drive and I don't want to put anyone out. I'm sure I'll be fine, really, but thank you." She was aware it all sort of fell out of her but had been caught a little off guard. "It's really no problem. Could you be ready in an hour?" Gibbons pressed on as he had been tasked with checking in on Adrian and providing a report, so had an ulterior motive. "I suppose I could be, yes," Lisa stuttered. Gibbons thanked her and made the arrangement to collect her from home.

Feelings she had been trying hard to suppress had come back with a vengeance now, bile crept to the back of her throat and she felt sweat forming on her forehead. It was going to happen, she was going to visit her husband in prison. It was such a surreal thing to come to terms with. They had been sitting around the dining table just a few days before and sharing a bottle of wine while watching a trashy film, but now she was being taken to prison. Prison.

It didn't matter how many times she repeated it to herself she couldn't normalise it at all. She went to the toilet, knelt down and retched into the bowl, tears running down her cheeks. She gathered herself, washed her face and grabbed her coat, seeing how much she was shaking when she stretched her hand out to remove it from the hook. Walking into the living room, she chose a seat on the sofa so she had a good view of the driveway, and when the blue saloon car pulled up she grabbed her housekeys and met the young officer at the front door. After their initial greeting, the six-mile trip was carried out mostly in silence as Lisa really didn't feel up to a conversation. Gibbons wasn't confident in striking one up either, so allowed his passenger to relax as much as she could.

On arrival at the prison she presented her ID, as did Gibbons. They were signed in at the front gate reception then escorted towards the visitor area. When she saw him her heart leapt and she was overcome with a mix of fear, anger and sympathy. He looked lost in his grey jogging suit and sitting on the orange plastic chairs, greyer than the last time she'd seen him, thinner and so desperately sad. She looked at Gibbons for some sort of permission to approach. He nodded gently to her and she had to stop herself from running over to him.

Adrian stood up and his face broke out into a broad smile which didn't make it to his eyes, which as she got closer could see were full of tears. They stood less than two feet apart for a few seconds, neither speaking, just taking in the situation. Then she slapped him hard across the face. He recoiled and stumbled back a step with the force and shock of the assault. It was all he deserved, he thought as he regained his balance, only to receive the same again, making his cheek sting. Gibbons looked over at the guard and gave a subtle shake of the head, stopping the man from making any move towards them. Lisa then burst into tears, the pain in her hand not really helping, and she shook her head, trying so hard to understand the complete jumble of thoughts racing through her mind now she was here and face-to-face with him. Gibbons walked a little closer and encouraged them both to take a seat. "We have as long as you need, OK, so take your time. I'm sure you have a lot to talk about." Lisa shot him a look to suggest he had no idea, then turned her attention to Adrian, sat opposite with a very red left cheek, biting his lip.

It took a little time for the conversation to start since neither really knew what to say initially. After a few minutes things began to move along. It was clear that Lisa needed to understand Adrian's motivation and what had brought everything to this, today. Adrian tried to explain as much as he could, bouncing from one part of the whole story to another, but trying to justify his actions. A wave of confidence came over him as he recalled his motivation, hoping Lisa would share the reasoning behind it all. It became clear by her facial reactions that she really was struggling with all this information, shaking her head each time he touched on specifics relating to how he had chosen people and why, the selection of the site, until she raised her hand to get him to stop talking.

"Adrian, I can't," she said, shaking her head. "Lis, I need you to-" She cut him off. "Don't call me that. I don't know who you are. I mean, Jesus, kidnapping people, a pit, a fucking pit Adrian!" she screamed at him, her face scarlet, eyes bright and tears running down her cheeks.

He backed up slightly. Lisa never lost her temper. In all the years they had been together she had barely even raised her voice. He blinked away his own tears and tried to come up with a response, but wasn't able to find any words that would land well. Lisa went to stand up. Adrian reached out to stop her, but she slapped his hand away and rose to her feet. "I didn't want to come," she announced from her position above him. "I made myself do it as I thought you needed me, that you were - I don't know -" Lisa raised her hands to shoulder height, struggling to organise her thoughts. "But you're deluded. Who are you? How have I not seen this coming in you? You're just-"

She turned away from him and started walking. "Lisa, please!" Adrian called out to her, and she stopped. "No, Adrian. No." She raised her right hand and pointed a trembling finger at him, before placing it on her lips. "No." "I want to leave, now," she said to Gibbons who was also on his feet. He noticed Adrian had stood and was walking towards Lisa. Adrian placed his hand on her back in an attempt to get her attention, and she spun around and struck him in the face for a third time. "Don't you touch me!" she said in a low voice, keeping her right hand where it had come to a stop after hitting her husband. "Don't you ever touch me." She pushed her way past Gibbons, who had to almost jog to catch up. He nodded at the guard to control Adrian, who was now trying to follow his wife to the door. Lisa was striding away and despite his pleading words, was taking no notice of Adrian.

"Take me home, please," she said to Gibbons, who

diligently complied with Lisa's wish and navigated them both out of the building and back to the car. He opened the front passenger door for her and closed it once he was sure she was in, then walked around to the driver's side, letting out a long breath through pursed lips. That was not what I was expecting, he thought to himself, considering how to explain it to Jim later.

Driving back to Lisa's house was even quieter than the journey to the prison. Lisa just stared out through the window, her head turned away from Gibbons the whole way. Once the car pulled up on the drive, she unclipped her seat belt, got out and slammed the door shut without a word.

Gibbons thought about just driving off, but his training stopped him and he turned off the engine and got out, meeting Lisa at the door as she was trying to get the key into the lock with shaking hands. She dropped the keys and swore, so Gibbons bent down and picked them up. "Allow me," he said and opened the door for her. She walked in leaving it open, so he followed her into the kitchen. "I'm really sorry," he said, and instantly regretted it, feeling Lisa might later believe he was accepting some sort of responsibility for the course of events. She took off her coat, let it drop onto a chair in the dining side of the room and turned to look at the office.

"Are all the meetings like that?" she asked, maintaining eye contact with a steely gaze. "Not many, but it's a difficult situation to walk into," he replied, taking the liberty of filling the kettle and switching it on. "I think you did really well, all things considered. It's a lot to take in," he offered in a conciliatory tone, trying to calm Lisa down a little. She nodded slowly and walked to a cupboard, taking out two mugs, pointing to the tea, coffee and sugar jars on the shelf and telling Gibbons where to find the spoons. She opened the fridge and handed him the milk. Lisa took in a sharp breath and drew herself up a little. "I don't know what to do," she said, looking at the floor and letting out the rest of the breath. She bit her top lip and locked eyes with Gibbons. "I can't tell the kids any of this." She almost laughed at the ridiculousness of the situation that had unfolded just thirty minutes earlier. "Can you imagine that conversation over their fish fingers tonight?" she snorted. "Kids, your dad's a-" but that was as far as she got. She leant forward to grab the worktop to prevent herself from falling, and Gibbons instinctively reached out for her arm. She made no attempt to pull away from him, glad of the additional support. He eased her towards the dining table and pulled out a chair and helped her into it, going back to finish the tea and brought her a mug, placing it in front of her. He took a seat to her right and waited for her to regain some composure.

Lisa sat at the table with her arms in front of her, palms down to steady herself. "I'll make sure there is someone here to help you, Mrs Burch," Gibbons said, once there had been a reasonable change in her breathing to signify she had calmed down a little. "It's Lisa," she said quite softly. "I don't think I can be Mrs Burch now, not now." She shook her head and closed her eyes. "Not anymore."

Once Adrian got to his cell that night the events of the day had been replayed a thousand times. So many different things he could have said, so many ways that should have gone, so many outcomes - and each one ended better, with Lisa throwing her arms around him, planting a great big kiss on his forehead and telling him that everything would be OK, that she would wait for as long as it took. But when he sat on the bunk all this evaporated in an instant, the sting still there on his face, the look in her eyes and the sight of her walking - almost running - away from him. His eyes scanned the cell for something to attach a makeshift rope to. He hadn't been able to go through with it in Devon, but things had got much, much worse. There had to be something to tie a sheet to that would take his weight, but it was obvious this was part of the design of the cells and his options were very limited.

He sighed. Tomorrow he would look for a way out - or maybe the people Gibbons had warned him about would take care of it for him. He could make them believe he had something, and when they found out he was bullshitting them, they would be given instructions to get rid of him.

He settled on that plan for now and tried to get comfortable on the narrow bunk.

FORTY-SIX

Bina had completed her report for Reg and submitted it with all the updated information on the axe that had been found. The full lab results had come back and the DNA was a match to their man in boxes. As she tidied away the day's work, Bina couldn't help thinking what an awful fate had befallen him. Her phone buzzed in her pocket but her hands were full so she let it go to voicemail, knowing she'd be able to attend to it later.

Across town, Gibbons was finalising his report on the day's visit between Lisa and Adrian, trying to keep some of the less appealing elements a little more low-key than had actually transpired. He couldn't quite shake the image from his head of a woman so angry and aggrieved that she would hit her husband in front of a police officer. Three times. He was just getting the last of it done when Jim came over to the desk he was using and sat beside him. "How do you think he'll cope?" Jim asked, nodding towards the report, clearly referring to Adrian. Gibbons mulled his response over before offering a considered reply. "To be honest, Sir, I think he is likely to be high-risk after today. I've already asked for there to be a watch on him and for any options in his cell to be dealt with- you know, sheets and things. But that must have been pretty tough for him. She really cut him off." The young officer looked deep in thought, obviously replaying some of the discussion that had taken place in front of him, and Jim could see why he was going to be a very good detective. He had compassion for those involved, and it showed. "You did well, Andrew. Now finish this in the morning if you'd rather and get home - it's been a hell of a day." Jim clapped Gibbons on the shoulder and went to leave.

"Sir," Gibbons said and turned in his seat. "I'll stay to finish this. I'd rather it was all done tonight, but I'm a bit concerned I may not have helped Lisa Burch today. I just think that I could have handled the meeting better."

Jim regarded the younger man in front of him, thought back to his earlier years as a DC and smiled to himself, then more outwardly. "Listen. That was never going to be an easy meeting for them two, and you could have taken them to dinner in a nice Italian and it wouldn't have made any difference. She learned some things about her husband today that will have shocked her, confused her and angered her to levels she probably didn't even know she had. She may well go home and over the next few days give it some thought and, who knows, maybe- not forgive him, but work through some of it and be there for him in one way or another. You did fine, don't worry.

The trial date is only a couple of weeks away, so you'll most likely see her again and she may thank you."

Gibbons gave a thin smile and brief nod. "Thanks, Sir," he said and returned to his paperwork. Jim nodded sagely and made his way out, trying Bina's number again as he walked.

This time she picked up. "Oh, hi - was that you a minute ago?" she asked with the leather fob of her keyring between her teeth. "Yes, are you hiding from me?" he joked, and she could hear it in his voice. "I am, I'm trying to make a covert exit from work and my phone keeps ringing and giving my location away" she chuckled. "I won't keep you, then," Jim said. "Just wanted to say I really enjoyed the other night and would love to return the dinner favour. I'll warn you now, my culinary skills are no match for yours." Bina winced silently and decided to come clean. "Well, actually, it was all M&S and I had a pud in reserve too, which I ate today at work." Jim laughed out loud and shook his head in mock dismay, even though Bina couldn't see him. "In that case, I'll have to see what Asda has prepared for us and bung something in the oven. Sound OK to you?" Bina grinned and almost skipped as she accepted the invitation, made her excuses and ended the call, nearly running to the car.

Jim slipped his phone into the inside pocket of his jacket and smiled. M&S, indeed - I need to watch her. Once at the supermarket he was aware that it was late, so the choice of something quick to cook - as well as tasty and ideally not pizza - was limited. A pang of guilt went through him. Bina had made such an effort for him, and he really didn't want to let her down. He rummaged about for a while in the chilled section but nothing really caught his eye.

When Bina arrived at Jim's the pizza was almost done, as was the garlic bread, a bottle of wine was open and airing and two glasses were on the counter. He opened the door looking a little sheepish. "It's pizza, I'm afraid - I didn't really get much inspiration at-" and she cut him off with a kiss planted right on his lips. "It really doesn't matter what we have to eat, Jim - it's you I'm here for. It's always been you, from the day we first passed each other in the lab. It's you, Jim." She gathered him in her arms and it felt like she wouldn't let him go - and he was absolutely fine with that. He poured the wine and they relocated to the living room.

Bina had her suspicions but they were realised when she took a look around. He kept a very tidy house. She had noticed in the front porch that the shoes were all orderly - everything seemed to have a place. Jim sat at the end of the sofa, leaning on the arm with Bina laying along the length of it, her back up against his chest, his arms around her and she felt more secure and comfortable than she could ever remember. With the slightest turn of her head she could see his eyes, sparkling with contentment. They talked about everything and nothing for most of the night, entwined in each other's arms, breaking apart only for sips of wine and for Jim to tidy stuff away in the kitchen.

It had gone midnight when Bina stood up. "I hope you don't mind, but I've brought a few things, we're not working tomorrow, hopefully, so I wondered if it would be OK." Her stomach had turned into a butterfly farm and she felt like a teenager again, awkward and incoherent. "We can have separate rooms, it's just I really don't want tonight to have to end in different houses. I'd love the morning to be with you." Jim really was lost for words but nodded and smiled and stood up too. "Well, look, yes, of course - I'd love that." Bina let out a small laugh of joy and excused herself to go to her car, returning within seconds with a small overnight bag. She closed and locked the door behind her.

Jim had opened another bottle of wine and stood in the kitchen looking like a kid who had spent the day in a toy shop. He took Bina's hand and they returned to the low light of the living room, and snuggled together again and she took in his scent, closing her eyes and smiling. By the time the bottle was empty it was time to go to sleep. They put the bottle in the bin and the glasses in the sink. Jim showed Bina where the bathroom was upstairs and the spare room, that he made sure had everything including fresh towels while Bina was freshening up.

He got into bed and lay there thinking about the evening and that Bina was just metres away, something he never thought would be possible. Then he heard her door open, and a tapping on his. He leapt out of bed, got to the door in just two strides and carefully opened it. Bina stood there nibbling her bottom lip. He took her hand and brought her close to him and then towards the bed. Once they got in together Jim held her in his powerful arms, her back to him, and he breathed in the smell of her hair and felt the softness of her skin against his.

On the other side of town, Seamus finally turned off the TV and got up to switch off the table lamp. He went to the kitchen, drew a glass of water from the tap and went off to the bathroom. He took a long look at himself in the mirror, ran his hand from his forehead to his chin and sighed. Who was that person and had they sold out? He continued his observation of the intruder while brushing his teeth and went into the bedroom. Following his usual routine he placed his phone on the wireless charging stand next to his bed as he pulled the duvet back so he could get into bed. He sat on the edge of the mattress to start with and picked his phone up again. Seamus opened the contacts list and scrolled down until he got to her number. He stared at the screen, his thumb hovering over the call button. He hadn't been tempted to call her for weeks now, but tonight he just wanted to hear her voice, to soothe him like she used to.

He bit at his top lip then ran his tongue over it. He then sniffed and shook his head, turning the phone off and placing it back on the stand. Not tonight.

FORTY-SEVEN

The trial was due to start the following day. John Muir had taken time with Adrian to prep him on the specifics, not just how the jury would likely respond to the offences but also how the judge would have needed to review what he had done. "Listen, you have been charged with four counts of kidnap and false imprisonment, fraud - so the identity theft and use of this identity for fraudulent insurance and vehicle registration documents - they will most likely roll all these up into one offence, so that is five and then the unlawful access to police data. This last one could be tricky for them to define and may be rolled into the fraud charge, but it's likely that they may impose consecutive sentences." Adrian was trying to take all this in and was simply nodding but not really understanding what was being said to him, and his solicitor had noticed. "Adrian, let me try and spell it out. Lesser offences will be looked at as maybe six to twelve months due to the culpability and harm range they will most likely use. They will take other things into consideration, so you have no prior convictions, you have assisted the police throughout their inquiries, you have shown a positive character and shown remorse during the final interviews. These are all good attributes and will count in your favour. However-"

This was the part Adrian wasn't really sure about, and right up to the last word it had been sounding quite positive. "However, what?" he asked Muir. "OK, offences I've explained so far could carry a maximum custodial sentence of two years, which may be suspended for twelve months given the mitigations. The kidnap and false imprisonment times four, though - this is where it gets complicated. We are looking at between two and seven years per offence. They will use the totality principle to ensure that they consider all offences, and the total effect of them on the sentencing to determine if they will apply consecutively or concurrently. They will assess everything holistically and use all this to make their sentencing decision."

Adrian was staring at Muir, trying to see the wood for the trees in all these words. "Depending on how they measure all the elements, including culpability, harm and your history will determine the sentencing mechanism and time. It is highly likely that they will recommend immediate custody and even at the lower limit of two years per offence, you would be expecting eight years. Upper limit for kidnap and false imprisonment is-" Muir hesitated and decided to soften the blow, "-a long time. So, let's look at our mitigation plan."

"What does that mean?" asked Adrian, still struggling to

take all this in. "It means we need to come up with a way to have your sentencing reduced from the start, so with your history and good conduct I'm recommending a guilty plea straight out of the gate. That will work very well in your favour and reduce the-"

"Are you kidding me? You want me to plead guilty- I mean what are you here for if all I need to do is walk in and say 'yeah, I did it all' - what are you talking about?" Adrian was clearly getting agitated and John Muir had anticipated this. "Adrian, listen to me. If we try to drag this out, there will be a long trial. You will have to listen to victim statements, you'll be in the dock for - who knows? - weeks. The victims and probably their families will be there and that can get ugly, so we need to reduce all that as much as possible and the best way to do this is a guilty plea. This will bring your sentence down and give you a slightly better path through this. OK? Now get some sleep, tomorrow is going to be a long day."

The following morning Adrian sat cross legged on the bunk in the remand cell staring at, rather than out of the window. He hadn't slept all that well which was no real surprise and nervously pulled at the sleeve of his prison issue top.

"Time to go" came a voice from the other side of his cell door and Adrian shook his head to bring some focus and slowly stood up. The escorting guard opened the door and gestured for Adrian to follow him. "Big day today, hope it goes well and we don't see you again" the man smiled as he led Arian along the corridor to the reception area. Through multiple sets of doors, all electronically unlocked, they made it to the waiting vehicle. It was a taxi, which Adrian thought was odd, but his escort attached the cuffs one on his right wrist, the other on Adrian's left and both men got into the car.

When Adrian made it to court he was taken to a small room where his solicitor was waiting for him. John Muir rose to his feet, thanked the escort and offered for Adrian to take the seat opposite. "So, had some time to think about what I said last night?" Muir said, leaning over the table between them.

The solicitor locked eyes with his client, raising his eyebrows to try and gain consent. Adrian sighed and hung his head, blowing out a long breath while shaking his head. "Fine, I'm in your hands, John. Please do the right thing." There was a sharp knock on the door and the Court Usher stuck his head through the now open door. "It's time, please, if you'll follow me." Adrian felt all the fear rising again as he stood along with John Muir and all three walked along the corridor to the court room. As they crossed the threshold, he thought he was going to pass out.

The Clerk called everyone to order and ensured all were standing while the Judge arrived and took his seat. On the instruction, the room was seated and Adrian was called into the dock, with the Prosecution Barrister invited to provide his opening after the case had been presented. "Thank you, Your Honour. As we have heard, the defendant Mr Adrian Burch is here on charges of kidnap and false imprisonment of four young men, the names of which had been selected following false access to police data. These men were abducted from the streets near their homes and incarcerated in an open pit at a derelict farm. "Additionally, Mr Burch falsified documents to falsely obtain, tax and insure a vehicle that was subsequently used to transport his victims from the location of their abduction to the place of incarceration. These were premeditated crimes, demonstrating that a lot of thought had gone into the planning and execution of each. His actions are those of a calculating and callous individual with little regard to the welfare of his victims."

Adrian listened with increasing dread as the barrister read out the opening statement and, even with John Muir's words in his head, it wasn't looking good. "Thank you, Mr Devonport," said the Judge when it was clear the Barrister had finished. He turned to John Muir. "May we have the opening statement from the defence now?" asked the Judge. "Your Honour, we understand that the court has decided a pre-sentence report is not necessary and we acknowledge this. We would like to enter a guilty plea against all charges. My client, Mr Burch, has no previous criminal history and has assisted the police in their inquiries from the start of their investigation. In addition to this, he has shown remorse towards the victims and their families for the stress and harm caused. He recognises his actions are not of his usual positive character."

Muir returned to his seat after thanking the Judge and looked over at Adrian, giving him an almost imperceptible nod. The Judge finished his note-taking and invited both representatives to the bench. "Gentlemen, I understand that the submission of a guilty plea will significantly reduce the time this court needs to stand on this case and appreciate that this will have a positive impact on the victims and the jury alike. However, I must advise that the offences recorded pass the custody threshold and it is likely even after deliberation that an immediate custodial sentence will be imposed on the defendant. I will review the case notes now and we will be in a position to proceed very shortly."

Muir and Devonport returned to their seats from the bench and the court clerk advised the room that the Judge was to take a few moments to review then would be able to address the court. Those few minutes felt like hours for Adrian. He maintained his gaze on John Muir, who was hastily scribbling notes and hadn't looked up for a while, which made Adrian even more nervous. The Judge called the Usher over and they had a whispered conversation, following which the Usher called the Clerk over and the latter called everyone to attention.

"Ladies and gentlemen," the Judge began. "You will have heard the Prosecution's opening statement and understood the severity of the offences that have been presented. These have clearly been premeditated and have inflicted serious harm and distress on those involved as well as serious injury or pain. There are also major aggravating factors to consider, that the location of incarceration was an isolated one, some distance from the homes of each victim, and there was no means of escape."

"It is also clear to me that there has been a significant degree of planning to have obtained the vehicle used, and to have fraudulently acquired the identification of a deceased person and obtained vehicle insurance and documents of proof of ownership by deception. These are serious offences and each carries a custodial sentence." Adrian was aware he was sweating as the Judge was explaining this to the court. It seemed to have more impact from him than it had done when the Prosecution Barrister had said almost the same thing. He was starting to sway and gripped the sides of the dock to prevent himself from falling. "However, I must take into account the mitigations presented by Mr Muir of the defendant's good character and no prior criminal history. That and an early guilty plea means we can deal with this today, and there is no need for a protracted trial. With all this in mind, I must move to sentencing. Mr Muir, before I close, do you have anything else you would like to add?" asked the Judge. Muir stood. "No, Your Honour." He gave a short bow of the head and retook his seat. "Thank you, Mr Muir," said the Judge. "Mr Devonport?"

The Prosecution Barrister stood and delivered the same response. "Very well then, Mr Burch. In light of your good conduct and history, as well as your guilty plea, I am prepared to offer a degree of leniency. That being said, the offences of which you have been charged are very serious, as is the harm you have caused - not only to your victims, but to their families and your own. In calculating the sentence I am about to apply to you, I have considered each of the factors that have been presented and applied the totality principle to ensure that the sentence is commensurate."

"Based on the severity of these offences, I feel that an example must be made here. You will serve a custodial term of three years for each of the four charges of kidnap and false imprisonment. For the offences of fraud, identity theft and accessing confidential data, obtaining legal documents by deception for the purpose of carrying out illegal activities, I will impose a custodial sentence of twelve months."

"I have considered the risk you may pose and the probability of reoffending in my decision. For the four offences you will serve these consecutively, and for the fraud and deception, this will be served concurrently. Therefore, you are to serve a maximum of twelve years at HMP Erlestoke. Bailiff, take him down."

Adrian's mouth fell open at the sentence decision and he seemed to be trying to speak, but no words came out. It was just as the Bailiff attached the handcuffs and turned him towards the door that he saw Lisa. She was in tears and just stood there staring at him. The last time he had seen her, she was a picture of anger but now it was sorrow and fear and it tore him apart. I'm so sorry he mouthed to her as he was led away but she just shook her head. He hoped it was in denial of what had just happened rather than in response to his words, but that was his last view of his wife.

Once he was in the transport van, the reality hit him. Even though he knew he was returning to Erlestoke, it was for twelve years. His daughter was almost twelve and throughout the journey he thought about all the events that had made up that time, the parties, the holidays, school trips and plays and he thought of the first time he'd held her and his son. He thought of all the things he wouldn't be part of now. He won't be there for any more holidays for twelve years. She would be in her twenties, his son would be twenty. They would learn to drive without him. His daughter might even marry before he got out. The van got through the gates and the door was opened, but Adrian couldn't stand up. His legs didn't want to work, in fact none of him did. The culmination of the last few hours, Lisa's face and the realisation of what he was going to miss pressed down on him and he simply couldn't move. The guard recognised this - it wasn't the first time he had experienced it in newly-sentenced inmates. He gently spoke to Adrian and encouraged him to get up, helping him to his feet. There was that look in the new arrival's eye.

Adrian was escorted to a new cell, as he was now an inmate rather than being on the remand wing. His new accommodation was marginally better to be fair, the bed seemed a little bigger, but Adrian noticed there were still few options substantial enough to bear his weight in the room that he could make a successful attempt of hanging himself from. He knew the overall layout of the place so made his way to the library to get the visitor process started. He needed to see Lisa again and be able to talk to her - maybe she could bring the kids. Would they be allowed, would they even want to come, would Lisa let them? That evening when he had returned to his cell he thought about whether he could ask for some photos or something to brighten the place up a bit. Maybe he could get the odd book too. He had been told that this place was a little more amenable to having some kind of comfort as a category C prison. He stretched out on the bunk and placed his hands behind his head. There was nothing he could do tonight. It had been a very long day with a lot to digest, and despite how he felt, he was exhausted.

He began to drift off to sleep, when the door opened and a figure walked across the small space to the bunk. “I believe you can get us access to the police computer system.” Adrian sat bolt upright and saw a bearded man standing before him. The visitor raised a hand. “No need to speak now, we will talk soon, but I’m sure you’ll help us.” He smiled, which made Adrian shiver. The man nodded, turned and left. Adrian wasn’t sure whether he should try to follow or just stay where he was. He opted for the latter, putting paid to his attempts at sleep for the next few hours. His door was closed from the outside and even though he knew he should, he didn’t feel secure at all.

FORTY-EIGHT

Lisa was only aware of what day it was since it was printed on the blister pack of her medication. By the time she had got the kids to bed and updated her parents on the outcome of the day she didn't know what to do with herself. She had spent almost ten minutes looking at the fridge earlier with all the photos on the door. Smiling family photos from holidays in Devon. She'd ripped them off and thrown them across the room; she couldn't bear to see his face and really didn't need any reminders of where he had run off to when all this had erupted. An hour later she was sat on the floor of the living room surrounded by photos she had insisted they had printed off, sorting them into small piles and placing some of her and the kids into a box. She had started to make a package to take to Adrian once she got the visitor request.

Lisa stopped at one of the photos. It was just the two of

them on their honeymoon at a restaurant she had pestered him to take them to. It was a nice little beachside affair, they had ordered cocktails and tapas and just talked and drank until the sun disappeared, then walked along the beach until it came back, emerging from the sea warming up their morning.

She could still feel the sand between her toes and hear their laughter. He could always make her laugh, he just had a way with words and could turn almost anything into a joke. She dropped the photo into the box and grabbed the pad and pen she had put on the floor next to her.

It was a few minutes before she could think of anything to say, but as soon as the first word took shape, the rest poured out of her. She told him about all the things she had been through, the sleepless nights and tears, what she had needed to say to the kids to stop them from being afraid for him. The first three attempts were screwed up and thrown across the room as she felt that she wasn't being fair. It was on her mind that his new situation was going to be just as difficult for him.

By the time she had gone up to bed, the box was sealed with a ribbon, the letter inside talked of her worries as well as how hurt she was, and that the kids needed reassurance somehow. But she ended it with a message of hope for him, that she did still love him and would visit as often as she could.

The pillow was wet from her tears as she moved from anger to deep sorrow as the night progressed trying to sleep but not succeeding at all.

Lisa looked at the empty side of the bed next to her and even though there had been many nights recently that Adrian hadn't been there, tonight was very hard to come to terms with.

Twelve more years ahead with this chasm in the room and in her heart. Getting up, Lisa went to one of the kid's rooms and collected a huge teddy bear and brought it back to bed.

Just the feeling of something against her chest brought her some comfort and she finally slipped into a troubled sleep.

ABOUT THE AUTHOR

Coming fashionably late to the party, I have been working in IT my whole career and recently began writing. Initially as a way to relax but it took me over and I found myself lost in the words.

Having an active interest in crime fiction and police documentaries I felt it was time to bring these two together and see what happened.

The Pit is the first in a series of DCI Seamus Corrigan novels, so watch this space.

Printed in Dunstable, United Kingdom

73173094R00198